Cloud Howe

Lewis Grassic Gibbon was the pseudonym under which James Leslie Mitchell wrote his Scottish novels. Born in 1901, near Auchterless in Aberdeenshire, he spent his boyhood mainly in Kincardineshire, the scene of *A Scots Quair*. At the age of sixteen he became a junior reporter on the *Aberdeen Journal* and between 1919 and 1928 he spent four years in the Army and six years in the RAF, during which time he travelled in Central America and the Middle East. In the seven years until his death in 1935 he wrote sixteen books, drawn from his childhood and travel experiences: these include *A Scots Hairst*, *Hanno* and *Nine against the Unknown*. For the latter part of his life he lived in Welwyn Garden City and was married with two children.

Cloud Howe

Book Two in the trilogy *A Scots Quair*

Lewis Grassic Gibbon

Pan Books London and Sydney

To George Malcolm Thomson

First published 1933
Published as part of the complete trilogy
A Scots Quair 1946 by Hutchinson & Co (Publishers) Ltd
This second book published 1973 by Pan Books Ltd,
Cavaye Place, London SW10 9PG
3rd printing 1978
All rights reserved
ISBN 0 330 23464 1
Printed and bound in Great Britain by
Hazell Watson & Viney Ltd, Aylesbury, Bucks

Contents

NOTE

Colquohoun is pronounced *Ca-hoon*,

and

Segget as with one hard g.

Foreword to the Complete Trilogy

By IVOR BROWN

Books about modern Scotland now commonly, and justly, include the name of Lewis Grassic Gibbon as one of the great interpreters of Scottish scene and character. His early death, at the age of thirty-four, and his rather peculiar pseudonym, which was used for only part of his work, have made him an elusive figure. Now that his notable trilogy of the hard life lived between the Grampians and the North Sea and in the granite towns and cities thereabout is being reprinted,* some information about his origins and his work is due to the reader. I am proud to have been asked to give it.

My interest in – which became a devotion to – this writer was due to various causes. My forefathers all sprang from the lands in Aberdeenshire, north of Don, where James Leslie Mitchell (the real name of Lewis Grassic Gibbon) was born. In London, thirty years after his birth, I became, all too late, his friend. I shared some of his opinions, disputed others, and found in him a spirit in tune with my own racial and local sympathies and my acquired philosophies. His utterance was of north-east Scotland in idiom and phrase. He was the voice of Scotland's past, almost of all antiquity in his great sense of pre-history and his addiction to primitive (the very opposite of barbaric and savage) men and things. He was a voice of humanity in his anger and compassion; his wrath flamed against oppression (he died in 1935, knowing full well what Fascism would do to the world). His pity for all poor and hunger-bitten men came out of his experience. He had lived with folk who lived hard, riving their food from an often grudging earth in an air that nips the blood.

Even more than any other of his qualities did I admire his superb mastery of words and rhythms, his spate of images, his

* Also available in Pan Books: *Sunset Song* and *Grey Granite.*

prose of the earth which continually dissolved into air to become the poetry of sky and cloud. Has anybody ever written
better about the mist of Scotland and the 'far-off mountains
turnéd into clouds', the steam of the land in summer, the sharp
savours of the root-fields after rain, the aroma of fir-trees on
the hillside, and the glitter of dew as it melts into the morning's canopy of jewelled Grampian air? Neil Gunn has said
that you can hear the earth itself speaking in Gibbon's prose.
I would add that the sky is in it too, a sky where the peesies
(lapwings) ribbon and cry, a sky where the whaups (curlews)
are eternally keening over the stones of the archaic men.

James Leslie Mitchell was born in February 1901, at the farm
of Hill of Segget, near Auchterless, in Central Aberdeenshire.
His mother, whose maiden name was Lily Gibbon, came from
Kildrummy. When he was only eight young Mitchell changed
his county, his father moving to a farm at Drumlithie in the
Mearns (otherwise known as Kincardineshire), the county
whence Robert Burns' father had migrated to Ayrshire. It is a
land of hills and the sea, containing the whole essence of Scotland in small compass, the large hills sweeping to the sky,
the farmlands sweeping to the cliffs. Here are the towns of
granite, the harbours of the herring-fleet, the cloth-mills, and
the crofts.

At the local school he was, I fancy, very lucky in his
dominie, Alexander Gray, who saw and knew how to shape the
immense promise in the boy. In his leisure the pupil was far
readier to escape with a book than to help the work on the
farm. At fifteen he went to Mackie Academy, Stonehaven,
where he was a gifted pupil, writing essays far above the
ordinary level. But he left after a year and found work as a
reporter on the *Aberdeen Journal*; later he moved to the
Scottish Farmer in Glasgow. At the age of twenty he fell ill
and came back for a short while to help in the fields in the
Mearns.

I was greatly struck later on by his width of reading and his
knowledge of languages. How he found time for it all, I never
knew. His boyhood must have been cruelly strenuous in self-

chosen bookishness, strenuous at the cost of his physique. It happens often so with the eager Scottish scholar. Leslie Mitchell was one of several Aberdonians whom I have known, greatly gifted in various ways, who spent themselves in studenthood and died in early manhood. At the age of sixteen, young Mitchell had even picked up enough Russian to try to interview M. Krassin in the latter's native language. Mitchell has related that Krassin was being deported from England by way of Aberdeen and that he met the cub-reporter's gallant Russian with English, explaining that in any case, he was not allowed to make a statement in any language. Meanwhile the young reporter dreamed of an Aberdeen Soviet and walked the grey city by the moon, thinking of Scotland's old pains and planning remedies to come. His mind ranged always, with a passionate eagerness, from the bright beginnings of mankind to its escape from present anguish.

After the illness followed eight years as a clerk in the Army and later in the RAF. That this brilliant boy should have wasted his time in military form-filling may seem strange, but he had no money and wanted to travel. It is on record that he did not mix well and was odd man out in the barrack-room, and one can well believe it. But the experience did get him out to the Middle East, where he could survey the greater relics of antiquity and muse upon the origins of society and of the martyrdom of man. It was there, he told me, that he met an archæologist who later took him to Central America, where he studied the remains of the Maya civilization, thus gaining the material for a book written later. He attributed some of his subsequent ill-health to that excursion: he told me once that his digestion had never recovered from the diet of maize on which he lived for some time amid the Maya ruins, following some years of a Service diet.

By 1928 he was free of Army forms. In 1935 he was dead. In seven years he wrote sixteen books; his fertility was tremendous, his energy hectic, his planning of a career absurd. (And still the myth endures that Aberdonians always know how to look after themselves.)

If he had gone back to his early craft of journalism he could have earned a steady moderate income and written a few books in his leisure, until he was able to live decently on books alone. But he slogged away at books and stories, dividing the day into three portions and expecting to write some 1,500 words in each. He tried to sell his short pieces to the wrong magazines till H. G. Wells noticed him and put him on the right lines. His books were, as a rule, written too quickly, but his quality was always there in one form or another. The Near East was a fruitful and a frequent background. The writer's life, though short and busy, was a blessed change from his old routine, and he was happily married, with children, a daughter and son, arriving later.

A Scots Quair was his salute to Scotland. A 'quair' is the same word as a 'quire', and means a set of papers or a volume. Mitchell himself marked that return by a change of name to Lewis Grassic Gibbon. The first book, Sunset Song, was published in 1932 and rapidly won the attention it deserved. Next year the tale of Chris Guthrie was carried further in Cloud Howe, which I find no less haunting. Grey Granite followed in 1934. This last gives the impression of being hasty and the end is unworthy of the whole. The great pattern appears to crumble in the author's hands, and the talent, which had been so finely maturing, suddenly seems younger and cruder. The book has some tiresome coarseness. Yet, being by a master, it has rarely beautiful things in it. When I said to Eric Linklater that it had disappointed me, he retorted that, whatever its faults, it had passages worthy of the great Scots ballads. And what greater praise could there be?

So here is the story of a small farm among the peesie-haunted 'parks' of the Mearns, a story linked with the early age of Scotland, a story returning continually to the standing stones of the ancient colonists who came, metal-hunting and exploring, from the Mediterranean to these far hills.

Two points of explanation must be made. Leslie Mitchell's philosophy of life was a belief in original innocence. The early, unpropertied men, who are usually regarded as warring savages, he believed to have been care-free and peaceable. (All the evidence about the real primitives, simple food-gathering folk, is on his side.) Then came, with the discovery of agriculture in Egypt and the misuse of the civilization which settled farming created, the flow of follies and corruptions, the worship of tyrannous gods and tyrannous kings, the cults of property and power, war, and all the miseries of modern man. To him the savage and the barbarian were the primitive in decay and his creed was a passionate assertion of the initial, the pre-savage, the primitive goodness which man must somehow recover.

This is no place to expound his whole doctrine of the archaic civilization, its diffusion, and its decay. It can be read in many of his books, in his contribution to *Scottish Scene* (a volume shared with Hugh MacDiarmid), in his record of the early explorers, *Nine Against the Unknown*, and in the earlier 'Leslie Mitchell' novels. I mention it here because the reader of this trilogy may be puzzled by the constant return to the standing-stones above Blawearie, the standing-stones which in his view linked Scottish earth to all enduring and universal things, symbol of the early men who were happy until they missed the way.

A second point needing explanation is the idiom and the rhythm of these books. Leslie Mitchell was born a peasant and his mind was divided about the peasant and his lot. At one moment he would hate the drudgery of the land; at another he was conscious of a powerful pride that the land was so closely and intimately his. 'My mother,' he wrote, 'used to hap me in a plaid in harvest time and leave me in the lee of a stook while she harvested.' These divisions of opinion, love of the earthy savours and the tang of the wind, resentment of the servitude under the 'on-ding' of the rain, hatred of the sweat and the shivering and the poverty, are constantly occurring in *Sunset Song* and *Cloud Howe*. There the Scottish peasants appear in all their roughness and coarseness as well as in their humours and their honour, just as the land itself appears in all its grudging and grinding dominion over labouring flesh as well as in the shimmering beauty of the Mearns upon a summer's day and in the foison of earth well dunged and well cropped by Scottish skill and endurance.

To utter this voice of the land and the landsman Mitchell chose a mannered, lilting style. When I first met this, it struck me as an affectation. But suddenly I realized what he was attempting and indeed achieving, which was 'to mould the English language into the rhythms and cadences of Scots spoken speech'. He used dialogue scantily, but in a sense he used it all the time. For his descriptions of men and places were the voice of one talking, say, the voice of Scotland itself. The vocabulary was a little antique, a trifle old-fashioned when it was first made. (So, they say, was that of Robert Burns.) That boy meets girl so often as 'childe meets quean' may irritate some. I am not here to defend all the means employed to achieve a certain result. That result was to make Scottish earth vocal, and I would claim that in the lilting, anapaestic prose of Lewis Grassic Gibbon you can indeed feel the swing of the horses at the plough, the rhythm of the wind upon the woods, the surge of the tumbling land where the mountains run down to the sea, and 'the speak' of the men who toiled and loved and quarrelled, the men of the little farms upon whose passing there is so noble a valediction at the close of *Sunset Song*.

The author has said that working in this convention helped him to turn out *Sunset Song* in six weeks. It kept his typewriter flowing. That was his surface talk. I believe that the rhythm did, in fact, come from deep fountains of his own feeling for the land and for its people. In any case, once the reader has settled down to the swing of it, he is likely to find the melody most apt to the subject and sweet to the senses.

In the autumn of 1934 Leslie Mitchell complained to me of increasing pains which he took to be due to a duodenal ulcer. Early in 1935 he underwent an operation for this affliction from which he did not rally. I shared the melancholy task of paying a tribute at his cremation at Golders Green. His ashes were later buried at Arbuthnott in the Mearns.

He was just thirty-four. He had never, I think, been able to spend time on any book. His life had been various, uneven, hustled. He was just touching success which would have given him leisure to stretch himself instead of rushing to his typewriter. He had begun a book which might have been a Scottish classic. At his wish what he had written was destroyed. But, at any rate, he had left this trilogy and in it were his head and his heart and the cunning of as quick a hand as ever put a landscape in a sentence. I do not think that the creator of Chris Guthrie, the colourist of the red-clay Guthrie fields and of the misty beauty of the Howe, and the recorder of 'the speak' of the Mearns in town and tavern, will easily be forgotten. Nor should he be.

IVOR BROWN

PROEM

The borough of Segget stands under the Mounth, on the southern side, in the Mearns Howe, Fordoun lies near and Drumlithie nearer, you can see the Laurencekirk lights of a night glimmer and glow as the mists come down. If you climb the foothills to the ruined Kaimes, that was builded when Segget was no more than a place where the folk of old time had raised up a camp with earthen walls and with freestone dykes, and had died and had left their camp to wither under the spread of the grass and the whins – if you climbed up the Kaimes of a winter morn and looked to the east and you held your breath, you would maybe hear the sough of the sea, sighing and listening up through the dawn, or see a shower of sparks as a train came skirling through the woods from Stonehaven, stopping seldom enough at Segget, the drivers would clear their throats and would spit, and the guards would grin: as though 'twere a joke.

But God alone knows what you'd want on the Kaimes, others had been there and had dug for treasure, nothing they'd found but some rusted swords, tint most like in the wars once waged in the days when the wife of the Sheriff of Mearns, Finella she was, laid trap for the King, King Kenneth the Third, as he came on a hunting jaunt through the land. For Kenneth had done her own son to death, and she swore that she'd even that score up yet; and he hunted slow through the forested Howe, it was winter, they tell, and in that far time the roads were winding puddles of glaur, the horses splashed to their long-tailed rumps. And the men of Finella heard of his coming, as that dreich clerk Wyntoun has told in his tale:

> As through the Mernys on a day
>   The kyng was rydand hys hey way
> Off hys awyne curt al suddanly
>   Agayne hym ras a cumpany

> In to the towne of Fethyrkerne
> To fecht wyth hym thai ware sa yherne
> And he agayne thame faucht sa fast,
> Bot he thare slayne was at the last.

So Kenneth was dead and there followed wars. Finella's carles builded the Kaimes, a long line of battlements under the hills, midway a tower that was older still, a broch from the days of the Pictish men; there they lay and long months withstood the folk that came to avenge the death of Kenneth; and the darkness comes down on their waiting and fighting and all the ill things that they suffered and did.

The Kaimes was left bare and ruined with walls, as Iohannes de Fordoun tells in his time, a Fordoun childe him and had he had sense he'd have hidden the fact, not spread it abroad. Some kind of a cleric he was in those days, just after the Bruce drove out the English, maybe Fordoun then had less of a smell ere Iohannes tacked on the toun to his name. Well, the Kaimes lay there in Iohannes' time, he tells that the Scots folk halted there going north one night to the battle of Bara; and one man with the Scots, a Lombard he was, looked out that morn as the army roused and the bugles blew out under the hills, and he saw the mists that went sailing by below his feet as the sun came quick down either slope of the brae to a place where a streamlet ran by a ruined camp. And it moved his heart, and he thought it an omen, in his own far land there were camps like that; and he swore that if he should survive the battle he'd come back to this place and claim grant of its land.

Hew Monte Alto was the Lombard's name and he fought right well at the Bara fight, and when it was over and the Bruce made King, he asked of the Bruce the lands that lay under the Kaimes in the windy Howe. These lands had been held by the Mathers folk, but they had made peace with Edward the First and given him shelter and welcome the night he halted in Mearns as he toured the north. So the Bruce he took their lands from the Mathers and gave them to Hew, that was well content, though vexed that he came of no gentle blood. So he sent a carle to the Mathers lord to ask if he had a daughter of age for wedding and bedding; and he sent an old carle that he well could spare, in case the Mathers should flay him alive.

For the Mathers were proud as though God had made their flesh of another manure from men; but by then they had come to a right sore pass in the mouldering old castle by Fettercairn, where hung the helmet of good King Grig, who first had 'stablished the Mathers there, and made of the first of them Merniae Decurio, Captain-chief of the Mearns lands. So the old lord left Hew's carle unskinned, and sent back the message he had more than one daughter, and the Lombard could come and choose which he liked. And Hew rode there and he made his choice, and was wedded and bedded to a Mathers quean.

But short was the time that he had for his pleasure, the English again had come north to war. The Scots men gathered under the Bruce at a narrow place where a black burn ran, the pass of the Bannock burn it was. And Hew was a well-skinned man in the wars, he rode his horse lathered into the camp, and King Robert called him to make the pits and set the spiked calthrops covered with earth, traps for the charge of the English horse. So he did, and the next day came, and the English, they charged right brave and were whelmed in the pits. But Hew was slain by an English arrow as he rode unhelmed to peer at his pits.

Before he rode south he had built a castle within the walls of the old-time Kaimes, and brought far off from his Lombard land a pickle of weavers, folk of his blood. They builded their houses down under the Kaimes in the green-walled circle of the ancient camp, they tore down the walls of that heathen place, and set their streets by the Segget burn, and drove their looms, and were well-content, though foreign and foolish and but ill-received by the dour, dark Pictish folk of the Mearns. Yet that passed in time, as the breeds grew mixed, and the toun called Segget was made a borough for sake of the Hew that fell at the Burn.

So the Monte Altos came to be Mowat, and interbred with the Mathers folk, and the next of whom any story is told is he who befriended the Mathers who joined with other three lairds against the Lord Melville. For he pressed them right sore, the Sheriff of Mearns, and the four complained and complained to the King; and the King was right vexed, and he pulled at his beard – *Sorrow gin the Sheriff were sodden – sodden and supped in his brew!* He said the words in a moment of rage, unthinking, and then they passed from his mind; but the lairds remembered, and took horse for the Howe.

There, as they'd planned, the four of them did, the Sheriff went hunting with the four fierce lairds, Arbuthnott, Pitarrow, Lauriston, Mathers; and they took him and bound him and carried him up Garvock, between two stones a great cauldron was hung; and they stripped him bare and threw him within, in the water that was just beginning to boil; and they watched while he slowly ceased to scraich, he howled like a wolf in the warming water, then like a bairn smored in plague, and his body bloated red as the clay, till the flesh loosed off from his seething bones; and the four lairds took their horn spoons from their belts and supped the broth that the Sheriff made, and fulfilled the words that the King had said.

They were hunted sore by the law and the kirk, the Mathers fled to the Kaimes to hide, his kinsman Mowat closed up the gates and defied the men of the King that came. So they laid a siege to the castle of Kaimes; but the burghers of Segget sent meat to the castle by a secret way that led round the hills; and a pardon came for the Mathers at last, the army withdrew and the Mathers came out, and he swore if ever again in his life he supped of broth or lodged between walls, so might any man do to himself as he had done to the Sheriff Melville.

And for long the tale of Segget grows dim till there came the years of the Killing Time, and the Burneses, James and Peter they were – were taken to Edinburgh and put to the question that they might forswear the Covenant and God. And Peter was old, in the torment he weakened, and by him his son James lay on the rack, and even when the thummikins bit right sore and Peter opened his mouth to forswear, his son was before him singing a psalm so loud that he drowned the voice of Peter; and the old man died, but James was more slow, they threw him into a cell at last, his body broken in many places, the rats ate him there while he still was alive; and maybe there were better folk far in Segget, but few enough with smeddum like his.

His son was no more than a loon when he died, he'd a little farm on the Mowat's land. But he moved to Glenbervie and there took a place, and his folk had the ups and downs of all flesh till the father of Robert Burnes grew up, and grew sick of the place, and went off to Ayr; and there the poet Robert was born, him that lay with nearly as many women as Solomon did, though not all at one time.

But some of the Burneses still bade in Segget. In the first few years of King William's reign it was one of them, Simon, that led the feud the folk of Segget had with the Mowats. For they still owned most of Segget, the Mowats, a thrawn old wife the lady was then, her sons all dead in the wars with the French; and her wits were half gone, it was seldom she washed, she was mean as dirt and she smelt to match. And Simon Burnes and the Segget minister, they prigged on the folk of Segget against her, the weaver folk wouldn't pay their rent, they made no bow when they met the old dame ride out in her carriage with her long Mowat nose.

And at last one night folk far from Segget saw a sudden light spring up in the hills; it waved and shook there all through the dark, and from far and near as the dawn drew nigh, there were parties of folk set out on the roads to see what their fairely was in the hills. And the thing they saw was the smoking Kaimes, a great bit fire had risen in the night and burned the old castle down to its roots, of the stones there stood hardly one on the other, the Segget folk swore they'd all slept so sound the thing was over afore they awoke. And that might be so, but for many a year, before the Old Queen was took to her end and the weaving entirely ceased to pay and folk went drifting away from the Mearns, there were meikle great clocks in this house and that, great coverlets on beds that lay neist the floor; and the bell that rung the weavers awake had once been a great handbell from the hall of the Mowats up on the Kaimes high hill.

A Mowat cousin was the heritor of Kaimes, he looked at the ruin and saw it was done, and left it there to the wind and the rain; and builded a house lower down the slope, Segget below, yew-trees about, and had bloodhounds brought to roam the purviews, he took no chances of innocent sparks floating up in the night from Segget. But the weavers were turning to other things now, smithying and joinering and keeping wee shops for the folk of the farms that lay round about. And the Mowats looked at the Segget burn, washing west to the Bervie flow, and were ill-content that it should go waste.

But it didn't for long, the jute trade boomed, the railway came, the two jute mills came, standing out from the station a bit, south of the toun, with the burn for power. The Segget folk wouldn't look at things, the Mowats had to go to Bervie for spinners, and a tink-like lot of creatures came and crowded the place, and danced and fought, raised hell's delight, and Segget looked on as a man would look on a swarm of lice; and folk of the olden breed moved out, and builded them houses up and down the East Wynd, and called it New Toun and spoke of the dirt that swarmed in Old Toun, round about the West Wynd.

The spinners' coming brought trade to the toun, but the rest of Segget still tried to make out that the spinners were only there by their leave, the ill-spoken tinks, with their mufflers and shawls; the women were as bad as the men, if not worse, with their jeering and fleering in Segget Square; and if they should meet with a farmer's bit wife as she drove into Segget to go to the shops, and looked neat and trig and maybe a bit proud, they'd scraich *Away home, you country cow!*

But the Mowats were making money like dirt. They built a new kirk when the old one fell, sonsy and broad, though it hadn't a steeple; and they lived and they died and they went to their place; and you'd hear the pound of the mills at work down through the years that brought the Great War; and that went by and still Segget endured, outlasting all in spite of the rhyme that some coarse-like tink of a spinner had made:

> Oh, Segget it's a dirty hole,
>   A kirk without a steeple,
> A midden-heap at ilka door,
>   And damned uncivil people.

I

CIRRUS

Segget was wakening as Chris Colquohoun came down the
shingle path from the Manse. Here the yews stood thick, in a
starlings' murmur, a drowsy cheep on the edge of the dawn;
but down the dark, as you reached the door, you saw already
lights twink here and there, in the houses of Segget, the
spinners' wynds, a smell in the air of hippens and porridge.
But she'd little heed for these, had Chris, she went quick as
she looked at the eastern sky, the May air warm in her face
as she turned, north, and went up the Meiklebogs road. So
rutted it was and sossed with the carts that there was a saying
in Segget toun: *There's a road to heaven and a road to hell,
but damn the road to the Meikelbogs.*

But that didn't matter, she wasn't going there, in a while
she turned by a path that wound, dark, a burn was hidden in
the grass, over a stile to the hills beyond. And now, as she
climbed swift up the slope, queer and sudden a memory took
her – of the hills above the farm in Kinraddie, how sometimes
she'd climb to the old Druid stones and stand and remember
the world below, and the things that were done and the days
put by, the fun and fear of the days put by. Was that why the
Kaimes had so filled her sky the twenty-four hours she had
been in Segget?

Now she was up on the lowermost ledge, it lay dark about,
the old castle of Kaimes, no more than a litter of ruined walls,
the earth piled high up over the stones that once were halls
and men-shielded rooms. There were yews growing low in a
corner outbye, they waved and moved as they heard Chris
come. But she wasn't feared, she was country-bred, she
wandered a little, disappointed, then laughed, at herself, to

herself, and the place grew still. Maybe it thought, as did Robert Colquohoun, that her laugh was a thing worth listening for.

She felt her face redden, faint, at that, and she thought how over her face the slow blood would now be creeping, she'd once or twice watched it, bronzed and high in the cheek-bones her face, and a kindly smoulder of grey-gold eyes, she minded how once she *had* wished they were blue! She put up her hand to her hair, it was wet, with the dew she supposed from the dark Manse trees, it was coiled over either ear in the way she had worn it now for over two years.

She turned round then and looked down at Segget, pricked in the paraffin lights of dawn. They were going out one by one as the east grew wanly blind in the van of the sun, behind, in the hills, a curlew shrilled – dreaming up here while the world woke, Robert turning in his bed down there in the Manse, and maybe out-reaching a hand to touch her as he'd done that first morning two years ago, it had felt as though he wakened her up from the dead. . .

So strange it had seemed a long minute she'd lain, half feared, with his hand that touched her so. Then he'd moved, quick breathing, deep in his sleep, and the hand went away, she reached out in the dark and sought it again and held to it, shy. It was winter that morning, they both had slept late from their marriage night; and, as the winter light seeped grey into the best bedroom of Kinraddie Manse, Chris Colquohoun, who had once been married to Ewan, and before that time was Chris Guthrie, just, had lain and thought and straightened things out, like a bairn rubbing its eyes from sleep. . . This was new, she had finished with that life that had been, all the love she had given to her Ewan, dead, lost and forgotten far off in France: her father out in the old kirkyard: that wild, strange happening that had come to her the last Harvest but one there was of the War, when she and another – but she'd not think of that, part of the old, sad dream that was done.

Had that other remembered the happening at all, his last hour of all in a Flanders trench?

And she thought that maybe he had not at all, you did this and that and you went down in hell to bring the fruit of your body to birth, it was nothing to the child that came from your womb, you gave to men the love of your heart, and they'd wring it dry to the last red drop, kind, dreadful and dear, and deep in their souls, whatever the pretence they played with you, they knew it a play and Life waiting outbye.

So she lay and thought, and then wriggled a little – to think these things on her marriage-morn, the hand she held now never held so before! And she peered in his face in the light that came, his hair lay fair on the pillow's fringe, fair almost to whiteness, his skin ivory-white, she saw his brows set dark in a dream, and the mouth came set in a straight line below, she liked his mouth and his chin as well, and his ears that were small and lay flat back, so, and the hand that had tightened again in his sleep – oh! more than that, you liked all of him well, with his kisses in the night that had only just gone, his kisses, the twinkle-scowl in his eyes: *And now it's to bed, but I don't think to sleep.* She had laughed as well, feeling only half-shy. *An awful speak, Robert, for Kinraddie's minister!* and he said *Don't ministers do things like that?* and she'd looked at him swift, and looked quick away. *Maybe, we'll see;* and so they had seen.

She stretched then, softly, remembering that, warm under the quilt her own body felt queer, strange and alive as though newly blessed, and she smiled at that thought, in a way it had been, one flesh she was made with a kirk minister! Funny to think she had married a minister, that this was the Manse, that she was its mistress – oh! life was a flurry like a hen-roost at night, the doors were banging, you flew here and there, were your portion the ree or the corner of a midden you could not foretell from one night to the next.

She got from bed then and into her clothes, agile and quick, and not looking back, if ministers ate as well as they loved, Robert would be hungry enough when he woke. Down in the kitchen she came on Else Queen, ganting as wide as a stable-door, she stopped from that, the Manse's new maid, a handsome quean, and she said *Hello!* Chris felt the blood in the tips of her ears, she saw plain the thing in the great lump's mind. *You call me Mrs Colquohoun, you know, Else. And you get up smart in the morning as well, else we'll need another maid at the Manse.*

Else went dirt-white and closed up her mouth. *Yes – Mem, I'm sorry,* and Chris felt a fool, but she didn't show it, and this kind of thing had just to be settled one way or the other. *My name's not Mem, it's just Mrs Colquohoun. Get the water boiling and we'll make the breakfast. What kind of a range is this that we've got?*

That was that, and she had no trouble at all with meikle Else Queen in Kinraddie Manse, though the speak went out and about the parish that Chris Tavendale, the new minister's new wife, had grown that proud that she made her maid cry *Mem!* every time they met on the stairs, a fair dog's life had that poor Else Queen, it just showed you the kind of thing that happened when a creature got up a bit step in the world. And who was she to put on her airs – the daughter of a little bit farmer, just, and the wife of another, killed in the War. Ay, them that were fond of their men didn't marry as close as that on the death of the first, the Manse and the minister's silver the things that the new Mrs Colquohoun had had in her mind.

Chris heard those stories in the weeks that went, if you bade in Kinraddie and any ill tale were told about you – and you fair had to be an angel in breeks if that weren't done and even then, faith! they'd have said there were unco things under your breeks – the very trees rose and sniggered it to you, the kye lowed the news from every bit gate. But she paid no heed, she was blithe and glad, happed in her Robert and the nearness of him, young Ewan as well, a third by the fire as they sat of a night and the storms came malagarousing the trees down the length and breadth of the shrilling Howe.

Behind and far up you would hear the hills quake, Robert would raise up his head and laugh, the twinkle-scowl in his deep-set eyes — *The feet of the Lord on the hills, Christine!*

Ewan would look up, staring and still, *Who's the Lord?* and Robert would drop his great book and stare in the fire, *That's a tough one, Ewan. But He's Something and sure, our Father and Mother, our End and Beginning.*

Ewan's eyes would open wider at that. *My mother's here and my father's dead.* Robert would laugh and upset his chair, *A natural sceptic — come out of that chair, there's over many of your kind already squatting their hams in the thrones of the mighty!*

So the two of them would crawl round the floor and would growl, play tigers and beasts of like gurring breeds, Ewan with his coolness and graveness forgot, Robert worse than a bairn, Chris sitting and watching, a book in her hand or darning and knitting, but not often those. Robert got angered when she sat and darned. *What, waste your life when you'll soon be dead? You're not going to slave for me, my girl!* And she'd say *But you won't like holes in your socks?* and he'd laugh *When they're holed we'll buy a new pair. Come out for a tramp, the storm's gone down.*

And out they would tramp, young Ewan in bed, the night black under their feet as cold pitch, about them the whistle and moan of the trees till they cleared the Manse and went up by the Mains, with the smell of the dung from its hot cattle-court, and the smell of the burning wood in its lums. You'd see and hear little about you by then, just the two of you swinging up the hill in the dark, till the blow of the wind would catch in your throats as you gained by the cambered edge of the brae.

Around them, dry, the whistle of the whins, strange shapes that rose and were lost in the dark, Robert would stop and would fuss at her collar, pretending he did it to keep out the cold. But she'd grown to know him, the thing that he'd want, she'd put up her arms round close by his throat, and hug him, half-shy, she was still half-shy. He'd told her that once and

Chris had been vexed, lying in his arms, for a sudden moment
she had touched him with lips fierce and sudden with a flame
that came up out of her heart, up out of the years when she
still was unwed: and he'd gasped, and she'd laughed *Do you
call that shy?* Then she'd been half-ashamed and yet glad as
well, and fell fast asleep till the morning came, and they both
woke up and looked at each other, and he said that she
blushed and she hid her face and said that one or the other
was a fool.

But best she minded of those night-time walks the first that
took them up to the hills, a rousting night in December's
close. They came at last on Blawearie's brae, and panting,
looked down on the windy Mearns, the lights of Bervie a lowe
in the east, the Laurencekirk gleams like a scattering of fag-
gots, Segget's that shone as the blurring of stars, these were the
lights of the jute mills there. So they stood a long while and
looked down the brae, Kinraddie below them happed in its sleep;
and Robert fell into a dreaming muse, as he often did, with his
mind far off. Chris said nothing, content though she froze,
after one peek at his stillness beside her. Queer with *him* here
on Blawearie brae, that once was hers, if they walked down
over that shoulder there they'd come to the loch and the
Standing Stones to which she had fled for safety, compassion,
so often and oft when she was a quean. . .

She could smell the winter smell of the land and the sheep
they pastured now on Blawearie, in the parks that once came
rich with corn that Ewan had sown and they both had reaped,
where the horses had pastured, their kye and their stock. And
she minded the nights in the years of the War, nights such as
this when she'd lain in her bed and thought of the times that
would come yet again – Ewan come back and things as before,
how they'd work for young Ewan and grow old together, and
buy Blawearie and be happy forever.

And now she stood by a stranger's side, she slept in his bed,
he loved her, she him, nearer to his mind than ever she had
been to that of the body that lay mouldering in France, quiet
and unmoving that had moved to her kisses, that had stirred

and been glad in her arms, in her sight, that had known the
stinging of rain in his face as he ploughed the steep rigs of
Blawearie brae, and come striding from his work with that
smile on his face, and his clumsy hands and his tongue that
was shy of the things that his eyes could whisper so blithe.
Dead, still and quiet, not even a body, powder and dust he
with whom she had planned her life and her days in the times
to be.

In a ten years' time what things might have been? She might
stand on this hill, she might rot in a grave, it would matter
nothing, the world would go on, young Ewan dead as his
father was dead, or hither and borne, far from Kinraddie: oh,
once she had seen in these parks, she remembered, the truth,
and the only truth that there was, that only the sky and the
seasons endured, slow in their change, the cry of the rain,
the whistle of the whins on a winter night under the sailing
edge of the moon—

And suddenly, daft-like, she found herself weep, quiet, she
thought that she made no noise, but Robert knew, and his arm
came round her.

It was Ewan? Oh, Chris, he won't grudge you me!

Ewan? It was Time himself she had seen, haunting their
tracks with unstaying feet.

But the Spring was coming. You looked from the Manse at the
hills as they moved and changed with each day, the glaur and
the winter dark near gone, the green came quick and far on the
peaks, the blink of the white snow-bonnets grew less, swallows
were wheeling about the Manse trees, down in the fields of the
Mains you could hear the click and spit of a tractor at work,
far up by Upperhill parks rise the baa of the sheep they
pastured now at Bridge End. It seemed to Chris when those
first days came that she'd weary to death with a house and
naught else, not to have fields that awaited her help, help in
the seeding, the spreading of dung, the turning out of the kye
at dawn, hens chirawking mad for their meat, the bustle and
hurry of Blawearie's close. But now as she looked on the land

so strange, with its tractors and sheep, she half-longed to be
gone. It had finished with her, that life that had been, and this
was hers now; books, and her Robert, young Ewan to teach,
and set a smooth cloth on the Manse's table, hide in the little
back room at the top and darn his socks when Robert didn't
see.

He was out and about on the work of the parish, marrying
this soul and burying that, christening the hopeful souls new-
come to pass in their time to marriage and burial. He'd come
back dead tired from a day of his work, Chris would hear him
fling his stick in the hall and cry out *Else, will you run me a
bath?* And because of those strange, dark moods she had met,
Chris seldom met him now on the stairs, she'd wait till he
changed and was Robert again, he'd come searching her out
and tell her the news, and snatch the book from young Ewan's
hand as Ewan squatted in the window-seat, reading. *A prig, a
bookworm!* Robert would cry as he flung the book the other
side of the room; and Ewan would smile in his slow, dark way,
and then give a yell and they'd scuffle a while, while Chris
went down and brought up the tea.

From that room you could see all Kinraddie by day and the
lights of Kinraddie shine as night came, Robert would heave a
great sigh as he sat and looked from Chris to Kinraddie below.
Wearied? she'd ask, and he'd say, *Lord, yes,* and frown and
then laugh: *Looks everywhere that would sour the milk! But
my job's to minister and minister I will though Kinraddie's kirk
grows toom at its head.* And would think a while, *It's near that
already.*

Faith! so it was, nothing unco in that, there was hardly a kirk
in the Mearns that wasn't, the War had finished your fondness
for kirks, you knew as much as any minister. Why the hell
should you waste your time in a kirk when you were young,
you were young only once, there was the cinema down in
Dundon, or a dance or so, or this racket or that; and your
quean to meet and hear her complain she'd not been ta'en to
the Fordoun ball. You'd chirk to your horses and give a bit

smile as you saw the minister swoop by on his bike, with his coat-tails flying and his wee, flat hat; and at night in the bothy some billy or other would mock the way that he spoke or moved. To hell with ministers and toffs of his kind, they were aye the friends of the farmers, you knew.

All the farmers now of Kinraddie were big, but they had as little liking as the bothy for the Reverend Colquohoun and the things he said, Would a man go up to the kirk of a Sabbath to sit down and hear himself insulted? You went to kirk to hear a bit sermon about Paul and the things he wrote the Corinthians, all of them folk that were safely dead; but Kinraddie's minister would try to make out that you yourself, that was born in Fordoun of honest folk, were a kind of Corinthian, oppressing the needy, he meant those lazy muckers the ploughmen. No, no, you were hardly so daft as take that, you would take the mistress a jaunt instead, next Sunday like or maybe the next, up the Howe to her cousin in Brechin that hadn't yet seen the new car you had bought; or maybe you'd just lie happed in your bed, and have breakfast, and read all about the divorces the English had from their wives – damn't, man! they fair had a time, those English tinks! You wouldn't bother your head on the kirk, to hell with ministers of the kind of Colquohoun, they were aye the friends of the ploughmen, you knew.

And Chris would stand in the choir and sing, and sometimes look at the page in her hand and think of the days when she at Blawearie had never thought of the kirk at all, over-busied living the life that was *now* to bother at all on the life to come. Others of the choir that had missed a service would say to her with a shy-like smile, *I'm so sorry, Mrs Colquohoun, I was late*; and Chris would say that they needn't fash, if she said it in Scots the woman would think, *Isn't that a common-like bitch at the Manse?* If she said it in English the speak would spread round the minister's wife was putting on airs.

Robert's stipend was just three hundred pounds, when he'd first told Chris she had thought it a lot, and felt deep in her a prick of resentment that he got so much, when the folk on the land that did all the work that really was work – they got not a third, with a family thrice bigger. But soon she was finding the money went nowhere, a maid to keep and themselves for-bye, this and that charity that folk expected the minister should not only help but head. And they didn't in vain, he'd have given the sark from his back, would Robert, if Chris hadn't stopped him, and syne given his vest. When he heard of a cottar that was needy or ill he'd wheel out his old bike and sweep down the roads, he rode with old brakes and they sometimes gave way, and then he would brake with a foot on the wheel, his thoughts far off as he flew through the stour, if he hadn't a broken neck it was luck. That was his way and Chris liked him for it, though she herself would as soon have thought of biking that way as of falling off the old tower by the kirk, and lippening to chance she would land on her feet.

Well, so, and most likely sparked up with glaur, he'd come to the house where the ill man lay, and knock and cry *Well, are you in?* and go in. And sit him down by the bed of the man, and tell him a story to make him laugh, never mention God unless he was asked, and that was seldom enough, as you knew, a man just blushed if you mentioned God. So Robert would talk of the crops and fees, and *Where is your daughter fee'd to now?* and *The wife looks fine*, and *I'll need to be off*. And syne as he went he'd slip a pound note into the hand of the sick bit man; and he'd take it and redden up, dour, and say *Thank you*; and after Robert went they'd say, *What's a pound? Him that gets paid as much as he does.*

Chris knew that they said that kind of thing, Else told her the news as they worked in the kitchen; and she knew as well how the news went out from the Manse of every bit thing that was there – Ewan, her son, how he dressed, what he said; and the things they said and the things they sang and how much they ate and what they might drink; when they went to bed and when they got up; and how the minister would kiss his wife, without any shame, in the sight of the maid – Oh, Chris knew most and she guessed the rest, all Kinraddie knew better

than she did herself how much she and Robert might cuddle in
bed, and watched with a sneer for sign of a son. . . And somehow, just once, you would hate them for that.

You knew these things, it was daft to get angry, you couldn't
take a maid and expect her a saint, especially a lass from a
cottar house, and Else was no worse than many another. So in
time you grew used to knowing what you did – if you put your
hair different or spoke sharp to Ewan or went up of an evening
to change your frock – would soon be known to the whole of
Kinraddie, with additional bits tacked on for a taste. And if
you felt sick, once in a blue moon, faith! but the news went
winged in the Howe, a bairn was coming, all knew the date,
they would eye you keen as you stood in the choir, and see
you'd fair filled out this last week; and they'd mouth the news
on the edge of their teeth, and worry it to death as a dog with
a bone.

But Chris cooked and cleaned with Else Queen to help, and
grew to like her in spite of her claik, she'd tried no airs since
that very first time, instead she was over-anxious to *Mem!*
Chris couldn't be bothered in a while to stop her, knowing well
as she did that in many ways she was a sore disappointment
to Else.

In other bit places where a quean would fee, with the long-
teethed gentry up and down the Howe or the poverty put-ons
of windy Stonehive, the mistress would aye be glad of a news,
hear this and that that was happening outbye, you'd got it
direct from so and so's maid. But Mrs Colquohoun would just
listen and nod, maybe, polite enough in a way, but with hardly
a yea or a nay for answer. And at first a lassie had thought the
creature was acting up gentry, the minister's wife: but syne
you saw that she just didn't care, not a button she cared about
this place and that, and the things that were happening, the
marryings and dyings, the kissings and cuddlings, the kickings
and cursings, the lads that had gone and the farmers that
broke; and what this cottar had said to his wife and what the
wife had thrown at the cottar. And it fair was a shock, the

thing wasn't natural, you made up your mind to give in your notice and go to a place where you wouldn't be lonesome.

So you'd have done if it hadn't been Ewan, the laddie that came from *her* first bit marriage, so quiet and so funny, but a fine little lad, he'd sometimes come down and sit in the kitchen and watch as you peeled the potatoes for dinner, and tell you things he had read in his books, and ask, *What's a virgin princess like – like you, Else?* And when you laughed and said, *Oh, but bonnier a lot*, he would screw up his brows, *I don't mean that, is she like you under your clothes, I mean?*

You blushed at that, *I suppose she is*, and he looked at you calm as could be. *Well, that's very nice, I am sure* – so polite you wanted to give him a cuddle, and did, and he stood stock still and let you, not moving, syne turned and went out and suddenly went mad in the way that he would, whistling and thundering like a horse up the stairs, with a din and a racket to deafen a body, but fine for all that, you liked a place with a bairn at play; though not aye making a damned row, either.

So you stayed at the Manse as the summer wore on, and you liked it better, and sometimes you'd stop – when outbye or gone up home for a day – in the telling of this or that at the Manse, and be sorry you ever had started the tale. And your father would growl *Ay, and what then?* and you'd say, *Oh, nothing*, and look like a fool, and whoever was listening would be sore disappointed. But you'd minded sudden the face of the mistress, or young Ewan, polite, who thought you looked nice; and it didn't seem fair to tell stories of *them*.

And then, in the August, you were ill as could be, and they didn't send you off home to Segget, as most others would, to the care of your folk. Faith! you half thought as the mistress came in and dosed you with medicine and punched up your pillows and brought you your breakfast and dinner and tea, that she was well pleased to do all the work, you heard her singing washing the stairs, the minister himself went to help in the kitchen, you heard of that through the half-open door, then laugh as the mistress threw water at him and the scamper of feet as he chased her for that. When next dinner came the minister himself came in with the tray and his shirt-sleeves up, you blushed, and tried to cover your nightie, he cried, *All safe, Else, you needn't be shy. I'm old and I'm married, though you're pretty enough.*

And somehow you just didn't tell that outbye, folk would have said that he slept with you next. So you lay in your bed and had a fine rest but that they tormented you to read books and brought great piles to put by your bed, and themselves were so keen that you fair were fashed, they would read you out bits, the mistress or minister, sometimes them both, and you never had had patience with books in your life. You could never get in them or past the long words, some thing there was that stood fast between, though you knit up your brows and tried ever so hard.

And you'd drop the damn book when a minute was past and listen instead to the birds in the trees, as the evening drew in and they chirped in their sleep, and the low of the kye in the parks of the Mains, and see through the swinging of the casement window the light of the burning whins on the hills, smell – you smelled with your body entire – the tingle and move of the harvesting land. And then you'd be wearied and lie half asleep, wondering what Charlie was doing tonight, had he taken some other quean out to the pictures, or was sitting about at some bothy fire? And would he come to see you as he'd written he'd come?

He came that Sunday, and the mistress herself it was brought him up, he stood with his cap in his hands and he blushed, and you did the same, but the mistress didn't. *Now sit down and talk and I'll bring you both tea.* And off she went, and you thought then, as often, she was bonny in a way, in a dour, queer way, with her hair dark-red and so coiled, and the eyes so clear, and the mouth like a man's, but shaped to a better shape than a man's, you stared at the door even after she'd gone, till Charlie whispered, *Do you think she'll come back?* And you said, *No, you gowk,* and peeked at him quiet, and he looked round about as slow as a sow and then cuddled you quick, and that was fair fine, and you wanted a minute to cry in his arms, because you were ill and weak and half-witted. You told yourself that and pushed him away, and he smoothed his hair and said, *You're right bonny*, and you said, *Don't haver*, and he said, *Well, I don't*.

The mistress and Ewan brought up the tea, then left you enough together alone for the two of you to have wedded and bedded, as you thought in a peek of a thought that came. And you looked at Charlie, he was sitting there douce, telling of his place, and the hard work there was, he'd as soon have thought ill as of dancing a jig. Like a fool you felt only half-pleased to know that, of course you didn't want anything to happen, but at least he should try to make out that *he* did, it was only nature a man should want that, especially if you looked as bonny as he said. So you were fell short with him in the end, and he took his leave and the mistress came up. And you suddenly felt a fool altogether, you were weeping and weeping, with her arm about you, safe you felt there and sleepy and tired. She said, *It's all right, Else, sleep, you'll be fine. You're tired now and you've talked so long with your lad*.

But you knew from her look she knew more than that, she knew the thing you yourself had thought; and you said to yourself when she left you that night, *If I ever hear any speak ill of the Colquohouns, I'll — I'll* — and afore you'd decided whether you'd blacken their eyes, or their character, or both, you fell fast asleep.

Sometimes a black, queer mood came on Robert, he would lock himself up long hours in his room, hate God and Chris and himself and all men, know his Faith a fantastic dream; and see the fleshless grin of the skull and the eyeless sockets at the back of life. He would pass by Chris on the stairs if they met, with remote, cold eyes and a twisted face, or ask in a voice that cut like a knife, *Can't you leave me alone, must you always follow?*

The first time it happened her heart had near stopped, she went on with her work in a daze of amaze. But Robert came from his mood and came seeking her, sorry and sad for the queer, black beast that rode his mind in those haunted hours. He said that the thing was a physical remembrance, only that just and Chris not to worry; and she found out that near the end of the War he'd been gassed by an awful gas that they made, and months had gone by ere he breathed well again, and the fumes of that drifting Fear were gone. And sometimes the shadows of that time came back, though his lungs were well enough now, he was sure, though 'twas in the months of his agony he'd known, conviction, terrible and keen as his pain, that there was a God Who lived and endured, the Tortured God in the soul of men, Who yet might upbuild the City of God through the hearts and hands of men of good faith.

But also Chris found it coming on Robert that here he could never do good or do ill, in a countryside that was dying or dead. One night he looked at Chris and said, *Lord! But for you, Christine, I was daft to come here. I'll try for a kirk in some other place, there's work enough to be done in the towns.* And thought for a while, his fair head in his hands. *Would you like a town?*

Chris said, *Oh fine,* and smiled reassurance, but she bit at her lips and he saw, and he knew. *Well, then, not a town, I'll try to find something betwixt and between.*

So he did ere a month was out, news came from Segget its minister was dead, Robert brought the news home: *I'm to try for his kirk.* And Chris said, *Segget?* and Robert said *Yes,* and Chris quoted the bit of poetry there was, somebody they said in Segget had made it:

> Oh, Segget it's a dirty hole,
> A kirk without a steeple,
> A midden-heap at ilka door
> And damned uncivil people.

Robert laughed, *We'll make them both civil and clean.* Chris said, *But you haven't yet gotten the kirk,* and he said, *Just wait, for I very soon will.*

Three Sundays later they set out for Segget, Robert to preach there and Chris to listen, it was April, quiet and brown in the fields, drowsy under a blanket of mist that cleared as the sun rose, leaving the hills corona'd in feathery wispings of clouds, Chris asked their name, and Robert said, *Cirrus. They bring fine weather and they're standing still. There's little wind on the heights today.*

And Chris on her bicycle suddenly felt young, younger far than she'd felt for years, Robert beside her on his awful bike, it made a noise like a threshing machine, collies came barking from this close and that, but Robert ground on and paid them no heed, scowling, deep in his sermon, no doubt. But once he swung round. *Am I going too fast?* and Chris said, *Fast? It's liker a funeral*, and he came from the deeps of his thoughts and laughed. *Oh, Chris, never change and grow English-polite! Not even in Segget, when we settle in its Manse!*

Syne he said of a sudden, a minute or so later, they were past Mondynes and Segget in sight: *Do you mind how Christ was tempted of the devil? And so was I till you spoke just now, I'd made up my mind I'd butter them up, in the sermon I preached — just for the chance of getting out of Kinraddie, settled in Segget, and on with some work. Well, I won't. . . By God, I'll give them a sermon!*

The old minister had died of drink, fair sozzled he was, folk said, at the end; and his last words were, so the story went, *And what might the feare's prices be today?* No doubt that was just a bit lie that they told, but faith! he'd been greedy enough for his screw, with his long grey face and his bleary eyes and his way that he had of speaking to a man, met out in the street or down by the Arms, as though he were booming from the pulpit himself: *Why didn't I see you in the kirk last Sabbath?* And a billy would redden and give a bit laugh, and look this way and that, were he one of New Toun. But more than likely, were he one of the spinners, he'd answer: *Maybe because I wasn't there!* in the awful twang that the creatures spoke; and go off and leave old Greig sore vexed, he'd never got over the fact that the spinners cared hardly a hoot for kirk session or kirk.

Ah well, he was a dead and a two-three came to try for his pulpit, more likely his stipend, two old men came, each buttered up Segget, you'd have thought by the way the creatures blethered the Archangel Michael could have come to Segget, and bought a shop, and felt at home as he sat at the back and sanded the sugar. Folk took that stite with a dosing of salts, then the third man came and some stories with him, 'twas the Reverend Robert Colquohoun of Kinraddie, he'd been down there only a bare two years, and half his congregation had gone, they'd go anywhere but listen to him, he was aye interfering and preaching at folk that had done him no harm, couldn't he leave them a-be? Forbye that he'd married a quean of the parish, and if there's a worse thing a minister can do than marry a woman that knows the kirk folk, it's only to suck sweeties under the pulpit in the time he's supposed to be in silent prayer.

Well, Mr Colquohoun, he didn't suck sweets, but he did near everything else, folk said, and most of Segget, though it thronged to hear him, had no notion to vote for the creature at all.

But when he was seen stride up to the pulpit, and he leaned from the pulpit rails and he preached, the elders were first of all ta'en with his way, and the old folk next with the thing that he preached, not the mealy stuff that you'd now hear often, but meaty and strong and preached with some fire – and man! he fairly could tell a bit tale!

For he took his text from a chapter in Judges, his sermon on Gath and the things that the Jew childe Samson did, how at last the giant was bound to a pillar but he woke from the stupor and looked round about, and cried that the Philistines free him his bonds; and they laughed and they feasted, paying him no heed, sunk in their swing-like glaurs of vice. Their gods were idols of brass and of gold, they lived on the sweat and the blood of men, crying one to the other, *Behold, we are great, we endure, and not earth itself is more sure. Pleasure is ours, and the taste of lust, wine in our mouths and power in our hands*; and the lash was heard on the bowed slave's back, they had mercy on neither their kith nor their kin.

And Samson woke and looked round again, he was shorn of his hair, bound naked there, in the lights of the torches, tormented and chained. And then sudden the Philistines felt the walls rock and they looked them about and saw the flames wave, low and sharp in a little wind; and again about them the great hall groaned, and Samson tore down the pillars of the roof, and the roof fell in and slew him and them. . . And Samson was rising again in our sight, threatening destruction unless we should change, and free both him and the prisoners chained in the littered halls of our secret hearts.

And maybe it was because it was Spring, new-come, the sun a long, drowsy blink in the kirk, and folk heard the voice of the Reverend Colquohoun like the wind they'd hear up under the hills, fine and safe as they listened below, and who could he mean by Samson but them, ground down by the rents they'd to pay the Mowats? Maybe it was that and maybe it was because folk aye had prided themselves in Segget in taking no heed of what others said, that they licked up the sermon like calves at a cog; and a fair bit crowd watched Robert Colquohoun, him and his wife, she seemed decent and quiet, mount on their bikes and ride home to Kinraddie.

Robert said to Chris, *That's the end of my chance. But I'm glad I preached what I felt and thought.* But Chris had a clearer vision than his, *They liked the sermon and I think they liked you. They hadn't a notion what the sermon meant – themselves the Philistines and someone else Samson.*

Robert stared. *But I made it plain as plain.* Chris laughed, *To yourself; anyhow, we'll see.* And they rode to Kinraddie, and the days went by, Robert didn't believe he would head the leet. But he found out, for fun, all he could about Segget, from papers and Else and lists and old books, there was less than a thousand souls in Segget, and most of them lost, if you trusted Else.

Half of the Segget folk worked at the mills – the spinners, as the rest of Segget called them; the others kept shops or were joiners or smiths, folk who worked on the railway, the land, the roads, and the gardens of Segget House. Robert found an old map of the place and renewed it, playing as a boy with a toy town.

Chris leaned on his chair and looked over his shoulder, his fingers nimble in limning New Toun (where the folk had gone when the spinners came), Old Toun and its winding jumble of lanes that bunched and clustered around the West Wynd. South was the Arms, in the Segget Square, the East Wynd dotted with a joiner's, a school, a tailor's shop, a grocery, a sutor's – *and the Lord knows what,* Robert said as his pen swooped down the Wynd to the Segget Square. Then it wheeled about and went up The Close to the post-office-grocery-shop combined, dotted the Segget smiddy beyond, and syne lost itself in the Segget slums. . . Chris saw on the northern out-skirts of Segget two dots for the Manse and the steepleless kirk, and over to the west another one still, Segget House, where the Mowats lived, the old mill-owner, new-dead, said Else, and his son, young Stephen at an English college.

And Robert would whistle as he looked at his map – *What mightn't a minister do in Segget, with the help of young Mowat or the folk of the schools? And sutors are atheists, bound to have brains, and extremely religious, all atheists are. One could do great things with a village League. . .*

Then he would laugh. *Just playing with bricks! Ewan, where are those toys you've outgrown?*

The news that he'd topped the leet at the poll was brought to Robert by an elder of Segget, it was Else who opened the door for the creature, she knew him well, but she didn't let on. It was wee Peter Peat, the tailor of Segget, his shop stood midway the wind of Easy Wynd, with his house behind it, he thought it a castle. And he spoke right fierce, and he'd tell a man, before you were well in the lithe of his door, that he made a fine neighbour to those that were good, the best of friends to

his friends, he was, but God pity the man that fell out with
him, he'd never forgive an injury, never. And he was the biggest
Tory in Segget, the head of the Segget Conservative branch,
and an awful patriot, keen for blood; but he'd loup in his shoes
as he heard his wife, Meg Peat that was slow and sonsy to
look at, come into the shop, she'd cry *Peter, I'm away. Mind
the fire and have tea set ready*; and he'd quaver, *Ay, Meg*, like
an ill-kicked cur. But soon's she was gone he'd look fierce as
ever, ready to kill you and eat you forbye, and running his tape
up and down your bit stomach as though he were gutting you
and enjoying it.

Well, here he was standing, fierce as a futret. *Is the Reverend
Mr Colquohoun indoors?* And Else said, *I'll see; what name
shall I tell him?* And he said *Gang and tell him Peter Peat's
here.*

Else went and found the minister in his study, and the
minister said *Peat?* and looked at the mistress; and the mistress smiled in the quiet way she had, and shook her head, and
the minister shook his. *Still, kindling or peat, I suppose I'd
best see him!*

Else went down the stairs to where Peter stood. *Come in,
and wipe your feet on the mat.* He looked as though he'd have
liked to wipe them on *her*, but he came in, fierce in his five feet
two, the minister was waiting and rose when he came. *I've
come from Segget*, Else heard the thing say, and the minister
answered as she closed the door, *Oh, yes? Well, won't you sit
down, Mr Peat?*

And then, half an hour or so after that, Chris heard the
closing of the Manse front door and syne the scamper of feet
on the stairs, she thought it was Ewan come in from his play.
But instead it was Robert, he burst into the room, his face was
flushed and he caught her arms, and plucked her up from the
chair she sat in, and danced her half round the great-windowed
room. She gasped, *What is't?* and he said *What, that? Peter
Peat, the tailor of Segget, of course.* Then he dropped in the
chair from which he had plucked her, and sat there panting,
still holding her hands. *Christine, you're now looking at*

Segget's minister. And he's promised that never as long as he lives he'll pray for All-but the Prince of Wales!

He told the story he'd gotten from Peter, and Chris heard it later amended by Else, a warning that folk in a pulpit speak plain. He was fell religious, wee Peter Peat, an elder of the kirk and twice every Sunday he'd nip up and down the pews with the bag; and look at you sharp to see what you put in. And once he cried out to Dalziel of Meiklebogs, that was stinking with silver but fair was right canny. *No, no, I'll not have a button from you!* And Meiklebogs reddened like a pig with rash, and dropped a half-crown in the bag by mistake, he was so took aback and affronted-like. That was back a good while, in the days of old Nichols, the last minister but one, he was, as proud and stuck-up as a hubbley-jock, English, and he never learned to speak right; and his prayers at first had fair maddened Peat. For when he came to the bit about Royalty, and he'd pray for the birn with might and with main, he'd finish up *And all but the Prince of Wales!*

Now Peat he was Tory and fond of the Prince, he went home to his wife in a fair bit stew, *What the hell ails him at the Prince of Wales that he blesses all but him, I would like to know?* And at last he tackled old Nichols on the matter, and the creature gave a bit sniftering laugh, and said to Scotch ears he supposed that *All-but* was how it sounded when he said *Albert.* And he spoke this slow, in a sneering bit way, as though he thought Scotch ears were damn poor ears, mostly bad in the need of a clean — when manners were being given out he hadn't even the manners to stay and receive his, Peter Peat said.

Chris woke on the morning of the move to Segget with a start of fear she had over-slept. It was May, and the light came round about five, red and gold and a flow of silver down the parks that she knew so well, she got from bed at the very first blink. Robert yawned and sat up and remembered the day, and dived for his clothes, no bath this morning she told him as each struggled into clothes. He said, *Ah well, I'm not very foul*, and she thought that funny, and giggled and tangled her hair with her dress; and he said, *Let me help*, and his help was a hinder, it was only an excuse to take her and kiss her, this day of all!

She pushed him away at last and he went, whistling, two steps at a time down the stair, Chris heard Else moving already in the kitchen and when she got down found breakfast near ready, and Else all excitement, and young Ewan up, his knickers pulled on the wrong way in his hurry. She'd to alter that and try answer his questions, and run to help Robert with the very last kist, full up to the brim with books and suchlike; and he swore at the thing and Chris sat on the top, and Ewan came running and jumped there as well, and it closed with a bang, and they all of them cheered.

They sat down to breakfast, famished already. Suddenly Else came running in – *Mem, it's started to rain!* with her face as though it were raining ink, and thick ink forbye. So Chris had to quiet her, and see Ewan ate, and Robert forbye, excited as Else. Then they heard down the road the burr of a lorry, and Else came again: *It's Melvin from Segget.*

So it was, they'd hired him to do the Manse flitting, and had heard his character redd up by Else. He kept the only hotel in Segget, the Segget Arms that stood in the Square, the other inn down at the foot of West Wynd had been closed when the local option came. Will Melvin had been right well pleased over that, he said if this was their Prohibition, then he for one was all for the thing. He'd a face like a cat, broad at the eyes, and he'd spit like a cat whenever he spoke; he aye wore a dickey and a high, stiff collar and a leather waistcoat, and leggings and breeks, and he drove the two cars on hire in Segget, and carted folks' coals and attended the bar when Jim the potman, that folk called The Sourock, was down with the awful pains in his wame.

Will Melvin had married fell late in life, an Aberdeen woman, right thin and right north, she kept a quick eye on the bar and the till. And if she heard a billy give a bit curse, as a spinner or a cottar might do from outbye, knowing no better, they weren't Segget folk, she'd cry out sharp in the thin Aberdeen: *None of your Blasting and Blaspheming in here.* So folk called her the Blaster and Blasphemer for short, and if thoughts could have burned she'd have needed to go and take out a life insurance for fire.

Well, here was Will Melvin, he sat in the kitchen, but got to his feet when Chris came in. *Good morning, Mem,* and Chris said *Good morning,* and he asked, *Will I start then to load her up?* meaning the lorry, Chris saw, not herself. And he said he had Muir, the gravedigger, to help, and Chris called in Robert, and he came and scowled because he was thinking of some other thing. But he said, *Hello, then, are we all ready? Would you like a dram before we begin?* Will Melvin said, genteel, *Just a drop,* and would have sat and waited for the dram by himself but that Chris asked, *Isn't there another with you?*

So John Muir was brought in from his seat in the lorry, he was big and cheery and buirdly, John Muir, a roadman of Segget, and the two had their dram, and John Muir as he drank began to tell them of the awful time he'd once had with a grave. He'd aye a horror of premature burial, a fell few there were that were buried like that, when you dug up the coffins of folk of old time and the boards fell agley you would sometimes see, through the shrouds, the bones all bulging and twisted, the creatures had struggled down there in the earth, not dead at all, gasping for breath. . .

Well, he'd been thinking of that one night as he went to dig a new grave by the kirk, it was windy weather on the winter's edge. He'd only finished digging the hole, and turned about, and straightened his back, when the earth gave way and his feet as well. Next minute his head went over his heels and flat in a puddle of red earth he went, right down at the bottom of the grave he had dug, his head half-jammed in under his shoulder. He nearly fainted with the awful shock, syne cried for help as loud as he could. But he heard long nothing, it was winter time, the light was waning up on the hills, he looked up and knew before long he'd be dead. And he cried again and as

luck would have it the old minister heard his bit yowl, and
came canny and slow down through the graves, and looked in
the hole where John Muir was lying. And he said: *Who is't?*
and John Muir was sore vexed. *Oh, we've been introduced,* he
cried back, *so stand on no ceremony — damn't, get a ladder!*

Maybe that was why he still gleyed that way and went with
a kind of twist to his shoulder, Chris thought; but Robert just
laughed and looked at his watch. *Well, this is a flitting, not yet
a funeral.* John Muir set down his glass and gleyed cheery. *Ah,
well, it'll end in that, come time,* you'd have thought he had
something wrong with his stomach. But he gleyed at Chris
cheery as a cock on a ree, and fell to with a will, him and Will
Melvin, and carried out tables and presses and chairs, and kists
and beds and boxes of dishes, and piled them up till the lorry
groaned. Will Melvin near did the same at the sound and went
spitting around like a startled cat. Then they drove off, Robert
went with them to help, Else went as well in the back of the
lorry, clasping the best tea-set to herself, and giving young
Ewan a wave as she went.

The rain had cleared and Chris watched the lorry lurch down
by the Mains in the flare of the sun, they'd got a fine day after
all for the flitting. She liked John Muir, if not Melvin much;
but then it was daft to judge folk at first sight. Young Ewan
came running and asked for a piece, they sat together in the
half-tirred rooms, and ate some biscuits and looked at each
other, with the bizz of a fly on the stripped window-panes.
Ewan asked why they were moving to Segget. Chris tried to
tell him, and he listened, polite, and then went out and drowsed
in the grass till he heard the lorry returning from Segget.

They loaded up the last of the stuff, John Muir climbed gleying up in its midst, and Chris locked the door and left the key
for the folk of the Mains to come up and get, hid in a little hole
in the wall. Then she went to the lorry where Melvin was
waiting, young Ewan beside him, and climbed in as well; and
the lorry wound out through the bending of yews where long,
long ago the knight Wallace had hidden as the English were
looking for him in the wars.

They saw not a soul as they passed the Mains, then they swung out into the road that led south; and so as they went Chris turned and looked back, at Kinraddie, that last time there in the sun, the moors that smoothed to the upland parks Chae Strachan had ploughed in the days gone by, the Knapp with no woods to shelter it now, Upperhill set high in a shimmer of heat, Cuddiestoun, Netherhill — last of them all, high and still in the hill-clear weather, Blawearie up on its ancient brae, silent and left and ended for you; and suddenly, daft, you couldn't see a thing.

But that went by, Chris glad to be gone; and the lorry switched from the main road's ribbon up by the old thatched toun of Culdyce, and she saw the Howe, spread out like a map, there was Drumlithie down in its hollow, a second Segget, but steepled enough. Mondynes that stood by the Bervie Water, Fettercairn, where the soldiers of the widow Finella had lain in wait to mischieve King Kenneth. All the parks were set with their hoeing squads, four, five, at a time they swung by the drills, here and there the hindermost man would stop, and straighten up slow, a hand at his back, to look at the lorry — whose could it be? And all the long line would straighten up, slow, and catch a glimpse of Chris, in her blue, and young Ewan in his, with his straight, black hair.

And there, as they swung by the Meiklebogs farm, the hills to the right, at last lay Segget, a cluster and crawl of houses white-washed, the jute-mills smoking by Segget Water, the kirk with no steeple that rose through the trees, the houses of the spinners down low on the left, though Chris didn't know that these were their houses. Then the lorry puffed up to the old kirk Manse, on the fringe of Segget, and Chris saw the lawn piled in a fair hysteria of furniture. She jumped down and stood a minute at gaze, in the shadows, the shadows the new yews flung, the grass seemed blue in the blaze of the heat.

Then as Melvin backed back the lorry and Ewan went running out over the lawn to the door, Robert came out and saw Chris and waved, and was pleased as though they'd been parted a year. He dropped the end of the press he'd picked up, near dropped it down on the toes of Muir (who gleyed as cheery as though 'twas a coffin) and cried to Chris, *Come and see the new study.* And nothing could content him but up she must go, leaving Melvin below to glower after the gowks.

Then two men came talking up the Manse drive, Dalziel of the Meiklebogs and one of his men, Robert went down to see who they were. Dalziel said, *Ay, you'll be the minister?* and smiled, he was bad in the need of a shave, of middle height though he looked a lot less, so broad in the shoulders, hands like hams; and he smiled slow and shy with his red, creased face, and he said that he'd seen the lorries go by, and he knew right well the sore job it was to do a flitting without much help. And all the time he was smiling there, shy, he looked to Chris like a Highland bull, with his hair and his horns and maybe other things: there was something in his shyness that made her shiver. Beside him Robert seemed like a boy from school, thin and tall with his slim, thin face; and back of Robert was Else as she looked, not slim at all but big and well-made, her head flung back in that way she had and a look on her face as much as to say, *Good Lord, what's this that has come to us now?*

Then they all fell to carrying in the Manse gear, and Chris fled here and there in the house, a great toom place that shambled all ways, there were stairs that started and suddenly finished and steps that crumbled away into gloom, down to old cellars that never were used. And sometimes you'd think you would come to a room, and you didn't, you came slap-bang on another, the windows fast-closed and stiff with the heat. Chris told where and how to place all the things, and Meiklebogs and Else carried up the beds, and set them together. Chris heard Else give orders and Meiklebogs answer, canny and shy, *You'll be the new minister's bit maidie?* Else said, *There's damn the MAIDIE about me;* and Chris didn't hear more, but she guessed a bit.

John Muir came to her, and asked where to put a press and a bed and some other things she'd brought from Blawearie the first flit she made. And she didn't know, in that crowding of rooms, till he said, *Would you maybe like the gear altogether?* and she said, *Just that, in a small-like room.* So he carried the bed up and back through the Manse, to a high-built room, it was three stairs up. The place was so lost that the cleaners had missed it, there were cobwebs looped from the walls like twine. But through the window, when you swung it out wide, you saw sudden hills rise up in your face, with below you the roll of long, grass-grown mounds. John Muir let down the bed with a bang, the great heavy bed that had once been her father's. Chris asked him what were the ruins up there, and he said, *You've heard of the Kaimes of Segget?*

Chris leaned from the window and looked to the west. *And what's that to the left, that hiddle of houses? — Where the spinners bide,* he told her, she stared, she had thought them abandoned byres or pig-sties. But Muir just gleyed and said they were fine — *good enough for the dirt that's in them. If you gave good houses to rubbish like them, they'd have them pig-rees in a damn short while. They're not Segget folk, the spinners, at all.*

Chris said *Oh!* and looked at him, quiet, then they went down to bring up the rest; and there was Meiklebogs met on the stair, smiling shy at that sumph of a maid. And John Muir thought, *You'd think he'd have quieted by now. A man that can't keep off the women by the time he's reaching to sixty or so should be libbed and tethered in a cattle-court.*

Near twelve they'd the most of the furniture in, all but a long table brought from the north, from the Manse of Robert Colquohoun's old father, solid and oak and a hell of a weight. And then Else called that the dinner was ready, Chris said they all must stay and have dinner. Robert said *Let's eat it out on this table.*

So Else served them the dinner in the shade of the yews, and sat down herself when she'd finished with that, Meiklebogs waiting to see where she sat, and sitting down next with a shy-like smile. Robert came out, getting into his coat, and stood at the end of the table a minute and bent his head, fair in the sunny weather, and said the grace, the grace of a bairn; and they bent and listened, all but young Ewan:

> God bless our food,
>> And make us good.
> And pardon all our sins,
>> For Jesus Christ's sake.

Then they all ate up, Muir, Melvin, and Meiklebogs, and the fee'd man that blushed and was shy, not just looked it. Chris liked him best, with that sudden compassion that always came on her as she looked at one of his kind — that conviction that he and his like were the REAL, they were the salt and savour of earth. She heard him, shy-like, say *Ay, I've a spoon*, as Else was asking, and knew by the way that he mouthed the *spoon* that he came from the North, as she did herself. And faith! so he did, like her 'twas from Echt, and he knew fine the place where once she had bidden. Cairndhu in the Barmekin's lithe. And he fair buckled up and he lost his shyness, *Ay, then, you're a Guthrie?* and she said that she was, and he said that they minded him long up in Echt, John Guthrie, her father, the trig way he farmed: and Chris felt herself colour up with sheer pleasure, her father could farm other folk off the earth!

Then she fell in a dream as she heard them talk, the rooks were cawing up in the yews, and you thought how they'd fringed your pattern of life — birds, and the waving leafage of trees: peewits over the lands of Echt when you were a bairn with your brother Will, and the spruce stood dark in the little woods that climbed up the slopes to the Barmekin bend; snipe sounding low on Blawearie loch as you turned in unease by the side of Ewan, and listened and heard the whisp of the beech out by the hedge in the quiet of the night; and here now rooks and the yews that stood to peer in the twisty rooms of the Manse. How often would you know them, hear them and see them, with what things in your heart in what hours of the dark and what hours of the day, in all the hours lying beyond this hour when the sun stood high and the yew-trees drowsed?

But she shook herself and came out of her dream, back to the table and the sun on the lawn, daft to go prowling those copses of night where the sad things done were stored with the moon. Here was the sun, and here was her son, Ewan, and Robert, the comrade of God, and those folk of Segget she had yet to know, and all the tomorrows that waited her here.

But that night she had slept in fits and in starts, waking early in that strange, quiet room, by the side of Robert, sleeping so sound. Then it was the notion had suddenly arisen, to come up to the Kaimes, as here she was now, watching the east grow pale in the dawn.

Pale and so pale: but now it was flushed, barred sudden with red and corona'd with red, as though they were there, the folk who had died, and the sun came washed from the sea of their blood, the million Christs who had died in France, as once she had heard Robert preach in a sermon. Then she shook her head and that whimsy passed, and she thought of Robert — his dream just a dream? Was there a new time coming to the earth, when nowhere a bairn would cry in the night, or a woman go bowed as her mother had done, or a man turn into a tormented beast, as her father, or into a bullet-torn corpse, as had Ewan? A time when those folk down there in Segget might be what Robert said all men might be, companions with God on a terrible adventure? Segget: John Muir, Will Melvin, Else Queen; the folk of the grisly rees of West Wynd—

Suddenly, far down and beyond the toun there came a screech as the morning grew, a screech like an hungered beast in pain. The hooters were blowing in the Segget Mills.

II

CUMULUS

Crossing the steep of the brae in the dark, by the winding path from the Manse to the Kaimes, Chris bent her head to the seep of the rain, the wet November drizzle of Segget. Then she minded a wall of the Kaimes still stood, and ran quick up the path to stand in its lee. That gained, she stood and panted a while, six months since she'd been up here in the Kaimes – only six months, she could hardly believe it!

It felt like years – long and long years – since she'd worked as a farmer's wife in Kinraddie. Years since she'd felt the beat of the rain in her face as she moiled at work in the parks. How much had she gained, how much had she lost? – apart from her breath, she had almost lost that!

She felt the wall and then leant against it, wrapped in her ulster, looking at Segget, in its drowse of oil-lamps under the rain. Safe anyhow to go home this time. . . And she smiled as she minded last time she had climbed to the Kaimes, and Segget had seen her go home – by the tale they told all Segget had seen her and stared astounded, a scandalled amaze—

But indeed, it was only Ag Moultrie that morning, as ill-luck would have it, who saw her go home. She had gone out early to the school to redd up, she went heavy with sleep and her great mouth a-agant, as you well might believe, though she didn't tell that. Folk knew her fine, all the Moultries forbye. Rob Moultrie had once been the saddler of Segget, his shop lay down by the edge of the Square. And as coarse an old brute as you'd meet, was Rob Moultrie, though a seventy years old and nearing his grave. 'Twas only a saddler's shop in name now, the trade had clean gone this many a year. There was still a britchen or so in the shop, and a fine bit bridle Rob

Moultrie had made in the days long syne when he still would work. But his trade had gone, and his sweirty had come, he was never a popular man in the toun; he couldn't abide the sight of the gentry, or the smell of the creatures either, he said, and that was why he was Radical still.

And if he went on a dander somewhere, along the road and he'd hear a car, toot-tooting behind him, would he get off the road? Not him, he'd walk on bang in the middle, dare any damn motorist try run him down. So sometimes he'd come back to Segget from a walk, step-stepping cannily along the bit road, with a two-three motorists hard at his heels, toot-tooting like mad, and the shovers red-faced. Mrs Moultrie would be looking from the window and see, and cry as he came, *Losh, Rob, you'll be killed!* And he'd stop and glower at her with his pocked old face, and his eyes like the twinkling red eyes of a weasel, and sneer, the old creature, shameful to hear. *Ay, that would be fine – no doubt you'd get up to your old bit capers. Get out of my way!* And he'd lift his stick, maybe more than do that, syne hirple over to his armchair, and sit there and stare in the heart of the fire or turn to the reading of his old bit Bible.

For he'd never forgiven Jess Moultrie, the fact that more than a forty years before, when he'd met her and married her, she'd been with a bairn. She told how it was before she would marry, and he'd glowered at her dour: *More fool that I am. But I'm willing to take you and your shame as well.* And he took her, and the bairn was born, young Ag, no others came and maybe that was why he still kept up the sneer at his wife. But she would say nothing, she was patient and bowed, little, with a face like a brown, still pool; and she'd say not a word. getting on with her work, making ready the supper for Ag when she came.

She cleaned out the school and the hall and such places, did Ag, and in winter made the school broth, as nasty a schlorich as ever you'd taste. She looked like a horse ta'en out of a plough, and her voice was a neigh like a horse's as well, and she'd try to stand up for her mother with old Rob. *Don't speak*

that way to my mother! she would cry, and he'd look at her
dour, *Ay, ay, no doubt she's precious in your sight. You had
only one mother, though three or four fathers*; and Ag more
than likely would start to greet then, she wasn't a match for
the thrawn old brute, though a good enough one for most
other folk. And faith! she'd a tongue for news that was awful.
Ake Ogilvie called her the Segget Dispatch, she knew everything that happened in Segget, and a lot that didn't, but she
liked best to tell of births and funerals and such-like things;
and how the daughter of this or that corpse no sooner looked
on the dead than broke down — *and fair roared and grat when
she saw him there.* So folk called her the Roarer and Greeter
for short.

Well, then, it was her, to get on with the tale, as she blinked
her way in that morning in May, saw a woman come down the
hill from the Kaimes, and stopped dumbfoundered: Who
could she be?

Ag was real shocked, for the Kaimes was the place where
spinners and tinks of that kind would go, of a Sabbath evening, and lie on the grass and giggle and smoke and do worse
than that — Ay, things that would leave them smoking in hell,
as the old minister said that they would. So no decent folk
went up there at night, this creature of a woman was surely
a tink. And Ag gave a sniff, but was curious forbye, and crept
canny along in the lithe of the dyke that hemmed in the
lassies' playground from the lads'. So she waited there till the
woman went by, hurrying bare-headed, with a stride and a
swing and a country-like gait. And then Ag Moultrie near
fainted with joy, though she didn't tell you that when she told
you the story, she saw that the woman was Mrs Colquohoun,
the wife of the new minister of Segget.

Well, afore the day was well started all Segget had heard
that the wife of the new minister had been seen by Ag Moultrie
up on the Kaimes, she'd been out all night with a spinner up
there, Ag had seen them cuddling and sossing in the grass.
Folk said, *By God, she's wasted no time; and who would the
spinner have been, would you say?* Old Leslie heard the story

in the smiddy and he said the thing was Infernal, just. Now, he minded when he was a loon up in Garvock — And the sweat dripped off him, pointing a coulter, and he habbered from nine until loosening-time, near, some story about some minister he'd known; but wherever that was and why it had been, and what the hell happened, if anything ever had, you couldn't make head nor tail if you listened; and you only did that if you couldn't get away.

Old Leslie was maybe a fair good smith: he was sure the biggest old claik in Segget. He'd blether from the moment you entered his smiddy, he'd ask how the wife and the bairns all were, and your brother Jock that was down in Dundon, and your sister Jean that was in a sore way, and your father that was down with the colic or the like, and your grandfather, dead this last fifty years.

And syne he'd start on your cousins, how they were, and your uncles and aunts and their stirks and their stots, their maids and all that were in their gates: till your hair would be grey and your head fair dizzy at the thought you'd so many relations at all. And his face would sweat like a dripping tap as he hammered at the iron and habbered at you and then he'd start some story of the things he'd done or seen or smelt when a loon up in Garvock, and the day would draw in, the night would come on, and the stars come out, he'd have shod all your horses and set all the coulters and you near were dead for lack of some meat; but *that* damned story wouldn't have finished, it would be going on still with no sign of an end, he'd start it the next time he saw you or heard you, though you were at the far side of a ten-acre field — as you took to your heels and run.

Well, about the only soul that couldn't do that was his son, Sim Leslie, the policeman of Segget. He had joined the police and had been sent back to Segget, and still bade with his father, he was used to the blether: and folk said if he listened with a lot of care, for a twenty years or so at a stretch, he at least might find out what really *had* happened that time when his father was a loon up on Garvock. Folk called him Feet,

Sim Leslie the bobby, he'd feet so big he could hardly coup, there was once he was shoeing a horse in the smiddy, an ill-natured brute from the Meiklebogs; and the creature lashed out at him fair and square and caught him such a clout on the chest as would fair have flattened any ordinary man. But young Sim Leslie just rocked a wee bit, his feet had fair a sure grip on Scotland.

Well, Feet heard the story of Mrs Colquohoun, from his father, as the two of them sat at dinner. And he kittled up rare, there was something in this, and maybe a chance of promotion at last. So he went and got hold of Ag Moultrie, the sumph, and pulled out his notebook with his meikle red fingers, and asked was she sure 'twas the minister's wife? And Ag said *Ay*, and Feet made a bit note; and then he seemed stuck, and he said, *You're sure?* And Ag said *Ay, I'm as sure as death*. Feet made another note, and scratched at his head, and swayed a bit in his meikle black boots. *It fair was her?* And Ag said *Ay*; and by then it seemed just about dawning on Feet it really was her and nobody else.

But Ag was real vexed, as she told to folk, she hadn't wanted to miscall a soul, *God knows I'm not a body to claik*; and she said when she'd finished with Feet and his questions she went home and sat down and just Roared and Grat, so sorry she was for the new minister. And she'd tell you some more how the woman had looked, her face red-flushed, with a springy walk; and if you were married you well could guess why all of that was – damn't man, 'twas fairly a tasty bit news!

That night Feet went up and prowled round the Manse, with his bull's-eye held in his hand and his feet like the clopping of a Clydesdale heard on the ground. He didn't know very well what he was there for, or what he would say if Mrs Colquohoun saw him; but he was awful keen on promotion. And he said he was fine at detective-work, like, and if honest merit were given its reward they'd make him a real detective ere long. And Ake Ogilvie said in his tink-like way *A defective, you mean? God, ay, and certificated!*

Well, Feet had prowled round to the back of the Manse, and

had stopped to give his head a bit scratch; when sudden the
window above him opened and afore he could move there
came a bit splash and a pailful of water was slung down his
back. He spluttered and hoasted and his lamp went out, when
he came to himself he was shaking and shivering, but the
Manse was silent and still as the grave. He thought for a
while of arresting the lot – ay, he would in the morning, by
God; and turned and went home, running home stretches to
change his bit sark, in case he might catch a cold from his
wetting.

And, would you believe it, next day as he sat in his office
writing up his reports, his mother said, *Here's a woman to see
you.* And Feet looked up and he knew the quean, Else Queen,
the maid at the Manse it was; 'twas said she'd been brought
up as a lassie in Segget, though her father had moved to
Fordoun since then, now she was fair a great brute of a
woman, with red eyes and hair, and cheeks of like tint. And
she said, *Are you Feet?* and Feet reddened a bit. *I'm Simon
Leslie the policeman of Segget. – Well, I'm the person that
half-drowned you last night; and I've come to tell you when
you want the same, just prowl round the Manse at such a like
hour.*

And she didn't stop only at Feet then, either. She made for
Ag Moultrie and told her the same, she would have her sacked
from her job at the school; and Ag broke down and just Roared
and Grat, she said she'd never said an ill word of any, but what
was the minister's wife doing on the Kaimes? *Looking at the
hills and the sunrise, you fool. Did you never hear yet of folk
that did that?* And Ag said she hadn't; and who ever had?
Folk shook their heads when they heard that tale, if the woman
at the Manse wasn't fair just a bitch, damn't! you could only
suppose she was daft.

Dite Peat heard the story and fair mocked at Feet. *What, you
that were once in the barracks?* he said, *and lived in Dundon,
and can't manage a woman?* And he told a story, 'twas down
in the Arms, about how once when he was living in London

he'd come here, he said, on a leave from the Front, he hired a bit lodging near Waterloo. – And old Leslie that was standing by said *Eh? Would that be the place the battle was at?* and Dite Peat said, *Oh, away to hell,* a coarse way to speak to an old bit man. – Well, Dite had put up in his London room, he saw the landlady was a gey bit quean, fair young and fair sonsy, her man at the Front. And he tried this way and that to get round her, keen for a woman but not a damn fool like some that come back on leave from the Front, they'd spend all their silver on whores, but not Dite, he wanted a gratis cuddle and squeeze.

Well, he waited and waited about for a bit, and half-thought of getting the woman at night, she was only English and they're tinks by nature, it wasn't as though she was decent and Scotch. But she locked up her door and went early to bed till there came one night that he heard her scraich, and he louped from his bed and he went to the door, and there she was standing down in the hall, in her night-gown, the tink, and white as a sheet. She'd a telegram held in her hands as she stood, and was gowking and gobbling at the thing like a cow, choked on the shaws of a Mearns swede. And Dite called down *What's wrong with you, then?* and she laughed and laughed as she looked up at him, she was young, with a face like a bairn, a fool, white, with no guts; like the English queans. And she said *Oh, it's just that my husband's dead,* and laughed and laughed, and Dite licked his lips, it fair was a chance, he saw it and took it.

Well, she wasn't so bad, but far over-thin; and God! she was fair a scunner with her laughing, every now and then she would laugh like an idiot, he supposed that the English did that in their pleasure. So he took her a clout or so in the lug, to learn her manners, and that quietened her down. Oh ay, she was tasty enough in her way.

Some folk in the Arms asked what happened next, did he bide there long? Dite said *Damn the fears. I nipped out next morning, afore she awoke. She might have tried on to get me to marry her.* And he went on to tell what tinks were the

English, they'd rob right and left if you gave them the chance. He gave them damn few, but once out in France—

That fair was a sickener, you put down your glass, or finished the dram and rose up and went out; and Will Melvin looked mad as he well could look, Dite sitting and telling a story like that, sickening customers away from their drinks. But you couldn't do much with a billy like Dite, a dangerous devil when he got in a rage. He looked a tink though he kept a shop, he and his brother, wee Peter the tailor hadn't spoken for years, though they lived next door. His father had lived with Dite till he died, Dite saw to that dying, some said helped it on.

The old man had been one of the roadmender childes, he worked with old Smithie and that fool John Muir, he'd come back with his wages at the end of the week and maybe he'd have spent a shilling on tobacco. And soon's he saw that Dite Peat would fly up and take him a belt in the face, most like, and send him to bed without any meat; and as he lay dying the old man cried to see his other son, wee Peter, the tailor. But Dite snapped *Be quiet, damn you and your wants. You'll see him in hell soon enough with yourself.*

That was hardly the way to speak to your father, him dying and all; and some folk stopped then going to his shop, spinners and the like, they said Dite should be shot; and collected below his windows one night and spoke of taking him out for a belting. But Feet, the policeman, came up and cried *Now, you'll need to be moving if you're standing about here*; and the spinners forgot the thing they'd come on, and took to tormenting the bobby instead, they carried him down the Drumlithie road and took off his breeks and filled him with whisky; and left the poor childe lying drunk in the ditch; and went back and fairly raised hell in the Arms, the Blaster and Blasphemer near scraiched herself hoarse, the spinners had new got a rise in their pay.

Ah well, that was how Dite Peat had escaped, spinners and their like wouldn't trade with him now, though most other folk weren't foolish as that. You went on as before and waited

the time when he and Ake Ogilvie would yet get to grips,
Ake hated Dite Peat as a dog hates a rat.

Chris found it took nearly a fortnight to settle, the whole of
the Manse wanted scrubbing and cleaning, she and Else Queen
were at it all hours, Robert laughed and locked himself in his
room. But he came out to help rig the curtains on rods, both
he and Else were handy and tall, they spent the most of one
long afternoon tacked up to the walls like flies in glue; and
Chris handed up rods and curtains and pictures, and this and
that, and hammers and nails; and Else and Robert would
cling to the walls, by their eyebrows sometimes, or so it would
seem, and push and tug and hammer and pant. Else was willing
and strong and enjoyed it, she'd poise on the edge of a mantel
and cry *Will that do, Mem?* and near twist her neck from her
shoulders to catch a look at some picture or other. Chris would
cry *Mind!* and Else: *Och, I'm fine!* and nearly capsize from her
ledge, and young Ewan, watching below, give a yell of delight.

But at last all things were trig and set neat. That evening,
with Ewan bathed and to bed, Chris found Else yawning wide
as a door, and sent her off to her bed as well. Chris felt she
was almost too tired to rest as she sat in a chair in Robert's
room; and Robert knew and came and made love; and that was
nice, and she felt a lot better. In the quiet and hush of the
evening below you could see the touns drift blue with their
smoke, as though it was they that moved, not the smoke.
Robert sat in his shirt-sleeves, smoking his pipe, planning his
campaign to conquer Segget, as Chris supposed, but she closed
her eyes. In a minute she'd get up and go to her bed.

But Robert jumped up sudden and picked up his coat. *I
know! Let's go and see Segget at night.*

Chris thought *If it wasn't that I am in love – Goodness, how
far I could tell him to go!* But she said not a word of that, but
went down, and he groped in the dark and found her coat, and
she his, and next they were out on the shingle, it crunch-
crunched under the tread of their feet, the moon had come
and was sailing a sky lilac, so bright that the Manse stood

clear as they turned and looked back, the yews etched in ink, beyond them the kirk that hadn't a steeple, set round with its row upon row of quiet graves, the withered grass kindled afresh to green, in long, shadowy tufts that whispered like ghosts. An owlet hooted up on the hill and through the quiet of the night round about there came a thing like a murmur unended, unbegun, continuous, the hum of the touns – and that was queer, most folk were in bed! Chris thought a thought and put it from her mind – an awful woman to have wedded a minister!

Then she slipped her arm in Robert's, beside him, Segget stood splashed in the light of the moon like a hiddle of houses a bairn would build. Their feet were quiet on the unpaved street, they smelt the reek of the burning wood, and Robert said sudden, his voice not a whisper, *It's like walking a town of the dead, forgotten, a ruined place in the light of the moon. Can you think that folk'll do that sometime, far off some night in the times to be, maybe a lad and his lass, as we are, and wonder about Segget and the things they did and said and believed in those little houses? And the moon the same and the hills to watch.*

Chris thought it most likely they would find these enough, the hills and the moon, and not bother about Segget, that lad and that lass in the times to be. So they passed quiet down through the wind of East Wynd, over to the right the hiddling of lanes where the spinners bade, nearer the road and black in the moon the school and the schoolhouse set round with dykes. They passed a joiner's shop to the left, Chris peered at the name and saw ALEC OGILVIE, then came to a place with shops all around, a grocer's shop with D. PEAT on the sill, fat lettering over a shoemaker's – HOGG; and a narrow little front that barked PETER PEAT. Beyond, to the right, a lane wound down to the post-office kept by Macdougall Brown, so Chris had been told, she hadn't been there.

East Wynd to the left was now bare of houses, beyond its dyke was the garden of Grant. And once they heard through the night a crying, some bairn frightened or waked in the dark, and

a voice that called it back to its sleep, all in a drowsy hush
through the night. *There's honeysuckle somewhere*, said Chris,
and stopped to smell, as they came to the Square, *over here by
the saddler's shop.*

But Robert was giving no heed to smells, he had stopped and
he said *My God, what a slummock!* And Chris saw the thing
that had now ta'en his eyes, the War Memorial of Segget toun,
an angel set on a block of stone, decent and sonsy in its stone
night-gown, goggling genteel away from the Arms, as though
it wouldn't, for any sum you named, ever condescend to believe there were folk that took a nip to keep out the chill. . .

Chris thought it was fine, a pretty young lass. But then as
she looked at it there came doubts, it stood there in memory
of men who had died, folk of this Segget but much the same
still, she supposed, as the folk she had known in Kinraddie,
folk who had slept and waked and had sworn, and had lain
with women and had lain with pain, and walked in the whistle
of the storms from the Mounth and been glad, been mad, and
done dark, mad things, been bitter for failure, and tender and
kind, with the kindness deep in the dour Scots blood. Folk of
her own, those folk who had died, out in the dark, strange
places of earth and they set up THIS to commemorate THEM
– this, this quean like a constipated calf!

Robert said *May God forgive them this horror! And look at
the star on its pantomime wand. But still it's a star; not a
bundle of grapes. Folk'll think it a joke when we've altered
things, this trumpery flummery they put up in stone!*

His dream again he could alter things here! *But what kind
of change, Robert, what can you do? Things go on the same as
ever they were, folk neither are better nor worse for the War.
They gossip and claik and are good and bad, and both together,
mixed up and down. This League of the willing folk of Segget
– who'll join it or know what you want or you mean?*

He leaned by the Angel, looked down at her, smiled, cool
and sure of his vision tonight. *Chris, if ever we've a child, you
and I, and when it grows up, it finds that that's true – what
you've said – then I hope it'll come here with Ewan, and a host*

*of others of their own generation, and smash this Memorial
into smithereens for the way that we failed them and left God
out. Change? It's just that men must change, or perish here in
Segget, as all over the earth. Necessity's the drive, the policeman that's coming to end the squabbling stupidities of old*—
Then he laughed. *What, sleepy as that? Let's go back.*

He fair had plenty on his hands that summer, Feet, the policeman, as the days wore to Autumn. First, 'twas the trouble in
the roadman's place, old Smithie and the hay he nicked from
coles and carted home at night to his kye. His house stood
side by side with John Muir's, both under the lee of the kirk
and the Manse, their back doors opened out on the land that
stretched east under the scowl of the hills to the lands that
were farmed by Meiklebogs. Muir kept no stock and he bought
his milk, but old Smith on the chap of dawn would be out, up
out of his bed and round to the byre, where his cows, and his
two young calves were housed, none knew where he bought
the fodder to feed them; and that wasn't surprising, he stole
the damned lot.

He'd look this way and that, he'd a face like a tyke, thin,
and ill-made, with a bushy moustache; and then, as swack as
you like he would loup, canny and careful in over a fence, and
made up a birn of somebody's hay; and be back and breaking
his stones as before when the next bit motor appeared on the
road. Syne at night he would load the lot on his bike and pedal
canny without any light, and nip up through Segget as the
Arms bar opened and folk had gone in for a bit of a nip, none
out to see; and syne he was home, and the cows, as hungry as
hawks, would low, old Smithie would give a bit low as well,
and stuff them with hay and pat at their shoulders, daft-like,
he near was crack about kye, he liked the breath of the
creatures, he said.

Folk said that the cows couldn't be so particular, else they'd
fair get a scunner at *his* bit breath. For he liked a dram and he
took what he liked, he'd no more than peek round the door of
an evening (though the house was his and all the gear in it)

than his daughter would cry *Here's the old devil home!* and her bairns, the bairns of Bruce the porter, would laugh and call him ill names as they liked. And he'd smile and stand there and mumble a while, though he wasn't a fool in the ordinary way; and syne he'd go down to the Arms in a rage and swear that before another night came he'd have Bruce and his birn flung out of his doors, he was damned if he'd stand their insultings longer.

Well, damned he was, for he kept them on, folk would once kittle up with excitement when they heard old Smithie get wild and say that, they'd 'gree with him solemn and say 'twas a shame for a man of Segget to stand what he did; and they'd follow him home when the Arms closed down and stand by the door to hear the din. But all that they'd hear would be Ellen his daughter, fat as a cow at the calving time, cry *Feuch, you old brute, and where have you been?* And Smithie would just mumble and gang to his bed.

He'd another daughter as well as his Ellen, he'd slaved to give her an education; and faith! so he'd done, and made her a teacher. She lived in Dundon and never came south. And the only thing Smithie said that he'd gotten, for all his pains and his chaving for her, was one cigarette: and that wouldn't light.

Well, that Saturday afternoon in July, old Smithie was wearied with chapping at stones, and instead of stealing some hay outbye and rowing it home strapped over his bike, he got on the bike and pedalled near home, till he came to the new-coled hay of Meiklebogs. And old Smithie got off and lighted his pipe and made on he'd got off for nothing but that. There wasn't a soul to be seen round about, the park was hidden, and old Smithie was quick, he nipped in over and pinched some hay, and was back with the stuff strapped on to his bike – so quick that you'd fair have thought it a wonder that his corduroy trousers didn't take fire. But no sooner had he gone than Dalziel jumped up, he'd been hiding all the while in the lee of a cole; and he ran to the close and got his own bike, and followed old Smithie and shadowed him home. Then he went down the toun and collected Feet, and they came on old

Smithie as he entered the byre, the bundle of stolen hay in his hands.

And Feet cried out *Mr Smith, I want you*; and old Smithie looked round and near dropped the birn. *Ay, do you so?* he quavered, and syne the old whiskered creature fairly went daft, he threw the birn in Meiklebogs' face. *Take your damned stuff. I wouldn't poison my kye with such dirt!*

Feet said, *Well, I doubt this'll be a case*, but old Smithie was dafter than ever by then. He said, *Make it two, and to hell with you both!* and went striding into his house as he hadn't, striding that way, gone in for years.

His daughter, that sumph that was Mistress Bruce, fair jumped as she heard the bang of the door, she cried: *You nasty old wretch, what's the din?* Old Smithie was fairly boiling by then, he said, *Do you know who you're speaking to, Ellen?* and she said, *Ay, fine, you disgrace to Segget*; and at that old Smithie had her over his knee, afore she could blink, she was stunned with surprise. She gave a bit scraich and she tried to wriggle, but she'd grown over fat and old Smithie was strong. And damn't! if he didn't take down her bit things and scone her so sore she grat like a bairn, her own bairns made at old Smithie and kicked him, but he never let on, just leathered his quean till his hand was sore, not so sore as her dowp. *That's a lesson for you, you bap-faced bitch*, he said, and left her greeting on the floor, and went down to the Arms, and near the first man he met there was Bruce, old Smithie by then like a fighting cock.

Bruce was a dark and a sour-like childe, but he looked near twice as sour in a minute when old Smithie took him a crack in the jaw. *What's that for?* Bruce cried, and Smithie said *Lip*, and came at him again, the daft-like old tyke. Well, you couldn't expect but that Bruce would be raised, he was knocking Smithie all over the bar when Mistress Melvin came tearing in. She cried in her thin Aberdeen, *What's this? Stop your Blasting and Blaspheming in here.* Bruce said, *I haven't sworn a damn word*, she said *That's enough, take your tink fights out, sossing up the place with blood and the like. If you've any quarrel to settle with your relations, go out and settle it where folk can't see.*

And Bruce said *Right*; and took old Smithie out, and gey near settled him entire you would say. It just showed you what happened to a billy that stole, there's a difference between nicking a thing here and there, and being found out and made look a fair fool.

And next Sabbath MacDougall Brown, the postmaster, came down to the Square and preached on stealing, right godly-like, and you'd never have thought that him and his wife stayed up of a night sanding the sugar and watering the paraffin – or so folk said, but they tell such lies. He was maybe a fifty years old, MacDougall, a singer as well as a preacher, i'faith! though some said his voice was the kind of a thing better suited to slicing a cheese. During the War he had fair been a patriot, he hadn't fought, but losh! how he'd sung! In the first bit concert held in the War he sang Tipperary to the Segget folk, with his face all shining like a ham on the fry, and he sang it right well till he got to the bit where the song has to say that his heart's right there. And faith, MacDougall got things a bit mixed, he clapped down his hand the wrong side of his wame: and Ake Ogilvie that sat in the front of the hall gave a coarse snicker and syne everybody laughed; and Mac-Dougall had never forgiven Ake that.

But he got on well with his post-office place, Johnnie his son was a bit of a fool and MacDougall sent him to take round the letters, it cost him little with a son that was daft and Mac-Dougall kept the cash for himself. Forbye young Jock he'd two daughters as well, the eldest, Cis, was bonny and trig, with a grave, douce face, she went to the College but she wasn't proud, a fine bit quean, and all Segget liked her.

Well, MacDougall had a special religion of his own, he wasn't Old Kirk and he wasn't of the Frees, he wasn't even an Episcopalian, but Salvation Army, or as near as damn it. He went on a Sabbath morn to the Square, and preached there under the lee of the angel, that the road to heaven was the way he said. He'd made two-three converts in his years in Segget, they'd stand up and say what the Lord had done, how before they'd met Him they were lost, ruined souls; but now God had made them into new men. And faith! you would think, if that was the case, the Lord's handiwork was failing, like everything else.

Well, that Sunday after the row at Smithie's, he was there at his stance where the angel stood, MacDougall himself with his flat, bald head, and beside him his mistress, a meikle great sumph, she came from the south and she mouthed her words broad as an elephant's behind, said Ake Ogilvie. She thought little of Cis, that was clever and bonny, but a lot of her youngest, the quean called Mabel – by all but her mother, she called her Maybull. Well, they both were there, and the daftie Jock, gleying and slavering up at the angel, and a two-three more, the gardener Grant and Newlands the stationy, them and their wives; with the angel above with her night-gown drawn back, right handy-like, in case it might rap against the bald pow of MacDougall Brown. Mistress Brown opened up the harmonica they'd brought, it groaned and spluttered and gave a bit hoast, syne they started the singing of their unco hymns, Newlands burring away in his boots and MacDougall slicing the words like cheese.

Syne MacDougall started to preach about stealing, with a verse from Leviticus for the text, though the case of old Smithie had supplied the cause; and they started singing another bit hymn, all about being washed in the Blood of the Lamb, the Lamb being Jesus Christ, said MacDougall, he was awful fond of hymns full of blood, though he'd turned as white as a sheet the time Dite Peat had come over to kill his pig and asked MacDougall to hold the beast down.

Well, they were getting on fine and bloody, and having fairly a splash in the gore, when MacDougall noticed there was something wrong, the words all to hell, he couldn't make it out. Syne his mistress noticed and screwed round her head, and she said *What is't?* and saw MacDougall, red as rhubarb, he'd stopped his singing. The rest of them had to do the same, for a

drove of the spinners had come in about, with that tink Jock
Cronin at their head, as usual, they were singing up fast and
fair drowning MacDougall, a coarse-like mocking at Mac-
Dougall's hymn:

WHITER than – the whitewash on the wall!
WHITER than – the whitewash on the wall!
Oh – WASH me in the water
Where you washed your dirty daughter.
And I shall be whiter than the whitewash on the wall!

MacDougall waited until they had stopped, then he cried to
Cronin *Have you no respect? – you, John Cronin – for the
Lord's Day at all?* And the tink said, *Damn the bit; nor have
you.* And MacDougall nearly burst to hear that, he'd lived by
the Bible all his life. And John Cronin said *You believe all that's
in it?* and MacDougall Brown said, *Ay, I have faith.* But Cronin
had fairly got him trapped now, he said *Well, it says in the
Bible that if you've got faith you can move a mountain. That'll
be proof. Move back the Mounth there in front of our
eyes!*

The spinners with him, a lot of tink brutes, all brayed up
then, *Ay, come on, MacDougall! Move a mountain – you're
used to move sand!* MacDougall habbered redder than ever,
then he cried *We'll now sing Rock of Ages.* Jock Cronin cried
Where's the rock of your faith? and as soon as MacDougall
and his converts began the spinners sang up their song as
before, about being whiter than the whitewash on the wall,
and about MacDougall's dirty daughter; and such a noise was
never heard before in the Sabbath Square of Segget.

Old Leslie came by and he heard the noise, and he knew
MacDougall and was right sorry for him. But when he came
over and tried to interfere, Jock Cronin cried *God, here's
Ananias!* And old Leslie walked away, fair in a rage, and went
up to the Manse to complain about them.

He arrived there just after the morning service, the minister
new back, and dinner-time done. And old Leslie said 'twas

Infernal, just, the way that they treated a man nowadays. In his young days if a loon like that Cronin had miscalled a man he'd have been ta'en out and libbed. Ay, he minded when he was a loon up in Garvock—

But the new minister rose up and said *Well, I'll hear that again, I've no time to waste*, with a look as black as though he could kill you. And afore old Leslie knew well what had happened he was out on the doorstep and heard the door bang.

Chris heard the door bang and she saw old Leslie, he was turning slow to go down the walk, crunching the shingle under his feet; and suddenly you saw the old man that he was, his back crooked into that queer-like shape, cruel and a shame to get rid of him so, suddenly you wanted to weep, but you didn't, biting your lips as you watched him go. Only a tiring old fool, as you knew, and he'd come on Robert in that mad, black mood. And yet—

Things like that caught you again and again, with a tightening heart, when you had no thought – Robert in weariness half an hour back, his head in his hands, as he said *What's the use?* Robert's head as he prayed to that God of his that you couldn't believe in, though you hid that away, what need to hurt Robert with something that never he or you could alter though you lived forever?

So, in the strangest of moments it would come, in a flame and a flash, a glimpse into depths that wrung your heart, you'd see the body of Else as she bent, a curve of pleasure that would curve yet in pain. You'd see – frightening the things if you cared to think in the dark of the night in the quiet of Segget, the hush of the yews out there on the lawn – the hopeless folly of all striving, all hope. Sudden, in a Segget shop, maybe, you'd glimpse a face like your father's, near, alive and keen with its bearded lips, and you'd think of your father, long ago dead, bones rotted from flesh in Kinraddie kirkyard – what had life availed him and all his long years when he hoped for this and he strove for that? He died a coarse farmer in a little coarse house, hid in the earth and forgot by men, as forgot as your

pains and your tears by God, that God that you knew could
never exist. . .

Only with Ewan you'd never these glimpses into the shifting
sands of life, bairn though he was there was something within
him hard and shining and unbreaking as rock, something like
a sliver of granite within him. Strange that his body had once
come from yours in the days when you were a quean unthinking, so close to the earth and its smell and its feel that nearly
he came from the earth itself!

From that we all came, you heard Robert say, but wilder
and stranger you knew it by far, from the earth's beginning
you yourself had been here, a blowing of motes in the world's
prime, earth, roots and the wings of an insect long syne in the
days when the dragons still ranged the world – every atom
here in your body now, that was here, that was you, that beat
in your heart, that shaped your body to whiteness and
strength, the speed of your legs and the love of your breasts
when you turned to the kiss of your Robert at night – these
had been there, there was nothing but a change, in a form, the
stroke and the beat of a song.

And you thought how long, long ago with Will, your brother,
that time he came home from France, before he went back
and was killed in France you'd said that the Scots were never
religious, had never BELIEVED as other folks did; and that was
fell true, and not only for you, MacDougall that brayed by
the angel in the square, the folk that came to the kirk on a
Sunday, Robert himself – even Robert himself!

There was something lacking or something added, something that was bred in your bones in this land – oh, Something: maybe that Something was GOD – that made folk take
with a smile and a gley the tales of the gods and the heavens
and the hells, the afterlives and the lives before, heaven on
earth and the chances of change, the hope and belief in salvation for men – as a fairy-tale in a play that they'd play, but
they knew the whole time they were only players, no Scots
bodies died but they knew that fine, deep and real in their
hearts they knew that here they faced up to the REAL at last,

neither heaven nor hell but the earth that was red, the cling of the clay where you'd alter and turn, back to the earth and the times to be, to a spraying of motes on a raging wind when the Howe was happed in its winter storms, to a spray of dust as some childe went by with his plough and his horse in a morning in Spring, to the peck and tweet of the birds in the trees, to trees themselves in a burgeoning Spring.

You knew, and you knew that they knew – even Robert, holding to God in his blackest hour, this God he believed was the father of men, pitiful. He was Pity and a Friend, helpless even in a way as men, but King and Hero, and He'd conquer yet with all the legions of hell to battle.

So Robert believed: but now, as you heard his feet coming down the stairs in haste, out of his mood and happy again, you knew that he knew he followed a dream, with the black mood REAL, and his hopes but mists.

Chris remembered that dream of her own – she'd been daft! she thought as she fled about next week's work. There was jam to make and she thought it fun, and so did Else, they'd boil pot on pot and fill all the jars, and forget about dinner. And Robert would come sweating in from the garden and cry *Losh, Christine, where have you been? I thought you promised to come out and help.What's wrong – nothing wrong with you, is there, my dear?* Chris would say *Only hunger*, and he'd say *Not love?* and the two would be fools for a moment till they heard the stamp of Else bringing in the tray. Syne they'd each slip into a chair and look solemn but once Else caught them and said to the minister *Faith, I don't wonder!* and looked at Chris; and Chris thought that the nicest thing ever *looked* about her.

Ewan ran wild, Chris seldom saw him all the length of the summer days, he was out in Segget, exploring the streets, Chris at first had been feared for him – that he'd fall in front of a horse, or a car, or one of the buses that went by to Dundon. She tried to tell him to be careful, then stopped, he'd take his chances with the rest of the world.

On the Saturday she and Robert looked up from their work in the garden, and stood and watched Ewan, hands in his pockets, no cap on his head, go sauntering out through the gates of the Manse, his black hair almost blue in the sun, and turn by the Meiklebogs, going to the Kaimes, Chris wondered what he could want up there?

Robert said *He's seeking the High Places already,* and laughed, and went on with his digging, Chris the same, sweet and forgotten the smell of the earth, you thrust with your spade, the full throw of your body, so, and the drill built up as you dug. Then the rooks came cawing and wheeling in by, and they both looked up from Segget to the Mounth, rain drumming upon it far in the heuchs, cattle, tail-switching, dots on the heath. Chris asked what the clouds were, up there by Trusta, they piled up dome on dome in the sky, like the roofs of a city in the land of cloud. Robert said *Cumulus; just summer rain*; and a minute later — *Look, here it comes!*

Chris saw it come wheeling like a flying of rooks, dipping and pelting down from the heights, she looked left and saw it through a smother of smoke, the smoke stilled for a minute as it waited the rain, all Segget turning to look at the rain. Then Robert was running and Chris ran as well, under the shelter of the pattering yews. There they stood and panted and watched the water, whirling in and over the drills, the potato-shaws a bend in the pelt, the patter like hail and then like a shoom, like the sea on a morning heard from Kinraddie, *the empty garden blind with rain.* And then it was gone and the sun bright out, and Chris heard, far, clear, as though it never had stopped; a snipe that was sounding up in the hills.

By noon they saw a drooked figure approaching. Chris heard Else cry *Are you soaked!* and Ewan answer *I was; but I dried,* he'd something in his hand. Turning it over he came up to Robert. *Look, I found this up on the Kaimes.*

Chris stopped as well to look at the thing, the three of them stood in the bright, wet weather, Robert turning the implement over in his hands, it was rusted and broken, the blade of a spear. *Did they use it for ploughing?* Ewan wanted to know, and Robert said *No, they used it for killing, it's a spear, Ewan man, from the daft old days.*

Then Else came crying them in for their dinner, and in they all went, as hungry as hawks. Ewan wanted to know a lot more about spears, 'twas a wonder he managed to ask all he did, him eating as well, but he managed both fine; he'd a question-mark for a brain, Robert said!

But the most of his questions he kept until night, when Chris bathed him and took him up to his room. Why did the stairs wind? Why weren't they straight? Would it be long till he was a man? Where was Christ now, and had Robert met Him? *That's an owl, why don't owls fly in the day? Why don't you go to sleep when I do? Does Else like Dalziel of the Meiklebogs much? I like the smiddy of old Mr Leslie, he says that when he was a loon up on Garvock he was never let gang anywhere near a smiddy, his mammy would have smacked his dowp; didn't she like it? I saw Mr Hogg, he said 'What's your name?' Why is there hair growing out of his nose? Mrs Hogg is fat, is she going to have a calf? Does she take off her clothes to have it, mother? Mother, have you got a navel like mine? I'll show you mine, look, there it is, isn't it funny – I'm not sleepy, let's sing a while. Why—*

He was sleeping at last, in the evening quiet, the Saturday quiet, the sun not yet gone. Chris went down to the garden and took out a chair, and leaned back in it with her arms behind her, drowsy, watching the gloaming come. Robert was up in his room with his sermon, he wrote the thing out when he'd thought of a theme – he would think of a theme of a sudden and swear because he hadn't a note-book at hand.

This afternoon it had come on him suddenly. *I know! That spearblade that Ewan brought – where the devil has he hidden the thing?*

At half past ten next morning, the Sunday, Chris heard John Muir and looked out and saw him, his shoulder a-skeugh in his Sunday suit, come stepping up the path from the kirk. *There's a fair concourse of the folk the day; and how are you keeping then, mistress, yourself?*

Chris said she was fine, and he gleyed at her cheery. *Faith, so you look, you take well with Segget. Well, well, if the minister hasn't any orders I'll taik away back and tug at the bell.*

Chris heard that bell in a minute or so beat and clang through the quiet of the air. It was time that she herself had got ready, she sought out her hymn-book and hanky and Bible, and inspected Ewan, and straightened his collar. Then the two of them hurried through the blow of the garden, and out of the little door let in the dyke, and into the little room back of the kirk. There the sound of the bell was a deafening clamour. Chris brushed Ewan down and went into the kirk, and put Ewan into a pew and herself went ben to the pews where the kirk choir sat, Mrs Geddes, the schoolmaster's wife, there already, smiling and oozing with eau-de-Cologne, whispered right low and right holy-like, *Morning. A grand day, isn't it, and such a pity so few have come up to hear the Lord's word.*

Chris said, *Oh, yes,* and sat down beside her, and looked round as the folk came stepping in, slow. Hairy Hogg, the Provost, and his mistress, Jean, they plumped in their seats and Hairy looked round and closed his eyes like a grass-filled cow. Then the wife and queans of John Muir came in, Chris had heard a lot about them from Else. Else said she could swear there were times when Muir wished he'd stayed where he was when he fell in that grave.

His wife was one of the Milton lot that farmed down under Glenbervie brae, she deaved John Muir from morning till night to get out of his job, a common bit roadman, and get on in the world and show up her sister, Marget Ann, that had married a farmer. But John Muir would say *Damn't, we all come to the same – a hole and a stink and worms at the end* and his mistress would snap, *Ay, maybe we do, but there's ways of getting there decent and undecent. And as for stinking, speak of yourself.* And, real vexed, she'd clout Tooje one in the ear, Tooje was her eldest, fairly a gawk, and then clout little Ted when she started to greet because she saw her sister

Tooje greeting; and John Muir would get up and say not a word but go dig a grave as a bit of a change.

Then Chris saw Bruce, the porter, come in, with the mark on his jaw where his goodfather hit him, then Leslie, the smith, paiching and sweating, he dropped his stick with an awful clatter. Then she saw Geddes, the Segget headmaster, sitting grim in a pew midway, his rimless specs set close on his nose, looking wearied to death, as he was. Robert had thought to make him an ally, but he'd said to Robert, *Don't be a fool, leave the swine to stew in their juice* – by swine he meant his fellow-folk of Segget. He would stand hymn-singing with his hand in his pocket, and rattle his keys and yawn at the roof.

Then Moultrie came in, a slow tap-tap, with his stick and his glare, and stopped halfway, his wife, Jess Moultrie, wait-ing behind, her hand on his arm, gentle and quiet. But when he moved on he shook her away. Chris had heard the story of him and of her and how he had never forgiven her her daughter, Ag, whom they called the Roarer and Greeter.

Then others came in, all in a birn, Chris didn't know some and of some was uncertain, she thought that one was Ake Ogilvie the joiner; and a trickle of folk from the farms outbye, a spinner or so, but they were fell few, and Dalziel of the Meiklebogs, red-faced and shy, funny how one couldn't abide him at all.

Syne John Muir finished with the ringing of the bell and came with his feet splayed out as he walked and his shoulder agley, down the length of the kirk; and went into the little room at the back. Robert would be there and Muir helped him to robe. Syne the door opened and John Muir came out, and swayed and gleyed cheerful up to the pulpit, and opened the door and stood back and waited. And Robert went up, with his hair fresh-brushed, and his eyes remote, and sat down and prayed, silent, and all the kirk silent as well, for a minute, while Chris looked down at her hands.

Then Robert stood up in the pulpit and said, in his clear, strong voice that hadn't a mumble, that called God GOD and never just GAWD. *We will begin the worship of God by the singing of hymn one hundred and forty. 'Our shield and defender, the Ancient of Days, pavilioned in splendour and girded with praise.' Hymn one hundred and forty.*

Folk rustled the leaves and here and there a man glowered helpless while his wife found the page; and the organ started with a moan and a grind and the kirk was a rustle with Sunday braws, folk standing and singing, all straight and decent, except young Ewan, a-lean in his pew and Geddes the Dominie, hand in his pouch.

Chris liked his hymn near as much as did Robert, most folk stuck fast when they came to pavilioned, Robert's bass came in, Chris's tenor to help, Mrs Geddes' contralto a wail at their heels. Then down they all sat; Robert said *Let us pray*.

Chris wondered what Robert was to preach today, his text was no clue when he gave it out. Folk shuffled in their seats, and hoasted genteel, and put up their hankies to slip sweeties in their mouths; sometimes Chris wished she could do the same, but she couldn't very well, the minister's wife. And all Segget lifted its eyes to Robert, he flung back the shoulders of his robe and began, slow and careful, reading from his notes; and then pushed them aside and began a sermon on that bit of a spear young Ewan Tavendale had found on the Kaimes. He'd brought the thing up in the pulpit with him, folk stopped in their sucking of sweeties and gaped.

And Robert told of the uses the thing had once had, in the hands of the carles of the ruined Kaimes; and the siege and the fighting and the man who had held it, desperate at last in the burning lowe as King Kenneth's men came into the castle: and the blood that ran on this ruined blade for things that the men of that time believed would endure and be true till the world died; they thought they were fighting for things that would last, they'd be classed as heroes and victors forever. And now they were gone, they were not even names, their lives and their deaths we know to be foolish, a clamour and babble on little things.

So might the men of the future look back, on this Segget

here, not of antique times, and see the life of our mean-like streets an ape-like chatter as the dark came down. For change, imperative, awaited the world, as never before men could make it anew, men of good will and a steadfast faith. All history had been no more than the gabble of a horde of apes that was trapped in a pit. *Let us see that we clean our pit-corner in Segget, there is hatred here, and fear, and malaise, the squabbling of drunken louts in the streets, poor schools, worse houses — we can alter all these, we can alter them NOW, not waiting the world.*

Robert had launched his campaign on Segget.

That sermon fair raised a speak in the toun, as soon's they got out Peter Peat said Faith! they'd fair made a mistake in getting this childe. You wanted a sermon with some body in it, with the hell that awaited the folk that were sinners, and lay on the Kaimes with their unwed queans, and were slow in paying their bills to a man. And what did he mean that Segget was foul? A clean little toun as ever there was, no, no, folk wanted no changes here.

Old Leslie said 'Twas Infernal, just, he minded when he was a loon up on Garvock—

Rob Moultrie said *Well, what d'you expect? He's gentry and dirt with his flat-patted hair; and speaking to God as though he were speaking to a man next door — and a poorman at that. Ay, a Tory mucker, I may well warrant, that would interfere in our houses and streets.*

Will Melvin said *Did you hear him preach against folk taking a dram now and then? And if he himself wasn't drunk then I'm daft, with his spears and his stars and his apes and his stite.*

That fairly got Hairy Hogg on the go. He cried *Ay, what was all yon about apes? And him glaring at me like a thrawn cat. If he comes from the monkeys himself let him say it, not sneer at folk of a better blood.*

Folk took a bit snicker at that as they went — damn't, the minister had got one in there! And afore night had come the story had spread, the minister had said – you'd as good as heard him – that Hairy Hogg was a monkey, just.

Well, it made you laugh, though an ill-getted thing to say that of old Hairy Hogg, the Provost. Faith, he fair had a face like a monkey, the sutor of Segget and its Provost forbye. He'd been Provost for years, not a soul knew why, or how he'd ever got on for the job; or what was the council, or what it might do, apart from listening to Hairy on Burns. For he claimed descent from the Burneses, Hairy, and you'd have thought by the way he spoke that Rabbie had rocked him to sleep in his youth. His wife had once been at Glenbervie House, a parlour-maid there and awful genteel; but a thirty years or so in old Hogg's bed had fair rubbed gentility off of the creature, she was common and rough as a whin bush now, and would hoast out loud in the kirk at prayers till the bairns all giggled and old Hogg would say, loud enough for the pulpit to hear, *Wheest, wheest, redd your thrapple afore you come here.*

She would make him regret that when they got home, she'd little time for any palavers, her daughter Jean that was nurse in London, or Alec her son that clerked down in Edinburgh. Old Hogg he would blow like a windy bellows about Jean and the things she'd done as a nurse. For when the bit King took ill with a cough she was one of the twenty-four nurses or so that went prancing round the bit royalty's bed, she carried a hanky, maybe, or such-like. But to hear old Hairy speak on the business you'd have thought she cured the King's illness herself, and been handed a two-three thousand for doing it. Yet damn the penny but her wages she got, said Mrs Hogg; what could you expect? The gentry were aye as mean as is dirt and wasn't the King a German forbye?

Young Hogg was at home now, on holiday like, he meant to attend the Segget Show. You had seen the creature, wearing plus-fours, east-windy, west-endy as well as could be, forbye that he said he had joined the Fascists. Folk asked what they were, and he said *they* were fine, Conservatives, like, but a lot more than that; they meant to make Britain the same as was Italy. And old Hogg was real vexed, he cried *But goodsakes!*

You're not going to leave your fine job, now, are you, and take to the selling of ice-cream sliders? And Alec said *Father, please don't be silly*; and old Hogg fair flamed: *Give's less of your lip. What could man think but that you were set, you and your breeks and your Fashers and all, with being a damned ice-creamer yourself?*

Alec said nothing, just looked at his quean, and she and him sniffed, she was real superior, a clerk like Alec himself down in Edinburgh. He'd brought her up on holiday to Segget, he called her his feeungsay, not just his lass; she wouldn't be able to stay for the Show, and if any soul thought that a cause for regret, he'd managed to keep a good grip on himself. The first time they sat down to tea in Hogg's house Alec finished his cup and looked round the table. *Where's the slop-basin, mother?* he asked, to show his quean he was real genteel. But his mother was wearied with him and his airs. *Slop it in your guts!* she snapped as she rose, *and less of your Edinburgh touches here!*

Segget Show was held in a park that was loaned to the toun by Dalziel of the Meiklebogs. He blushed and looked shy, *Oh ay, you can have it*, when Hairy Hogg went out there and asked him. 'Twas a great ley park with a fringe of trees, the hills up above, the Kaimes to the left; and early on the evening afore Segget Show there were folk down there marking out this and that, the lines of the tents and the marquees and such, the circle where the bairns would run their bit races and folk that thought they could throw the hammer could stand and show what their muscles were made of. Folk came to Segget Show far and about, from Fordoun and Laurencekirk, Skite and Arbuthnott, early on the Saturday Segget awoke to the rattle of farm carts up through East Wynd, down past the Manse, and so to the park, carts loaded with kail and cabbage and cakes, and hens and ducks in their clean straw rees, and birns of bannocks and scones for show, and the Lord knows what that folk wouldn't bring to try for a prize at the Segget Show.

It was wet in the morning, folk looked out and swore, but

by noon the rain had cleared off and soon, as the lines of folk held out from Segget, there came a blistering waft of the heat, men loosed their waistcoats, some took off their collars and paid their shillings and went in at the gates, all except a crowd of the spinners. They suddenly appeared near the big marquee, and Sim Leslie, him that the folk called Feet, went over and looked at the bunch fell stern, he hadn't seen them pay at the gate. But he wasn't keen on starting a row, just looked at them stern: and the spinners all laughed.

There fair was a crush as the judges began, Hairy Hogg was one, the minister another, Dalziel of the Meiklebogs the third. They started in on the hens to begin with, a lot from Mac-Dougall Brown's of the post-office. MacDougall stood by, looking proud as dirt, he'd won first prize for his Leghorns for years. So he fell near fainted when he got a green ticket, the second prize only and not the red first; and he said to whoever stood by to listen that it was that minister had done this to him, he was scared at the way that MacDougall drew folk away from the Auld Kirk's preaching and lies. But faith! his Leghorns looked none so well, he'd been mixing lime in their feed and the birds had a look as though they'd like to lie down and burst. But they daren't, with MacDougall's eye upon them, they stood and chirawked, as though kind of discouraged when they saw that they'd ta'en only second prize.

By then the judges were through with the hens, the ducks as well, a childe from a farm out near by Mondynes had ta'en every prize there was to be took. Syne the judges turned into the big marquee, to judge the baked stuff and the flowers and the like. The minister was speaking as they went inside; Hairy Hogg turned round to hear what he said; and prompt his elbow knocked over the dish that was set with cakes of Mistress Melvin. The landlady of the Arms looked at the Provost as though she'd like to bash in his head, with a bottle, and syne carve him up slow with its splinters; but she daren't say anything, seeing it was him, and he'd given the Melvins the catering to do.

So the Blaster and Blasphemer just smiled, genteel, and got

down and picked up her cakes from the grass, the minister got down and helped her; and smiled (what was the creature laughing about?). But Hairy Hogg said, for the marquee to hear, *I want stuff set out plain and decent, not pushed right under my nose when I judge.* He spoke as though he were the Lord God Almighty, and the bannocks sinners on the Judgement Day.

They couldn't make up their minds on the pancakes, there were two fine lots, one rounded and cut, neat-shaped and fine as ever you saw, the other lot not of much shape at all, but bonnily fired, and the judges stopped, and each ate a bit, of the well-cut at first, they weren't so bad, but looked better than they tasted. Syne the judges bit at the ill-cut cakes, they fairly melted in a body's mouth, the minister had eaten up one in a minute, and Meiklebogs nodded, and Hairy Hogg nodded, and the Reverend Mr Colquohoun gave a nod.

So old Jess Moultrie had the first prize, faith! that was fairly a whack in the face for that Mistress Geddes with her fine-shaped cakes, and her blethering of lectures at the WRI. She was daft on the WRI, Mrs Geddes, she said that folk in a village like Segget wanted taking out of themselves. So she and some others started the thing, they'd collect at all hours, the women of the place, and speak about baking and minding the bairns, and how to make pipes from the legs of old sofas; and hear lantern-lectures on Climbing the Alps. Well, damn't! she'd have to do a bit of climbing herself ere she learned to bake cakes like the Moultrie wife.

By three nearly everything there had been judged, most of the folk had scattered by then, to see the games in the ring that Ake Ogilvie had set up for nothing, the previous night. And well so he might, damn seldom he worked, you couldn't get near to his joiner's shop for the clutter of carts, half-made and half-broken, lying about, and the half of a churn, a hen-coop or so and Heaven knows what – all left outside in the rain and sun while Ogilvie sat on a bench inside and wrote his ill bits of poetry and stite – he thought himself maybe a second Robert Burns.

He was broad and big, a fell buirdly childe, and it seemed fell queer that a man like that couldn't settle down to the making of money, and him the last joiner left in the place. But he'd tell you instead some rhyme or another, coarse dirt that was vulgar, not couthy and fine. He was jealous as hell of the real folk that wrote, Annie S. Swan and that David Lyall: you could read and enjoy every bit that they wrote, it was fine clean stuff, not sickening you, like, with dirt about women having bairns and screaming or old men dying in the hills at night or the fear of a sheep as the butcher came. That was the stuff that Ake Ogilvie wrote, and who wanted to know about stuff like that? You did a bit reading to get away from life.

Well, Ake Ogilvie, him and his poetry and dirt, there he was, on the edge of the ring. And inside the ring, round about the hammer, were a pickle of those that would try a bit throw. And Feet cried *Back, keep out of the way,* and went shooing bairns at the ring's far side; and folk clustered around fair thick to look on, old Leslie and Melvin the judges here.

The first to throw was a man from Catcraig, Charlie Something-or-other his name, and he swung himself slow and steady on his feet and syne took a great breath and leaped in the air, and swung, and syne as his feet came down his arms let go and the hammer flew out and flashed in the air and spun and then fell — ay, a gey throw, folk cheered him a bit. But one of his galluses had split with the throw and he blushed to the eyes and put on his coat.

Syne another childe threw, a farmer he was, the hammer went skittering out from his hand, he laughed in an off-hand way as to say he was just taking part to encourage the others. Syne folk saw that the third was that tink Jock Cronin, one of the spinner breed, he picked up the hammer and waited and swung, and louped, and the thing went a good foot beyond any of the earlier throws that were made. 'Twould be a sore business if the Cronin should win. His friends all shouted, *That's the stuff, Jock!* they were fair delighted with their champion's throw, with their rattling watch-chains and their dirty jokings,

the average spinner knew as much of politeness as a polecat
knows of the absence of smell.

The worst of the lot, folk said, were the Cronins, they bade
in West Wynd, a fair tribe of the wretches, old Cronin had
once been a foreman spinner till he got his bit hand mashed
up in machinery. He'd fair gone bitter with that, they told,
and took to the reading of the daftest-like books, about
Labour, Socialism, and such-like stite. *Where would you be if
it wasn't for Capital?* you'd ask old Cronin, and he'd say *On
the street — where the capitalists themselves would be, you
poor fool. It's the capitalists that we are out to abolish, and
the capital that we intend to make ours*. And he'd organized
a union for spinners and if ever you heard of a row at the mills
you might bet your boots a Cronin was in it, trying to make
out that the spinners had rights, and ought to be treated like
gentry, b'God!

The worst of the breed was that young Jock Cronin, him
that had just now thrown the hammer. The only one that
wasn't a spinner, he worked as a porter down at the station,
folk said that the stationmaster, Newlands, would have sacked
him right soon if only he'd dared, him and his socialism and
the coarse way he had of making jokes on the Virgin Birth;
and sneering at Jonah in the belly of the whale; and saying
that the best way to deal with a Tory was to kick him in the
dowp and you'd brain him there. But Jock Cronin worked as
well as he blethered, the sly, coarse devil, and he couldn't be
sacked; and there he stood with a look on his face as much as
to say *That's a socialist's throw!*

It was Newlands, the stationmaster, himself that came next,
you hoped he'd beat the throw of the porter. But faith, he
didn't, he was getting fell slow, maybe it was that or he wasted
his breath singing at the meetings of MacDougall Brown, the
hammer just wobbled and fell with a plop, if they didn't do
better at the second round and third it was Cronin the porter
would grab the first prize.

But syne folk started to cheer, and all looked, 'twas the
Reverend Mr Colquohoun himself, being pushed inside the

ring by his wife. Ay, that was well-intended of him, now, you
gave a bit clap and syne waited and watched. And the minister
took off his coat and his hat and smiled at the childe that held
out the hammer, and took it and swung, and there rose a gasp,
he'd flung it nearly as far as the Cronin's.

The second bout he landed well over Jock Cronin's, plain it
was between the spinner and him, the spinners stopped laughing, crying, *Come on, then, Jock! You're not going to let a
mucking preacher beat you?* The Reverend Colquohoun looked
at them and laughed, and syne spoke to Cronin, and *he*
laughed as well, not decent and low as a man would do that
spoke to a minister, but loud out and vulgar, he wished folk
to think that he was as good as any minister that ever was
clecked. Then the childe with the galluses threw once again,
but he'd never got over the blush or the galluses, he landed
fell short and went off the field, and Else Queen, the maid at
the Manse, was his lass, and she laughed out loud; and that
was ill-done.

Syne Ake Ogilvie threw — ay, not a bad throw, but shorter
than Cronin's, Ake did it with a sneer. Syne Cronin again, and
the hammer was flung with the whole of his weight and his
strength and it fell, crack! a bare foot short of his very first
throw. And as the minister stood up, arms bared, you knew
well enough that he couldn't beat that; and then everybody
knew that he wasn't going to try, he maybe thought it not
decent for a minister to win, he swung the hammer to give it a
good throw, but safe and not as far as Jock Cronin's.

But the spinners had broken into the ring, a birn of them
down at the farther end; and as the Reverend picked up the
hammer and got ready to swing, one of them cried, you
couldn't tell which, *Jesus is getting a bit weak in the guts.*

The minister gave a kind of a start, you thought for a
minute that he wouldn't throw. But instead he suddenly
whirled him about, and spun and swung and had flung the
hammer, so quickly you hardly saw what he did. And the
hammer swished and twirled through the air, like a catapult
stone or a pheasant in flight, and landed a good three feet or

more beyond the farthest throw of the Cronin: and struck on a great meikle stone that lay there, and stotted and swung, the handle swung first, into the middle of the spleiter of spinners.

They jumped and ran and the hammer lay still, and there rose such a yell from the folk that watched, your lugs near burst in the cheering and din. The minister's face had reddened with blood, the veins were like cords all over his face; and then he went white as ever again, and put on his coat and went out of the ring, folk cried, *That was a fine throw, minister,* but he didn't say a word, just went off with his wife.

Chris said, *What's wrong?* Then she saw his hanky as he took it away from his lips; it was red. He said, *Oh, nothing. Gassed lungs, I suppose. Serves me right for trying to show off.*

Chris said, *You didn't; I thought you were fine.* Robert said, *I'm afraid not, only a fool. There, I'm all right, don't worry, Christine. Come on, we've to watch Ewan running his race.*

The bairns' races were the next things set. Ewan Chris watched line up with the others, Geddes the schoolmaster in charge of the lot, disgusted as ever he looked with the job. They'd marked out a track through the middle of the ring, John Muir stood down at the farther end, the bairns had to run to him and then back. Chris watched Ewan, he was eating a sweetie, calm as you please, his black mop blue in the sun, his eyes on the Dominie, he didn't care a fig. But as soon as Geddes cried *Run!* he was off, he went like a deer, his short legs flying, the other bairns tailed off behind, and Ewan was first to reach Muir and go round him, swinging round gripping at John Muir's trousers; and as he went by the place where Chris stood, he looked at her and grinned calmly as ever, and shifted the sweetie to the other side of his mouth, and looked back, and slowed down, no need to race. He was up at the Dominie first, at a trot, folk round about asked who he was, as black as all that, he was surely foreign?

Then somebody knew and saw Chris stand near, and cried out *Wheest!* but Chris didn't care; she watched Ewan take the prize and say *Thanks,* calm still, and put the shilling in his

pocket, and come walking back to look for her, and stand grave
in front of her as she smoothed down his collar. Robert gave
him a shake and he smiled at that (the smile that so sometimes
caught your heart, the smile you had known on the lips of his
father). Then Robert said, *Well, since we've won all the prizes,
let's go and look for tea in the tent.*

And the three of them set out across the short grass, through
the groupings and gatherings of folk here and there, the show
was fairly a place for a claik, one gossip would now meet in
with another she hadn't seen since the last Segget Show, and
would cry *Well, now, it's Mistress MacTavish!* And Mistress
MacTavish would cry back *her* name, and they'd shake hands
and waggle their heads and be at it, hammer and tongs, a twelve
months' gossip, the Howe's reputation put in through a mangle
and its face danced on when it came through the rollers.

There was a great crush in the tent they entered, but Melvin
came running and found them a table, the gabble of the folk
rose all round about, they nodded to the minister and minded
their manners, and reddened when they thought that he looked
at them, and took a sly keek at the clothes Chris wore – faith!
awful short skirts for a minister's wife. Mrs Hogg was sitting
at a table with her son, him that she'd told to slop slop in his
guts, his quean had gone back, and folk saw the damned
creature trying to catch the minister's eye. But the Reverend
Mr Colquohoun didn't see you were torn two ways with scorn
of the Manse for being so proud, and with sheer delight at
seeing the Hoggs get a smack in the face.

Then it was time for the band to begin, folk trooped out to
see in the best of spirits, well filled with biscuits and baps and
tea; but weren't such fools as to go over close to the board
where John Muir and Smithie were standing, crying, *Come on
folk, now, will you dance?* Behind them the Segget band played
up. Ake Ogilvie there at the head of it, fair thinking himself of
importance, like, with Jim that served in the bar of the Arms
and folk called the Sourock because of his face, tooting on his
flute like a duck half-choked, and Newlands the stationy cuddling his fiddle a damn sight closer than ever his mistress, or

else she'd have had a bairn ere this – not that you blamed him,
she'd a face like a greip, and an ill greip at that, though you
don't cuddle faces. And Feet was there, he was playing the
bassoon, he sat well back to have room for his boots and
looked as red as a cock with convulsions. God ay! it was worth
going up to the board if only to take a laugh at the band.

But not a childe or a quean would venture up on the thing
till at last Jock Cronin, that tink of a porter that came of the
spinners, was seen going up and pulling up a quean. She
laughed, and turned her face round at last, and folk fair had a
shock, it was Miss Jeannie Grant, she was one of the teachers,
what was she doing with a porter, eh? – and a tink at that, that
called himself a socialist, and said that folk should aye vote
for labour, God knew you got plenty without voting for't.

Socialists with queans – well, you knew what they did, they
didn't believe in homes or in bairns, they'd have had all the
bairns locked up in poor houses; and the coarse brutes said
that marriage was daft – that fair made a body right wild to
read that, what was coarse about marriage you would like to
know? . . . And you'd stop from your reading and say to the
wife, *For Heaven's sake, woman, keep the bairns quiet. Do
you think I want to live in a menagerie?* And she'd answer you
back, *By your face I aye thought that was where you came
from*, and start off again about *her* having no peace, she
couldn't be sweir like a man, take a rest; and whenever were
your wages going to be raised? And you'd get in a rage and
stride out of the house, and finish the paper down at the
Arms, reading about the dirt that so miscalled marriage – why
shouldn't they have to get married as well?

Well, there were Jock Cronin and Miss Jeannie Grant, they
stood and laughed and looked down at the folk. Syne some
spinners went up, as brazen as you like, giggling, and then a
ploughman or so, syne Alec Hogg that was son of the Provost,
he had up Cis Brown that went to the College, thin and sweet,
a fell bonny lass, she looked gey shy and a treat to cuddle. So
there were enough at last for a dance, and Ake waved his arms,
and they struck up a polka. There was fair a crowd when the

second dance came, you felt your back buttons to see were they holding, and took a keek round for a lass for the dance: and the queans all giggled and looked at you haughty, till you asked one, bold, and then she'd say *Ay*.

Charlie, the childe from Catcraig, went to Else, the maid from the Manse, and said *Will you dance?* and she said *Can you?* and he blushed and said *Fine*. Else was keen for a dance and she left Meiklebogs, he looked after her shy, like a shy-like stot, as she swung on the board, a fair pretty woman. God, you hardly saw her like nowadays, queans grown all as thin as the handles of forks, and as hard forbye, no grip to the creatures; and how the devil they expected to get married and be ta'en with bairns you just couldn't guess, what man in his senses would want to bed with a rickle of bones and some powder, like?

Well, Else was up with the Catcraig childe, it was *Drops of Brandy* and the folk lined up, Else saw the minister, he smiled like a lad with the mistress herself further down the line. Ake waved his arms and you all were off, slow in the pace and the glide, then the whirl, till the brandy drops were spattering the sky the board kittled up and the band as well, and you all went like mad; and Else's time when she did the line she found the minister the daftest of the lot, he swung her an extra turn right round, and he cried out *Hooch!* and folk all laughed – ay, fairly a billy the new minister, though already he'd started interfering with folk, and he'd preached so unco, a Sunday back, that old Hairy Hogg was descended from monkeys. . . Had he said that, then? Ay, so he had, old Hogg himself had told you the speak, it was hardly the thing to have said of the Provost, fair monkey-like though the creature was. . .

And just at the head of the dance as Else flew round in the arms of her Catcraig childe, he gave a kind of a gasp and his hand flew up to his waistcoat and Else cried *What?* And the childe let go and grabbed at his breeks, his other bit gallus had fair given way, he lipped from the board with his face all red, and went home fell early that evening alone, not daring to stay and take Else Queen home.

The teas were all finished and Melvin had opened up one of the tents for the selling of drams, folk took a bit dander up to the counter, had a dram, and spoke of the Show and looked out – at the board, the gloaming was green on the hills, purple on the acre-wide blow of heather. There was a little wind coming down, blowing in the hot, red faces of the dancers, you finished up your dram and felt fair kittled up; and went out and made for the board like a hare, damn't! you might be old, but you still could dance, you hoped the mistress had already gone home.

There was old Smithie, well whiskied by now. He cried each dance till he got to the Schottische, he stuck fast on that and shished so long you thought the old fool never would stop, his whiskers sticking from his face in a fuzz, like one of the birns of hay he would steal. And just as he paused to take a bit breath his eyes lit down on his goodson, Bruce, and he stopped and said *What the devil's wrong with you, you coarse tink, that lives in my house, on my meal, and snickers like a cuddy when a man tries to speak?*

Bruce glunched up, dour, *Be quiet, you old fool*, and that fair roused the dander of Smithie to hear. *Who's a fool? By God, if I come down to you* – and he made a bit step, just threatening-like, but he was over-near the edge of the board to be threatening, even, next minute he was off, on top of Ed Bruce, folk were fair scandalized and crowded about, snickering with delight to see the daft fools, old Smithie and Bruce, leathering round in the grass. But down came the minister and pushed folk aside, angry as could be, and folk stared at *him. Get up there, confound you, the two of you!* he cried, and in a jiffy had old Smithie up in one hand and Bruce in the other, and shook them both. *Haven't you more sense than to behave like a couple of bairns! Shake up and shut up!*

And so they did, but before the night was well done the speak was all over the Howe of the Mearns that the new minister of Segget had come down and bashed Ed Bruce in the face and syne Smithie, and cursed at them both for ten minutes without stopping. And a great lot of folk went to kirk next

Sunday that never went afore, and never went again, for no other purpose than to stare at the minister, and see if he'd be shamed of the coarse way he'd cursed.

Well, that was the Segget Show and Games, by eight and nine the older folk were crying ta-ta and taiking away home, the farmers in their gigs spanked down by Meiklebogs, the Segget folk dandered home low in the light, it lay like the foam of the sea on the land, soft, in a kind of blue, trembling half-mist, a half-moon, quiet, came over the hills and looked down on the board where the young still danced. Else sought out the mistress — should she take Ewan home? But the mistress shook her head, *I'll do that. Dance while you're young, but don't be too late*; and she smiled at Else the fine way she had, she looked bonny with that dour, sweet, sulky face, the great plaits of her hair wound round her head, rusty and dark and changing to gold, Else thought *If I were a man myself I'd maybe be worse than the minister is — I'd want to cuddle her every damned minute!*

Young Ewan was beside her, he stood eating chocolate, he had eaten enough to make a dog sick, as Else knew well, but he looked cool as ever, the funny bit creature, and said *Ta-ta, Else. Will Mr Meiklebogs squeeze you under my window?* Else felt herself flushing up like a fire, *Maybe, if I let him*, and Ewan said *Oh, do*, and would maybe have said more, for bairns are awful, but that the minister had hold of his arm — *Come on, or I'll squeeze YOU, Ta-ta, Else.*

So the three went home through the night-quiet park, Robert and Chris the last of the elders to leave. It came sudden on Chris, with her feet in the grass, her hand in Ewan's, that that's what they were — old, she who was not yet thirty years old! Old, and still how you'd like to dance, out under the brightening coming of the moon, drop away from you all the things that clung close, Robert and Ewan and the Manse — even Chris — be young and be young and be held in men's arms, and seem bonny to them and look at them sly, not know next hour who would take you home, and not know who would kiss you or what they would do. . . Young as you never yet had been young, you'd been caught and ground in the wheels of the days, in this dour little Howe and its moil and toil, the things you had missed, the things you had missed! The things that the folk had aye in the books – being daft, with the winds of young years in your hair, night for a dream and the world for a song. Young; and you NEVER could be young now.

Like a sea you had never seen plain in your life, you heard the thunder and foam of the breakers, once or twice, far off, dark-green and salt, you had seen them play, spouting and high on a drift of the wind, crying in the sun with their crested laughters, hurrying south on the questing tides. Youth, to be young—

High up and over the Kaimes two birds were sailing into the western night, lonely, together, into the night Chris watched them fade to dots in the sky.

The whispers went round the minister had gone, the plough-men and spinners gave a bit laugh and took a bit squeeze at the queans they held; and some of the folk that were hot with their collars pulled the damned things off and threw them in the hedge. In Will Melvin's bar was a roaring trade, old Hairy Hogg's son and Dite Peat were there, the both of them telling the tale, you may guess, Alec Hogg of the things he had seen in Edinburgh, Dite Peat of the things he had done in London. God! 'twas a pity they'd ever come back. Meiklebogs came taiking into the bar, near nine that was, folk cried: *Will you drink?* and he answered back canny, *Oh, ay; maybe one*; and had two or three, and looked shyer than ever. Dite Peat roared *With that down under your waistcoat, you'll be able to soss up the Manse quean fine*. Meiklebogs looked a wee bit shyer than before, and gave a bit laugh, and said, *Fegs, ay*.

Else had danced every dance since the dancing began. When Charlie from Catcraig, the fool, disappeared, Alec Hogg had taken her up for a while, and half Else liked him and half she didn't, he felt like a man though he spoke like a toff. He asked in his clipped-like way, *You're Miss Queen?* as though he thought it should be a *mistake*. Else answered careless, *Oh, ay,*

so I've heard. You're the son of old Hairy Hogg, the Provost?
He grinned like a cat. *So my mother says,* and Else was fair
shocked, a man shouldn't make jokes about his own mother.
So after a while she got rid of the creature, and the next dance
she had was with Ogilvie the joiner, he'd left the band for Feet
to conduct, he swung her round and round in a waltz, his own
eyes half-closed near all that time. If he thought your face
such a scunner to look at, why did he ask you up for a dance?

Then Feet cried *The Last,* and there was John Muir he'd
grabbed Else afore any other could get near, and he danced
right well, Else warmed up beside him, he cried out, *Hooch!*
and she did the same, if he dug graves as well as he danced,
John Muir, he should have had a job in a public cemetery. As
Else whirled she saw the blue reek of Segget, and the dusk
creep in, it was warm and blue, and the smell of the hay rose
up in her face; there was the moon, who was taking her home?

She was over big and scared off the shargars; but one or two
childes she knew keen enough for a slow-like stroll up to
Segget Manse. But they looked at Dalziel, that was waiting
by, and turned away and left Else alone. And the old fool said,
with his shy-like smile, *Ay then, will I see you home, Else lass?*

Else said *You may, since you've feared all the rest!* but he
smiled as canny as ever and said *Ay,* he didn't seem to mind
that she was in a rage. The dances were ended and the folk
were going, streaming from the park as the night came down,
the band with their instruments packed in their cases, and
their queans beside them, them that had queans, them that
had wives had the creatures at home, waiting up with a cup of
tea to slocken the throats of the men that had played so well
for Segget that afternoon. Here and there in the park a bit
fight broke out, but folk paid little heed, they just gave a smile,
that was the way that the Show aye ended, you'd think it queer
in a way if you didn't see a childe or so with his nose bashed
in, dripping blood like a pig new knived.

Jock Cronin and his spinners had started a quarrel with the
three fee'd met at the Meiklebogs. Jock Cronin said ploughmen should be black ashamed, they that once had a union

like any other folk, but had been too soft in the guts to stick by it, they'd been feared by the farmers into leaving their union, the damned half-witted joskins they were. George Sand was the foreman at the Meiklebogs, a great meikle childe with a long moustache and a head on him like a Clydesdale horse. He said, *And what the hell better are the spinners? They've done a damn lot with their union and all? I sit down to good meat when the dirt are starving*, and another Meiklebogs man cried the same. *Ay, or a porter down at the station? What the hell has your union done for you? I've more money in my pouch right the now, let me tell you, than ever you had in your life, my birkie. I could show you right now a five and a ten and a twenty pound note.*

Jock Cronin said sneering-like, *Could you so? Could you show me five shillings?* and the childe turned red, he hadn't even that on him at the time, it had been no more than an empty speak, and he felt real mad to be shown up so. So he took Jock Cronin a crack on the jaw, by God it sounded like the crack of doom. Jock Cronin went staggering back among the spinners, and then the spinners and ploughmen were at it, in a minute as bonny a fight on as ever you saw in your life at Segget Show. You'd be moving off the Show-ground quiet with your quean, till you saw it start and then you'd run forward, and ask what was up, and not stop to listen, for it fair looked tempting; so you'd take a kick at the nearest backside, hard as you liked, and next minute some brute would be bashing in your face, and you bashing his, and others coming running and joining; and somebody trotting to Melvin's tent and bringing out Feet to stop the fight.

He was well loaded up with drink by then, Feet, and he'd only a bit of his uniform on. But he ran to the fighters and he cried *Hold on! What's all this jookery-packery now? Stop your fighting and get away home.*

But the coarse brutes turned on poor Feet instead, it was late that night when he crawled from the ditch and blinked his eyes and felt his head, the moon high up in a cloudless sky, the field deserted and a curlew crying.

All the folk had gone long ere that, even the youngest and daftest of them gone, home from the Segget Show in their pairs, there were folk at that minute on the Laurencekirk road, a lad and his lass on their whirring bikes, the peesies wheeping about in the moon, the childe with his arm around the quean's shoulder, the whir of the wheels below their feet, the quean with her cheek against the hand that rested shy on her shoulder, so, home, before them but still far off; and the dark came down and they went into it, into their years and to-morrows, they'd had that.

Some went further in business, if less in mileage. Near Skite a farmer went out to his barn, early next morning, and what did he see? Two childes and two lasses asleep in his hay. And he was sore shocked and went back for his wife, and she came and looked and was shocked as well, and if they'd a camera they'd have taken photographs, they were so delighted and shocked to see two queans that they knew in such a like way, they'd be able to tell the story about them all the years that they lived on earth; and make it a tit-bit in hell forbye.

Cis Brown had asked her father MacDougall if she could stay on late at the dance; and he'd said that she might, his favourite was Cis; and so she had done and at the dance end she had looked round about and had blushed as she wondered would anyone ask her to walk home to Segget? She was over young, she supposed, for all that, a college quean with her lessons and career, and not to waste her time on a loon. And she wished then she wasn't, and then looked up and saw a spinner, a boy beside her, about the same age as herself, she thought. He was tall like a calf, and shy and thin, he looked at her and he didn't look — *Are you going up home?*

She said she was and she thought as she said it, *What an awful twang those spinners speak!* She was half-ashamed to walk home with one. But so they got clear of the stamash of the fighting, saying never a word as they went through the grass. Then the boy gave a cough, *Are you in a hurry?* and Cis said *No, not a very great hurry,* and he said *Let's go down by*

*the Meiklebogs corn and home through the moor to the Segget
road.*

So she went with him, quiet, by the side of the park, the
path so narrow that he went on ahead, the moon was behind
them up in the Mounth, below them stirred the smell of the
stalks, bitter and strange to a quean from Segget, she bent and
plucked one in the dark, and nibbled at it and looked at the
boy. Behind them the noise of the Show grew faint: only for
sound the swish of the corn.

Then the path grew broader and they walked abreast, he
said sudden, but quiet, *You're Cis Brown from MacDougall's
shop aren't you?* Cis said *Yes*, not asking his name, he could
tell her if he liked, but she wasn't to ask. But he didn't tell, just
loped by her side, long-legged, like a deer or a calf, she
thought, leggy and quick and quiet. They heard as they passed
in that cool, quiet hour the scratch of the partridges up in the
moor, once a dim shape started away from a fence with a
thunderous clop of hooves in the dark, a Meiklebogs horse
that their footsteps had feared.

Syne they came to the edge of the moor, it was dark, here
the moon shone through the branched horns of the broom,
the whins tickled your legs and Cis for a while couldn't find
her way till the boy said *Wait. I know this place, I often come
here.* And his hand found hers and she felt in his palm the
callouses worn by the spindles there, he'd some smell of the
jute about him as well, as had all the spinner folk of the mills.

Water gleamed under the moon in a pool. Cis stopped to
breathe and the boy did the same, she saw him half turn round
in the moonlight and felt suddenly frightened of all kinds of
things – only a minute, frightened and curious, quick-strung
all at once, what would he do?

But he did not a thing but again take her hand, still saying
nothing, and they went through the moor, the low smoulder
of Segget was suddenly below them, and below their feet
sudden the ring of the road. She took her hand out of his then.
So they went past the Memorial up through The Close to the
door of the house of MacDougall Brown; and Cis stopped and

the boy did the same, and she knew him, remembered him, his name was Dod Cronin. And he looked at her, and looked away again; and again, as on the moor, queer and sweet, something troubled her, she had never felt it before for a soul – compassion and an urgent shyness commingled, sixteen herself and he about the same, daft and silly to feel anything like this! He slipped his hand slow up her bare arm, shy himself, he said something, she didn't know what. She saw him flush as she didn't answer, he was feared, the leggy deer of a loon!

And she knew at once the thing he had asked. She put up her hand to the hand on her arm, and next minute she found she was being kissed with lips as shy, unaccustomed as hers. And a minute after she was inside the door of MacDougall's shop, and had the door closed, and stood quivering and quivering alone in the dark, wanting to laugh and wanting to cry, and wanting this minute to last forever.

Else Queen of the Manse had held home with Dalziel. As they gained the road he turned round and said, with a canny glance back to where folk were fighting: *Would you like to come ben the way for some tea?* Else was still in a rage, she didn't know why, or with whom, or how it began, so she snapped: *No, I wouldn't, then. Do you know what the hour is?* Meiklebogs looked shy-like – she knew that he did, she could guess the soft-like look on his face, she felt half inclined to take it a clout – and said: *Oh ay, but I thought that maybe you would like to slocken up after the dancing about.*

She might as well do as the old fool said, even though there'd be no one else at Meiklebogs. Oh ay, she had heard the gossip of Segget, about Dalziel and his various housekeepers, though he did his own cooking now, as folk knew: It was said that two hadn't bidden a night, two others had come to the Meiklebogs alone and left in their due time, each with a bairn, a little bit present from the shy Meiklebogs. Well, that didn't vex Else, the stories were lies, old Meiklebogs – he was over shy ever to find out what a woman was like, unless it was out of a picture book, maybe: and even then it was like he would blush the few remaining hairs from his head. And even were there something in the Segget gossip she'd like to see the creature alive that would take advantage of *her* – just let him.

So she nodded, *All right, I'll come for a cup*. Meiklebogs said *Grand,* and the two went on, the moon was behind them, in front was the smell from the coles out still in the hayfield, tall, they'd had a fine crop that year of the hay. As they came near the house there rose a great barking and, Meiklebogs' meikle collie came out. Meiklebogs cried *Heel!* and the beast drew in, wurring and sniffing as they passed through the close. In the kitchen 'twas dark and close as a cave, the window fast-snecked, the fire a low glow. Meiklebogs lit a candle, *Sit down, will you, Else? I'll blow up the fire and put on the kettle.*

So he did, and Else took off her hat, and sat down and looked at the dusty old kitchen, with its floor of cement and its eight-day clock, ticking with a hirpling tick by the wall; and the photo of Lord Kitchener that everyone had heard of, over the fireplace, a dour-looking childe. 'Twas back in the War-years that Meiklebogs had got it, he'd cycled a Sunday over to Banchory, to a cousin of his there, an old woman-body; and she'd had the photo new-bought at a shop. Well, Meiklebogs had fair admired the fine thing, he thought it right bonny and said that so often that the woman-body cousin said at last he could have it. But it was over-big to be carried in his pouch, and the evening had come down with a spleiter of rain. But that didn't bog Meiklebogs, faith, no! He took off his jacket and tied the damn thing over his shoulder with a length of tow; and syne he put on his jacket above it. And the cousin looked on, and nodded her head: *Ay, the old devil's been in a pickle queer places. But I'm thinking that's the queerest he's ever been in.*

The dresser was as thick with dust as a desert, Else bent in the light of the candle above it, and wrote her name there, and Dalziel smiled shy. *Will you get down two cups from the hooks up there?*

Else did, and brought saucers as well, he gleyed at them:

Faith, I don't use them. I'm not gentry. Else said: *Oh, aren't you? Well I am.*

He poured the tea out and sat down to drink it. And faith! he found a good use for his saucer, he poured the tea in it and drank that way, every now and then casting a sly look at Else as though he were a mouse and she was the cheese. But she didn't care, leaning back in her chair, she was tired and she wondered why she'd come here, with this silly old mucker and his silly looks; and why Charlie had made such a fool of himself. Meiklebogs took another bit look at her then, she watched him, and then he looked at the window, and then he put out a hand, canny, on to her knee.

It was more than the hand, a minute after that, he louped on her as a crawly beast loups, something all hair and scales from the wall; or a black old monkey; she bashed him hard, right in the eye, just once, then he had her. She had thought she was strong, but she wasn't, in a minute they had struggled halfway to the great box bed. She saw once his face in the light of the candle, and that made her near sick and she loosed her grip, he looked just as ever, canny and shy, though his hands upon her were like iron clamps. She cried *You're tearing my frock*, he half-loosed her, he looked shy as ever, but he breathed like a beast.

Ah well, we'll take the bit thing off, Else.

Robert had gone to moil at his sermon: Chris heard the bang of the door upstairs. Ewan was in bed and already asleep, hours yet she supposed ere Robert came down. The kitchen gleamed in the light of the moon, bright clean and polished, with the stove a glow, she looked at that and looked at herself, and felt what she hoped wasn't plain to be seen, sticky and warm with the Segget Show. She'd have a bath ere she went to bed.

The stove's red eye winked as she opened the flue, and raked in the embers and set in fresh sticks; and on these piled coals and closed up the flue. In a little she heard the crack of the sticks, and went up the stairs to her room and Robert's, and took off her dress and took off her shoes, not lighting a light; the moon was enough. The mahogany furniture rose-red around, coloured in the moonlight, the bed a white sea, she sat on the edge and looked out at Segget, a ghostly place, quiet, except now and again with a bray of laughter borne on the wind as the door of the Arms opened and closed. Far down in the west, pale in the moon, there kindled a star that she did not know.

She stood up and went over and looked in the glass, and suddenly shivered, cold after the dancing; and drew the curtains and lighted the lamp, and took off her clothes in front of that other who watched, and moved in the mirror's mere. She saw herself tall, taller than of old, lithe and slim still with the brown V-shape down to the place between her breasts, she could follow the lines of the V with her fingers. And she saw her face, high cheek-boned and bronze, quiet and still with the mask of the years, her mouth too wide but she liked her teeth, she saw them now as she smiled at the thought her mouth was too wide! She loosed the pins in her hair and it fell, down to her knees, tickling her shoulders, faith! it was worse than a mane, a blanket, she'd cut it one day, if Robert would let her. She caught it aside and suddenly remembered a thing she'd forgot, forgotten for years, and looked for the dimple she once had had, and found it, there still, and saw her face flush faint as she minded, now that she thought of the thing at all, she'd been told that first night two years ago that the dimple was there—

Funny and queer that you were with a man! You did this and that and you lay in bed, there wasn't a thing of you he might not know, or you of him, from the first to the last. And you could speak of these things with him, and be glad, glad to be alive and be his, and sleep with your head in his shoulder's nook, tickling his chin, you supposed, with your hair – you could do all that and blush at the memory of a daft thing said on your wedding night!

Then she remembered she'd wanted a bath. She seemed to have stood there dreaming for hours, and found her dressing-

gown and her slippers, and went down the stairs and turned
on the taps. The water came gurgling out with a steam, she
saw her face in the shaving-glass, and stared at it – something
happening tonight?

She splashed for a little thinking of that, the water about
her stung quick at first; she saw herself fore-shortened and
fragile, but fair enough still, so she supposed – yes, she would
think that if she were a man! She lifted an arm and the water
ran down it, little pellets, they nested under her cheek, and
'twas then she thought of the thing she would do. Yes, she
would do it this very night! . . . And because that wouldn't
bear thinking about, here, she splashed herself and got out,
Robert's mirror blinded in a cloud of steam. She opened the
bathroom door and listened, there was no one to hear or see
for this once, she caught up her gear and ran quick up the
stairs, in the moving pattern of splashed moonlight high from
the window set in the gable, and gave a gasp as she felt a hand
on her shoulder, the arm came tight, she was kissed. Robert
coming down had seen the light splash as she opened the bathroom door.

She struggled away, *I've no clothes on!*

He said that he'd half suspected that, teasing her a minute,
then let her go. Then he said he'd go down and get ready their
supper, and went lightly down the stairs as a lad, it was Chris
who now stood still and looked down, high in her breast her
heart beating fast. She would, and this very night she would,
in spite of what he had told her and taught her!

She dressed and went down through the quiet of the Manse,
Robert popped his fair pow round the edge of the door, *Supper
in the kitchen, or shall we be grand?* She said she would like
the kitchen as well and pushed him into a chair as she spoke,
and took off Else's apron he'd draped on his trousers, and set
to the making of supper herself. He sighed and stretched out
and lighted his pipe, and drew at it, looking out of the window.
There's something in the night – or is it in you? He stood up
and walked to the window and peered, and came back and
looked at Chris for a while; and put out a finger upon her

forearm. *Funny to think that was once monkey-hair!*

She said that it wasn't, whatever his ancestors had been, hers were decent, like Hairy Hogg's, hers (they'd both heard the story). Robert chuckled over that as he sat down again, the only result of his sermon so far to drop a blot on the Provost's escutcheon. Hopeless, the Provost, and most of the others, Geddes, poor chap, had mislaid his guts; but he'd form that Segget League even yet, wait till this young Stephen Mowat came home!

Chris asked when that was but Robert didn't know, he thought very soon, then grew puzzled again. *Funny, there really is something about,* and Chris said, *Maybe,* and keeked at him sly, as he sat there and puzzled, and restrained herself from suddenly and daftly cuddling him tight. When she opened the kitchen window wide there came a faint scent on the tide of the wind, from the garden, the jonquils and marigolds glowed faint and pale in the light of the moon.

Then Chris set the table and they both sat down, it was fine to work in her kitchen untrammelled, good though Else was as a general rule, if it wasn't for the fact that the Manse was so big they could have done well without a maid here. She said that to Robert, he said *Yes, I know, I feel that way myself — for tonight! As though I could turn our Segget myself into Augustine's City of Gold. . . Something in the night that's making us like this,* and stopped and stared, *Why, Chris, you look different!*

She said he was silly — or 'twas maybe the bath! Then she felt herself colour with his eyes upon her. He shook his head, *An unusual bath!— A mental one? They're uncommon in Segget.*

He said *That's the first time I've ever heard you bitter,* and she said she didn't feel bitter, she was fine; and they washed up and dried in the moonlight quiet, together and content and yet more than that, once he brushed her shoulder as he went to and fro, carying the dishes over to the dresser; and he stopped and scowled, sore-puzzled upon her, *It must be that monkey-hair that's electric!*

And then they had finished and a mood came on Chris. *Let's go out in the garden.* And they both went out in the honey-dark shadows that the hedgerow threw, warm, a little mist crept up from Segget, under the nets in the strawberry patches the berries were bending their heads full ripe, Chris knelt by a bed and found one that was big, and ate half herself, Robert the other, seeing it waiting there on her lips. And, as he laughed and kissed her for that, something caught them both to a silence, foolish and quiet by the strawberry beds. The rooks chirped drowsily up in the yews as they passed beneath to the sheltered wall where love-in-a-mist and forget-me-nots bloomed blue and soft even now in the night, under the wall that led to the kirkyard, just low enough for Chris to look over.

And so for a little she stopped and looked, that third Chris holding her body for a while, how strange it was she stood here by Robert, so close that the warmth of his body warmed hers — when in such a short time she would die down there on a bit of land as deserted and left. They were gone, they were quiet, and the tears that were shed and the folk that came and the words that were said, were scattered and gone and they left in peace, finished and ended and all put by, the smell for them of forget-me-nots and the taste of a strawberry eaten at night and the kiss of lips that were hard and kind, and the thoughts of men that had held them in love and wondered upon them and believed in God.

All that had gone by, now under the gold of the moon the grass rose from those bodies that mouldered in Segget, the curlews were calling up in the Kaimes, the hay lay in scented swathes in the parks, night wheeled to morning in a thousand rooms where the blood that they'd passed to other bodies circled in sleep, unknowing its debt. Nothing else they had left, they had come from the dark as the dustmotes come, sailing and golden in a shaft of the sun, they went by like the sailing motes to the dark; and the thing had ended, and you knew it was so, that it would be with you in the end. And yet — and yet — you couldn't believe it!

Robert teased. *Choosing a place for your coffin?* and Chris

said *Just that, but don't plant me deep*, and he said with a
queer sudden fear in his voice, he startled Chris and she turned
to look, *Lord God, how I'd hate to be 'planted' myself! If I die
before you, Christine, see to that, that I'm sent for burning to a
crematorium. I'd hate to be remembered once I am dead*. Chris
thought in a flash how Segget would take it, should he die and
she get him a funeral like that. *They'd say, most likely, that
I'd poisoned you, Robert, and were trying to get rid of the
evidence, you know*. He laughed, *So they would!* and then
laughed again, a second laugh that was dreary, Chris thought.
*My God, were there ever folk like the Scots! Not only THEM
— you and I are as bad. Murderous gossip passed on as sheer
gospel, though liars and listeners both know it is a lie. Lairds,
ladies, or plain Jock Muck at the Mains — they'd gossip the
heart from Christ if He came, and impute a dodge for popular-
izing timber when He was crucified again on His cross!*

Chris said *That's true, and yet it is not. They would feed
Christ hungry and attend to His hurts with no thought of
reward their attendance might bring. Kind, they're so kind. . .
And the lies they would tell about how He came by those hurts
of His—*

*And yet you don't believe in a God. I've never asked you, but
do you, Chris?*

She bent her head as she answered, No, not looking at him;
but his laugh was kind. *You will sometime, however you find
Him.*

Then he looked at his watch, it was nearly midnight; and
suddenly Chris forgot the sad things. She ran away from him
and he came after, playing hide and seek, daft bairns both, in
the play and wisp of the moonlight's flow, till Chris lost breath
and he caught her up: and she suddenly yawned and he said,
Bedtime. And Chris minded now the thing she had planned,
and lingered a minute behind his step, shy as a bride to go with
him.

The room was in shadow, for the moon had veered, Robert
moved about quiet and lighted the lamp, his close-cropped
hair lay smooth on his head till his clothes ruffled it up as he

pulled them off. He looked over at Chris, *I'm not sleepy at all.* And said in a voice that he sometimes used *You look very sweet, Christine, tonight. Did you know?*

She reached up then and put out the light, and changed in the dark though he laughed and asked why. She answered nothing, slipping in beside him between the cool sheets; and lying so, still, she heard her heart hammer.

He lay quiet as well, then the curtain flapped and bellied in the breeze and you saw like a shadow the smile on his face, it was turned to you and you turned to him; and he said in a minute, *Why Christine!* solemn, and his hands came firmly under your chin to hold you so and to kiss you, stern. And you knew that you stood on the brink of that sea that was neither charted nor plumbed by men, that sea-shore only women had known, dark with its sailing red lights of storms, where only the feet of women had trod, hearing the thunder of the sea in their ears as they gathered the fruit on that waste, wild shore...

So; and his lips were in yours, and they altered, and you were gladder than you'd been for years, your arm went round his bared shoulder quick . . . and suddenly you were lying as rigid as death. Robert said, *Tired out, after all, Christine?*

For months after that she remembered that moment, her voice hadn't come from her lips for a minute; then she said, *Just a bit,* and heard him draw breath, and she said again, soft *Not TOO tired, Robert,* and had set her teeth fast after that, for an age, the thunder of that sea cut off by a wall, as she herself was, by a wall of fire; but she said not a word of either of these, stroked his hair where it clung to his brow; and he put his head on her breast and slept, after a while: and the house grew still.

She'd sleep soon herself, she'd put that damn dream by, the dream of a bairn fathered by Robert – not now, maybe never, but she could not tonight, not with memory of that scar that was torn across the shoulder of this living body beside her, the scar that a fragment of shrapnel had torn – but a little lower it would have torn his body, grunting, into a mesh of blood, with broken bones and with spouting blood, an animal mouthing in mindless torment. And she'd set herself to conceive a child – for the next War that came, to be torn like that, made blood and pulp as they'd made of Ewan – *Oh, Ewan, Ewan, that was once my lad, that lay where this stranger's lying the night, I haven't forgotten, I haven't forgotten, you've a Chris that lies with you there in France, and she shan't bring to birth from her womb any bairn to die as you for a madman's gab...*

Quiet, oh, quiet, greet soft lest he wake, who's so kind and dear, who's so far from you now. But you'll never have a bairn of his for torment, to be mocked by memorials, the gabblings of clowns, when they that remained at home go out to praise the dead on Armistice Day.

Faith, when it came there was more to remember in Segget that year than Armistice only. There was better kittle in the story of what happened to Jim the Sourock on Armistice Eve. He was aye sore troubled with his stomach, Jim, he'd twist his face as he'd hand you a dram, and a man would nearly lose nerve as he looked – had you given the creature a bad shilling, or what? But syne he would rub his hand slow on his wame, *It's the pains in my breast that I've gotten again*; and he said that they were fairly awful sometimes, like a meikle worm moving and wriggling in there. Folk said he fair did his best to drown it, and God! that was true, the foul brute would go home, near every night as drunk as a toff, and fall in the bed by the side of his wife, she'd say *You coarse brute, you've come drunken again*; but he'd only groan, with his hand at his stomach, the worm on the wriggle like a damned sea-serpent.

Well, the Sourock and his mistress kept a pig, and the night of November the tenth Dite Peat closed up his shop and came over to kill it. He fair was a hand at a killing, was Dite, and the pig looked over its ree as he came, and knew fine what the knife and axe were for. So it started to scraich, and Dite grinned at the brute, *Wait a minute, my mannie, I'll let that scraich out*. And the Sourock's wife, that was standing by, felt queer as she saw that look on his face, she thought him a tink, but he fair could kill, not useless entirely like that gawpus Jim.

So she asked Dite in for a dram ere he started, and down he sat with his dram and his cake, and he drank down the one like a calf with its milk and ate up the cake like a famished dog. Syne he said it was over late tonight to cut up the beast out there in the ree, he'd come over the morn and see to that, Armistice Day would be a fine time to do a bit cutting about among flesh – *Fegs, mistress, I've seen humans carved up like pigs, like bits of beef in a butcher's shop, and it fair looked fine, as I often thought, you couldn't wonder at those cannibal childes*—

The Sourock's wife asked if he'd like to see her sick, Dite said, *Be sick as you like, I won't mind; you've an uneasy stomach for a potman's wife.* And she broke down and grat then and said what a fool she had been to marry a creature like Jim, her that was a decent bit parlourmaid once, with her wages her own and her fine new clothes, Jim had sworn in those days he was fair tee-tee, now he drank like a drain and stank like one, too, he wouldn't care a fig though he came of a night and found her lying dead in her bed. Dite thought, *B'God, if he'd sense he'd dance!* but he didn't say that, he didn't care a damn for the Sourock's wife or the Sourock's troubles, why should you care about any man's troubles, there were damn the few that had cared for yours – not that you'd asked them, you could manage them fine.

So he rose up and said, *Well then, I'll go and have a bit play with that beast in the ree.*

She asked if he'd manage the thing by himself, she was off for the night to her sister in Fordoun, soon's she'd laid his supper for the Sourock, not that she supposed the sot would eat it, he'd come home and just stiter to his bed, as usual. Dite said he would manage fine on his own, and went out, and the Sourock's wife a bit later heard the grunt of the pig turn into a scream, nasty to hear, and then it came shrill, and she put on her hat and took her bit bag and went out and down by the ree as she went, not wanting to look and see Dite at his work of killing her pig for the winter dinners. But something drew her eyes in over the ree, there was Dite Peat, he was covered with sharn, he'd tripped in a rush he had made at the pig, now he'd cornered it up at the back of the ree. Its mouth was open and its bristles on end, and it whistled through its open jaws like the sound of the steam from an engine in Segget station.

So she didn't look longer, went hurrying on, it had been a fine beast, the pig, she remembered, would stand on its trough with a pleased-like grumph as she scratched the bristles on its back and lugs, fair a couthy beast, though scared at the rats, it had once near tripped her as she stood in its ree, she thought the creature was aiming at her; but instead it had caught a glimpse of a rat and was trying to get behind her for safety. So she turned the corner by Moultrie's shop and heard up in Segget the pig scream again, and she found herself hoast, like a fool of a bairn, with water in the nose – where was her hanky? And she suddenly thought of Dite Peat as a rat, a great rat with its underhung jaw and cruel eyes, creeping on the pig that was frightened at rats and had run once frightened to hide behind her – och, she was daft or soft or just both, and damn it! she couldn't get at her hanky.

But Dite had cornered Jim's pig at last, as it swithered its head he saw it set fine, and swung the bit axe, the blade of it up, the pig screamed again and fell at his feet with a trickle of blood from its snout and its trotters scraping and tearing at the sharn of the ree. So Dite turned the brute over, slow, with his axe, and took out his knife and cut its throat, slow, and held the throat open to led it bleed well. Syne he slung it on his shoulder and took it to the kitchen, and hung it on a hook and left it to drip.

It was fell dark then, as he slung the brute up, its flesh was still warm, and it minded him well of the bits of folk that a shell would fling Feuch! in your face with a smell of sharn, out in the War – He had liked it fine; there was something in blood and a howling of fear that kittled up a man as nothing else could. So he left the pig to drip in the dark, and it moved quick once, when the sinews relaxed, and Dite gave a laugh and gave it a slap.

'Twas near to ten when he took a bit dander back again to the Sourock's house, a blatter of rain was dinging on Segget, sweeping and seeping up over the Howe, lying at night on the winter's edge with its harvests in, potato-crops with dripping shaws in the rigs of red clay. Dite pulled down his cap and lifted the sneck and went into the house of Jim the Sourock. He cracked a match and looked at the pig, it was getting on fine, had near finished to drip, he would leave it now till the morn's night. And then – he was aye a coarse brute, was Dite Peat, though you couldn't but laugh when you heard the tale – a grand idea came into his head, and he sat down and thought it all out and syne laughed, and took down the pig he had killed from its hook and slung it over his shoulder and went ben to the bed the Sourocks slept in, a great box-bed that was half-covered in.

Dite threw back the blankets and put the pig down, near the side of the bed where Sourock's wife slept – all the wives of Segget slept at the front, a woman aye sleeps at the front of the bed where she can get quicker out than a man, that's sense, for the lighting of the morning fire or getting up in the dark to be sick, as a woman will, when she's carrying a bairn, and not disturbing her man from his rest.

So Dite dumped down the pig in the bed, and covered it up, careful and canny. And he took a bit dander up through Segget, to freshen himself, as he said, for the night; and syne he went home, for he was fell tired.

'Twas an hour or so later ere the Sourock came home, he'd had to clear up the bar in the Arms, and lock the doors and hand over the silver, and stoke up a fire for a traveller childe that was spending the night in the Arms' best room. What with one thing and another that night, the drinks he had ta'en and the heat of the Arms, Jim came through Segget with a head fair spinning. As he crossed the Square he keeked at the angel, and damn't! there were two of the things up there, he stared at them fairly stern for a while; not decent for angels to cuddle like that. But then he decided he was fell drunk, and shook his head, two angels still there, and went slithering up through the lurching East Wynd.

Well, he got home at last through the drift of the rain, there was hardly a light to be seen in Segget, it cuddled up close in its beds and slept, with its goodmen turned to the wall and its wives wearied with a day of bairns and of claik, the bairns lying three-four in a bed, though five or six among the tink spinners, they bred like lice and they slept like them, too, Ake Ogilvie said – an ill bit speak, a man couldn't help the bairns that came, sometimes a woman was just of the kind that would take if you gave her no more than a squeeze, the next was cannier: you just couldn't tell.

Well, Jim the Sourock had been lucky so far, a fell good thing, one Sourock enough; but he wasn't thinking that or aught else, for a while he couldn't lay hands on his sneck. But he got it at last and let himself in, and sat down on the chair that stood by the door, and gave a great paich and rubbed at his middle.

Syne he loosened his boots, not bothering with a lamp, he knew better than that, he might fire the damned house; so he got his boots off and left them lie there, and made for the bedroom, holding to the wall, he would know the way in his sleep by now. Then the first thing happened that jaggered his night, his knees went bang 'gainst the side of a tub; he tumbled half-way into the tub, the bottom was full of some sticky soss, the Sourock swore and lurched up to his feet and wiped his hands on the seat of his breeks, he supposed that the wife had been washing fell late – the careless bitch to leave the tub there!

Well, he edged round about it and got to the door, and stitered inside and grumbled out loud, *Do you know you've near broken my neck, eh, woman?*

His wife said nothing, that wasn't surprising, considering that she was five miles off. But the Sourock had forgotten all about that, he went shoggling and stitering about the room, pulling off his breeks and his socks, nothing else, he aye slept in his drawers and kept fine and warm. Syne he made for the bed and went in by the foot, his left hand on the hump he took for his wife. So he pushed back the blankets and got in below, and felt about with his feet a while to lay them on his wife and get himself warm. But damn the warmth could he find the night, so he reached out to give the creature a joggle – *Jean, are you wake?*

Well, the hump said nothing and the Sourock by then had his head a bit cleared through the fall in the tub. And he felt in a rage – *Here, answer me, can't you? What's wrong with the like of you, eh, the night?* And he put his hand under the blankets to feel her, so he did, and nearly shot out of bed. *Jean – God, Jean, but you're awful cold!*

She said nothing at all and he sudden felt ill. He put out his hand, she was cold as a stone – worse than that, the hair frozen hard on her skin, the Sourock was dribbling and yammering by then. *Jean, Jean, waken up; you're near frozen stiff!* And at last he could bear the thing no longer, and got from his bed and found a match and lighted it up and pulled back the blanket. And he saw a great gaping throat in the light, and the spunk went out, his yell maybe blew it.

That was the story he'd tell to folk. For the rest, you gathered he pulled himself together, and went out to get some body go for the doctor: he was maybe a bit fuddled, but he knew what he wanted and was keeping quite calm, or so he would swear. That maybe was so and maybe it wasn't, 'twas strange anyway if he felt like that, that when Peter Peat heard a bellow and yammer and somebody beat on the door of his house like the angel of God on the Judgement Day – and Peter got from his bed and looked out, there was no angel but Jim the Sourock, in his sark, with no boots or breeks on either, his face and neck all covered with blood. And he yammered in the light of Peter Peat's candle – *Let's in, Peter Peat. Oh, God, let me in!*

But Peter wasn't near such a fool as do that. *Go home to your bed,* he said, *and keep quiet. Is this a time to disturb decent folk? Go home and sleep by your good-wife's side* – And he couldn't say more, the creature of a Sourock was fairly daft, he decided, for he yelped like a dog hard-kicked, and vanished from the range of Peter Peat's eyes; and Peter closed down the window and went back, canty, to sleep by his meikle wife's side, like a calf cuddling up to a haystack, folk said.

The Sourock was fair demented by then, he tried the house of old Hairy Hogg, and the Provost came down and keeked through the slit that was set in the door for letters, fair gentry. And to the Sourock cried *Let me in, oh, I'm feared*. And old Hogg said *In? To your sty, you drunkard! You're a fair disgrace to Scotland and Segget. Go home like a decent man to your wife*. The Sourock vanished so quickly at that that the Provost was fair convinced he'd obeyed — ay, there still were folk had the power to rule, them that come of the Burns' blood.

Well, where do you think that Jim ended up? Down in the house of MacDougall Brown. MacDougall let him in and heard his bit story. Cis got from her bed and came down to hear. MacDougall cried on her to go back, but she wouldn't, she said *All right, I won't look* — not decent for a lassie to look on a man when he hadn't on breeks, or not at least till she'd married one herself, syne she'd think, said Ake Ogilvie, his breeks fair the best bit of the bargain, and the Scythian childe that invented the things the greatest benefactor of the human race.

Well, Cis boiled some water to wash the Sourock, and MacDougall, it fair must have been a sore wrench, made tea for the creature and he drank it up, and his stomach for once didn't turn at the taste. And he felt a bit better and washed his foul neck, telling how his wife lay with her throat cut. MacDougall said, *Ay, she has met the Lord, as you yourself one day must do. Repent and come to the arms of Jesus* — that's what he'd planned from the first, you gathered. Well, the Sourock said that he would, by God, he'd fair be tee-tee from that minute, he would; and MacDougall was pleased as punch and near kissed him, he was awful fond of bringing souls to God, was MacDougall, and threatening the souls with the pains of hell if they traded at any other shop but his.

So he loaned a pair of his breeks to the Sourock, and out the pair of them went together, and went canny up to the Sourock's

house and ben to the room where the red corpse lay, Mac-
Dougall carrying the lantern he'd lit. And he lifted the lantern
and glowered at the thing that was lying there in the Sourock's
bed, and cried *Hoots, man, this is no the mistress* and pulled
back the blankets and showed Jim the pig. And the Sourock
glowered at it, *Well, then, I'm damned. Man, but it fair looked
her image to me.*

They were into Armistice Day by then, though neither Mac-
Dougall nor the Sourock cared, they shifted the pig and went
to their beds, the rain held on through the night, and morning
came soaking laired across the clay parks, the parks that be-
girdle Segget in red, in a wheep of gulls driven in from the
coast, if you drove into Segget that day you'd have seen enough
glaur around to make you believe the tale that they never took
a good wash in Segget till the harvest was over and the bills
all paid. That was no more than a speak, you knew, but it made
a fine hit at the Segget folk, them so damned proud of their
Burgh and Kaimes, and their new bit kirk that hadn't a steeple,
not so proud of their mills and the spinners that made up the
most of their population. And faith, by the time Armistice was
out, it was less proud than ever of its spinners, Segget.

The day had cleared by eleven o'clock, and folk came taiking
in round the angel that stood so bonny in Segget Square. Ay,
fairly a gey bit gathering, impressive – except for the smell,
Ake Ogilvie said. But he aye was sneering something like that,
the coarse brute, why couldn't he let folk a-be? And you saw
him there in the midst of the lave, with his medals pinned on
his waistcoat flap, and his hands in his pockets, looking at the
angel as though he wouldn't sleep with the lass though she
tried to come down and crawl into his bed.

Sim Leslie, the bobby, that folk called Feet, tried to form a
half-circle here, the Provost to the right, all hair and horns,
with his popping bit eyes and his ancestor Burns, he was telling how Burns was a patriot childe, aye ready to shed his blood
for the land. Ake Ogilvie said *Ay. He slew a fell lot of the
French – with his mouth. He was better at raping a servant*

quean than facing the enemy with a musket. And Hairy Hogg
said that was a foul slander, Ogilvie mad with jealousy, just,
because the dirt that he wrote himself was worse than dirt,
compared with the Bard; and Ake said he'd rather be just plain
dirt than slush on a dung-heap, disguised as a flower; and
young Alec Hogg, that was home from Edinburgh, cried *Cannot
you leave my father alone?*

Ake looked him up and down with a long, cold stare. *I never
touch dung except with a fork, but give's none of your lip, or
I'll break my rule.* Alec Hogg cried *Try it!* and maybe in a
minute there would have been a fine bit fight on the go, right
there by the angel in Segget Square, folk round about looking
shocked as could be and edging nearer for a better look, when
they saw the minister coming from East Wynd, and the choir
coming with him; and folk cried, *Wheest!*

'Twas him, the minister, that had started the thing and had
you all out in the Square today, old Greig, that filled the pulpit
afore him, hadn't bothered to hold any service at all, he'd
over-much sense to catch cold in the Square. But the Reverend
Mr Colquohoun was fell keen, he'd badgered folk to close up
their shops and gotten the mills to close down as well, he fair
was a go-ahead billy, like, though some folk said he was more
than that, he'd barely started interfering yet. 'Twas said he'd
already the kirk session against him, with his preaching for
this and that daft-like reform: and he'd badgered Hairy Hogg
near from his wits – or what little wits were left the old Provost – about the town council and where it might meet, and
what it could do, and who were the members, and why didn't
they light Segget at night, did they know the drains in West
Wynd were bad, when were the mills inspected and how? . . .
Folk said the next thing you'd find him keen on would be
shifting the Kaimes for a seat in his yard, ay, if the creature
went on at this rate he'd soon have all Segget on his hands to
fight.

A raw wind blew down the Howe through the Square and
fluttered the minister's robes as he prayed, his thin white face
down-bent as he prayed, his prayer just said in an ordinary

voice. It made a man kind of uneasy to hear the way that he spoke to God like that — not as any other ministers would do, as though they'd only half-swallowed their dinners and had the remainder still in their throats.

No, no, the Reverend Colquohoun spoke plain, some liked it that way, you were damned if you did: and he asked the mercy of God on a world unawakened yet from a night that was past. And he said that God had made neither night nor day in human history. He'd left it in the hands of Man to make both, God was but Helper, was but Man himself, like men he also struggled against evil, God's wounds had bled, God also had died in the holocaust in the fields of France. But He rose anew, Man rose anew, he was as undying as God was undying — if he had the will and the way to live, on this planet given to him by God. *A pillar of cloud by day and a pillar of fire by night* — they had hung in the sky since the coming of men, set there by God for the standards of men, clouds and the shining standards of rain, the hosts of heaven for our standard by night . . . A trumpet had cried and unsealed our ears; would it need the lightning to unseal our eyes?

And after a bit you stopped listening to that, you didn't know much about preaching and the like, but was that the way a minister should speak? You were damned if you thought so: fair heathen it sounded. And you took a canny bit keek round about, at the throng of the Segget folk that were there — hardly a spinner, where were the dirt? There was Mrs Colquohoun, anyway, bonny in a way, with a sulky-like face, a common bit quean the minister had wifed, folk that had known her well in Kinraddie said she had once been as blithe as bonny; but now she was altered out of all manner, if they met her and spoke to her and cried, *Chris!* she would smile and be friends enough, but different somehow — ay, she'd grown damned proud.

Well, there she was, and her son as well, the son of her first bit man you had heard, with a cool, dark face, but not a bad bairn. Nearby was the Provost and next him, his son, the Fasher, rigged out in his baggy breeks. MacDougall Brown was

well to the fore, not that he'd fought in the War, but he'd
sung; and Peter Peat, the tailor, a terrible patriot; and Dite,
the foul tink; and Dominie Geddes, and the three women
teachers; and the porters and stationy, Smithie and Ake. Will
Melvin you could see near the Station folk, John Muir and
Bruce and a birn of the like. Syne the minister held up his hand
for quiet, and you knew that it was eleven o'clock.

And faith! The quiet would have been fell solemn, but for a
great car that came swishing up, from the south, and turned,
and went up East Wynd. Folk had stood still like stooks of
rags, but they moved then and stared at the thing go by – all
but the minister, he stood like a stone. Then he said, low and
clear, *We will now sing the hymn 'Our God, our help in ages
past'.*

You cleared your throat and looked right and left, felt shy
to be such a fool as stand there and sing without a bit organ
to help; and the first few words were a kind of growl till you
heard the minister himself sing up. And just as folk were
getting in the swing, the dirt of spinners came down to the
Square.

They came marching down through the Close from West
Wynd, a twenty or thirty of the ill-getted creatures, with their
mufflers on, not in decent collars, their washy faces crinkled
with grins, marching along there four by four. In front of the
lot was that tink John Cronin, and over his shoulder he carried
a red flag, and the spinners behind him were laughing and
joking, two-three of them women, the shameful slummocks.
Well, your mouth fell open, as it damn well might, you had
never yet seen such a sight in Segget; and you stopped your
singing, and so did some more, and some after that, till the
only folk left were the Reverend Colquohoun, and his wife, and
Cis Brown, and that gawpus Else Queen. And then Ake Ogilvie
that hadn't yet sung took a look round about and started to
sing, as loud as could be, as though he'd new-awakened; he
did it to be different from others as usual.

But afore folk could pipe up again to the thing the spinners
were close and Jock Cronin cried *Halt!* And they swung round

about him and stood in a circle, and next minute they'd started singing themselves, loud as could be, and fair drowning the hymn, a song about shrouding their dead in red, and about their bit limbs being stiff and cold; and God alone knows what kind of stite.

Well, that fairly finished the Memorial Service. The minister had turned as white as a sheet, he finished his singing and so did his wife, here and there a man in the crowd cried out, *Have you no manners?* – speaking to the spinners. And Feet, the policeman, went over to them, *Now then, you're causing a disturbance*, he said, he was awful proud of that word, was Feet, that he'd got in a book on how bobbies should speak. But they took no notice, just stood round and sang, till he pushed through the ring round that tink John Cronin; then they stopped and Cronin said *Well, Feet, what's up?*

Feet was fair roused, a patriot-like childe, he hadn't been out to the War himself, they wouldn't let him go with feet like that in case he might block up the trenches, folk said. But he'd fair been one for the War all the same, and he wasn't to see its memory insulted by a pack of tink brutes that didn't wear collars – them and their song about flinching and sneering from a scarlet standard and God knows what. Who ever heard of a scarlet standard – Just a tink way of calling their betters bloody. . . So he said to Jock Cronin, *Aren't you black ashamed to break in on the War Memorial service?* And Jock Cronin said No, *we're not, you see, Feet, we all had a taste of the War ourselves. Take a keek at our chests now, Feet my lad, and then have a look at your own and see if there's anything on it the like of on ours!*

And then you saw plain what he meant, he himself, and all of the spinners that had marched to the Square, had War-medals pinned on their jackets or waistcoats, they were all of them men who had been to the War: except the three women, and they wore medals sent on to them after their folk were dead. Well, that fair staggered Feet, and you felt sorry for him, especially as you had no medal yourself, you hadn't been able to get to the War, you'd been over-busy with the shop

those years, or keeping the trade going brisk in the Arms, or
serving at Segget as the new stationmaster. And well you might
warrant if the King had known the kind of dirt that those
spinners were he wouldn't have lashed out as he'd done with
his medals.

But Jock Cronin pushed his way past Feet, and jumped on
the pedestal under the angel, and cried out *Comrades — not
only mill folk, but others as well that I see down there: WE
went to the war, we know what it was, we went to lice and
dirt and damnation: and what have we got at the end of it all?
Starvation wages, no homes for heroes, the capitalists fast on
our necks as before. They're sacking men at the mills just now
and leaving them on the bureau to starve — that's our reward,
and maybe it's yours, that's the thing we must mind today.
Not to come here and remember the dead, they've a place
that's theirs, and we'll share it some time, they're maybe the
better compared with some that live here in Segget worse-fed
than beasts. It's the living that's our concern, you chaps. Come
over and join us, the Labour Party. You first, Mr Colquohoun,
you were out there, you've sense.*

And as the impudent brute ended up he waved his hand to
the Reverend Colquohoun, and for a minute after that there
was such a quiet you could near have cut it and eaten it in
chunks, it was that damned solid, while all the folk stared.
Syne the minister just turned his back and said, cool, *I think
we'll go home, Chris,* to his wife; and she nodded and said
nothing, they were both cool and calm. It made a man boil to
see them so meek, damn't! if you had been a minister, would
you let yourself be insulted like that? No, you wouldn't; and
neither any minister in the days before the coming of the War,
the War had fair been a ruination, letting tinks like the Cronins
find out that their betters ate and smelt just the same as themselves.

Well, next there was near a fight broke out. Ake Ogilvie cried
to Jock Cronin, *Oh ay, and where the hell did YOU serve in the
War?* And Jock Cronin said, *Up in the front, my lad, not
scrounging behind with the Royal Engineers. — No, you hadn't*

enough brain for them you poor fool, Ake Ogilvie said, and would maybe have said more, if the minister hadn't turned round and cried, *Ogilvie!* And Ake went off, and the spinners all laughed. Some folk stayed near to hear what they'd say, most decent bodies went over to the Arms and spoke of the things they'd have done to the spinners if they'd stayed behind in Segget Square.

Chris ran nearly all the way from the Square, Mr Geddes and his teachers were coming for lunch (as they called it, but they ate it just as a dinner); and the meat was cooking in the Manse's oven. Else you could see flying on in front, as anxious as you, you'd left Robert behind, he'd laughed and slowed down and lighted his pipe. But you ran up under the drip of the yews through the Manse front door and through to the kitchen, and there was Else with her face like a fire, leaning panting up by the kitchen back door, and a burning smell from the open oven. Else cried *Well, I was just in time!* and pointed to the chicken out in its ashet, it had just begun to burn at the top. And you said *That was fine, you're a blessing, Else. Sit and rest a minute.* Else took a look at herself in the glass, *I've a face like that flag the spinners were carrying. Did you ever see such nasty brutes?*

Chris said they hadn't much manners, she thought. But she'd never before seen men with that flag, or heard them singing the song about it – hirpling and sad, but it caught you somehow, there was something in it that you knew was half-true, true with a truth that drew your mind back to Chae Strachan far in your younger days, who had said the mission of the common folk was to die and give life with their deaths forever... Like Robert's God, in a way, you supposed.

And maybe that was Robert's own thought, Chris came on him in the sitting-room, standing and staring queerly at Segget, harsh-blue, rain-driven, in its clouded noon. Chris put up a hand on his shoulder. *Not vexed? The service was fine, and I liked what you said.* Robert squeezed her hand, *My vanity's vexed. That's all, I suppose, and those spinner chaps – a perfect devil if they're right, Christine.* Chris said *How right?* and he said *Their beliefs — a war of the classes to bring fruit to the War. Remember the Samson I preached that day I tried for the kirk of Segget, Christine? I suppose we saw him in the Square today, with a muffler on and a thin, starved look. If his betters won't mend the world, HE may!*

Then his gaze drew in, *Lord, here they come. His betters — well, well. They're just at the door.*

Chris herself went and opened the door, Mrs Geddes came gushing in over the mat, Miss M'Askill behind, sharp as a needle, the second teacher at Segget school. She eyed Chris up and down as a ferret might, *How d'you do, Mrs Colquohoun? Disgraceful exhibition down in the Square!* Chris had heard of Miss M'Askill from Else, straight as a pole and nearly as bare, and she wore her hair in two great plaits, low down on her brow, and it gave her a look like a stirk with its head in a birn of hay; and whenever she saw a new man in the toun she'd stare at him till the man would blush, up and down in the line of her stare; and she'd give a bit sniff (or so said Else), as much as to say *What, marriage with you?*

But damn the soul had offered that yet, not even for a night at the furthest gait, Ake Ogilvie had said he would rather sleep with a Highland steer in the lee of a whin. Chris tried hard not to remember that, she would laugh if she did: and so she did not, but shook hands instead with Miss Ferguson next, her that they called The Blusher in Segget. And she started to blush as though someone had couped a jar of red ink on her head at that minute, the blush came thicker and thicker each second, till Chris felt so sorry she blushed as well. Then Miss Jeannie Grant, dapper and trig, with a fresh, fair face, *Hello, Mrs Colquohoun! What did you think of the fun in the Square?* Last, Mr Geddes, he looked at you bitter, as though he thought you poor stuff like the most of mankind, and shook your hand limp, and trailed after the others, his hands in his pockets, till he tripped on a toy of Ewan's in the hall, a wooden horse, and it fell with a clatter and Ewan came running out to see why.

Mr Geddes had nearly fallen with the thing. Now he picked it up, a great splinter of wood torn out of its side. Ewan said

What a fool, man, why didn't you look? and Chris cried *Ewan!* Mr Geddes grinned. *He's right enough, I suppose I'm a fool. I'm sorry, young man.* Ewan said *So am I.*

Chris wanted to giggle, but again did not, instead looked solemn as a funeral, near – or two funerals if you counted one of John Muir's; and separated the Dominie and Ewan ere worse came; and shooed Mr Geddes in after his wife.

Robert was there, he'd greeted them all, and was standing by with the sherry decanter. Mr Geddes had lost the smile plucked out for Ewan, like a last swede plucked from a frozen field, he said bitter as ever, *A drop, Colquohoun,* and sat down and looked round the room as though he thought damn little of any thing in it.

And then Ewan started to sing outside, in the moment when folk were sipping their sherry; and Miss M'Askill near dropped her glass. Chris got to her feet and felt herself blush, silly to do that, and she called out *Ewan!* and he cried back *Yes?* and opened the door. And Chris felt a fool, the whole room looking at her. *Why were you singing that song just now?*

Ewan said, polite, *I like it, mother. I think it's a bloody fine song, don't you?*

Else saved the situation, as usual. They heard her feet in the hall, Ewan vanished, and the door was snibbed with a sudden click. Miss M'Askill said it was dreadful, dreadful, those spinners corrupting even the children. Didn't Mrs Colquohoun think the authorities ought to take steps to putting it down?

Miss Jeannie Grant was sitting by Robert, showing a fine length of leg, nice leg, she said *What's 'it'? Put a stop to singing the Red Flag, do you mean?* And Miss M'Askill said, *Yes, that for one thing, there are plenty of others – the ongoings in general of those paid agitators.* And Miss Jeannie Grant said, *Well, I'm an agitator, but I get no pay. Where do the others get theirs? I'd like to apply!* And Miss M'Askill looked at her so awful, 'twas a wonder she didn't shrivel up there and then. But instead she just winked blithe at Chris, and drank up her sherry and had some more.

Syne they were all speaking of the scene in the Square, Geddes said bitter that the spinners had behaved as you would expect such cattle to do, neither better nor worse than other Scotch folk. All Scots were the same, the beastliest race ever let loose on the earth. Oh no, he wasn't bitter, he'd got over that, he'd got over living amongst them, even: their gossip that was fouler than the seeping of a drain, there was hardly a soul in a village like Segget but was a murderer ten times over in word — they hadn't enough courage to be it in deed. Spinners were no worse than the rest, or not much. As for this business of a Segget League, well, he voted Tory himself every time, and no league could remain non-political long. His advice: Colquohoun leave the lot alone, if there's anything a hog hates it's cleaning its sty.

Robert asked Miss Ferguson what she might think, Miss Ferguson blushed till Chris feared for her vest, her underthings would sure be on fire in a minute, she stammered that she didn't know, for sure, some of the spinners' children were cruel, they'd get a girl in the playground and tease her, or worse than that — and Miss Ferguson blushed some more, a torrent, till Chris in pity looked away, and thought herself of her own schooldays and those things that were WORSE in the reek of the playground, hot and still on a summer day and a crowd of loons round about you, laughing, with bright, hot eyes and their short, fair hair, and cruel, eager fingers . . . but she hadn't much minded, she'd been able even then to look after herself, it needed a sudden twist of her mind to think, appalled, that Ewan might do that, might stand by some girl and pry beastly in things—

She switched to listening to the talk again, Mrs Geddes was having all the say now, the three teachers had no other course, very plain, but listen to the Dominie's wife with attention. And Mrs Geddes said what was really wrong, with the whole of Segget, not only the spinners, was Refusal to Cooperate in Fellowship. But the WRI was to combat that, and she really didn't think that this League was needed. The WRI was to organize socials, and teach the mothers all kinds of fresh things – basket work, now, that was very interesting. . . And she shone and wobbled like a jelly from a mould, and Geddes' look of contempt grew deeper.

Miss Jeannie Grant put her sherry-glass down. *I don't see anything your League can do. But the Labour Party can here in Segget, if only we make the branch strong enough;* and she looked as sweet as an apple as she said it, and young and earnest, and Chris half liked her, as though she stood on a hill and looked down on her own youth only beginning to climb, half-liking its confidence, pitying its blindness. But she thought for that matter, again and again (and more than ever since their coming to Segget) that she was older than most she met, older even than Robert himself – older than all but her own son Ewan!

Then they heard Else stamping out in the hall, and she rang the bell and they went through to dinner, Mrs Geddes calling it lunch, of course, she was so genteel Chris thought it a wonder she should ever open her mouth for food. But she fair put away a good plateful and more, for the chicken was golden and cooked to a turn, Robert sat and carved when he'd said the grace, the grace that Chris thought so childlike and kind:

> God bless our food,
> And make us good,
> And pardon all our sins,
> For Jesus Christ's sake.

Syne Miss M'Askill was asking Chris, sharp, *Are you fond of social work, Mrs Colquohoun?* and Chris said *Not much, if you mean by that going round and visiting the kirk congregation.* Miss M'Askill raised up her brows like a chicken considering a something lying on the ground, not sure if it was just a plain empty husk, or an interesting bit of nastiness, like. Mrs Geddes said she was very disappointed, she'd hoped they'd have Mrs Colquohoun to help – with the work of the WRI, she meant; and why didn't Mrs Colquohoun like visiting? And suddenly Chris understood her and hated her – she

minded the type. oh, well, well enough! So she smiled sweet
at her and said *Oh, you see, I wasn't always a minister's wife.
I was brought up on a croft and married on one, and I mind
what a nuisance we thought some folk, visiting and prying
and blithering about socials, doing everything to help us, or
so they would think – except to get out and get on with the
work!*

Robert's face went queer, a half-laugh, a half-scowl, but
Miss Jeannie Grant was delighted, she said *And get off your
backs, you could surely have added! You're a socialist the
same as I am, you know.* Chris shook her head, she knew
nothing about it, sorry already she had spoken like that, Mrs
Geddes had gone quite white for a minute, Chris knew she had
made an enemy in Segget. The Dominie stared at his plate with
a sneer; Miss M'Askill looked at Robert, brows up; Mrs Ferguson looked at her plate and blushed; only Ewan ate on,
as calm as ever, except when he said, *Can I go now, please?*

Chris caught Miss M'Askill's eye when he'd gone, it said,
plain as plain, *A very spoilt child.* And you supposed that it
really was true, the truth as she'd see it, who'd never had a
child, who didn't know the things that bound you to Ewan, as
though his birth-cord still bound you together, he tugged at
your body, your heart, at your womb, in some moments of pity
it was sheer, sick pain that tore at you as you comforted him.
But THAT you could never explain to a woman who'd never
had a bairn, had never, you supposed, yet lain with a man,
known all the shame and all the red splendour and all the dull
ache and resentment of marriage that led to the agony and
wonder of looking on the face, sweet and blind as the eyes of
love, of a child new-born from your body's harbour. . . And
Chris roused herself, *Mr Geddes – pudding?*

Robert was trying to keep the talk going, but some thing
had spoiled the talk at the table – herself, Chris supposed,
with telling the truth. And she thought *They're just servant-
queans, after all, with a little more education and a little less
sense –* these, the folk Robert had thought could save Segget!
It was hardly likely he thought so now; what would he do with

his League and his plans? Still wait for young Stephen Mowat
to come home?

Suddenly in the midst and mid of them all – the words she
now used, the thoughts she thought, the clothes she wore and
the things she ate – Chris would see her father's face from
long syne, the jutting beard and the curling lip – *Come out of
that, quean, with your dirt of gentry!* And because she knew in
a way it was true, the gentry that or but little more, sometimes she'd stop in the middle of a talk, in the middle of a
walk, in the middle of a meal, and stare for so long that
Robert would say, *We've lost her again! Ewan, bring back your
mother!*

That feeling came over her later that day, when it brought
Stephen Mowat to tea at the Manse. Though none of them
guessed the fact at the time, it had been his car that passed
the service at eleven o'clock in Segget Square; but ere well the
car had reached Segget House the news had spread all around
the toun, young Stephen Mowat had come home at last, from
wandering about in foreign parts after leaving his English
university. And his shover told as they passed the Square
young Mowat had looked and seen the angel, and had groaned
aloud, *Oh God, even here – another bitch in a flannel shift!*
The shover said they'd seen birns of the statues as they
motored up from England that week, lasses in bronze and
marble and granite, dancing about on pedestal tops, he'd
thought them bonny, Mr Stephen hadn't, he said that Britain
had gone harlot-mad, and stuck up those effigies all over the
place, in memory no doubt of the Red Lamps of France.

And the shover said he should know about queans, young
Mowat, considering the number he'd had since he'd left the
college a six months back. No doubt he'd soon have them at
Segget House, he intended to bide there and fee a big staff,
and bring back the good old days to the toun. He was going
to look after the mills for himself, the estate as well, and the
Lord knows what.

Chris heard all this when the school-folk had gone, from
Else, when she went to the kitchen to help. But Else needed

no help, she'd a visitor there, Dalziel of Meiklebogs it was. He smiled shy and rose when he saw Chris come in, and she told him to sit, and Else poured out the news. Chris didn't feel excited, but she thought Robert might. *Well, that'll be fine, no doubt, for Segget. Oh, have we made any cakes for tea?*

Else said they hadn't, but they damned soon would. *Out of the way, there, Meiklebogs, now!* and pushed him into a chair, he sat canny, his cap in his hands, and watched while she baked. Chris went back to Robert and told him the news.

He said *Mowat home? It's an answer to prayer. And just as I heard the black dog come barking! Let's celebrate!* And he caught Chris, daft, and twirled about the room in a dance. So they didn't hear the knocking at the door, Else did, and went and brought Stephen Mowat in. They came to the door of the sitting-room and watched, till Chris saw them and stopped, and Robert did the same. And Else said, *Mr Mowat, Mem,* and vanished.

He'd a face that minded her of a frog's, he was younger than herself by a good few years, with horn-rimmed spectacles astride a broad nose, and eyes that twinkled, and a way of speaking that in a few days was to stagger Segget. His brow went back to a cluster of curls, he was charming, you supposed, as a prince should be, and very likely damn seldom is; and he said he was pleased to be back in Segget, looking at Chris as though she were the reason, Chris had never met in with his like before and stood and looked at him, cool in surprise, taller than he was, he was to say later he felt he was stared at by Scotland herself.

And once, when drunk, he was to say to the Provost that she couldn't get over her blood and breed, she was proud as all the damned clodhoppers were, still thought in her heart they were the earth's salt, and thought the descendant of a long line of lairds on the level with the descendants of a long line of lice. And he said by God, had it been a four hundred years back he'd have tamed that look quick enough in his bed, maybe she lost something of her sulkiness there. And Provost Hogg boasted and said *Not a doubt;* and started to tell of his ancestor, Burns. And Mowat said, *Who? Oh, Robbie Burns? A hell of a pity he couldn't write poetry*, and the Provost was vexed, but then, 'twas the laird, just joking-like; and he was the *laird*.

Chris heard of that later, she'd have needed second sight to know of the gossip that would be in the future: she said she was glad to see him, she wasn't, neither glad nor sad, a funny little thing, was this what Robert depended upon? Funny that the like of him for so long had lived on the rent of folk like hers. Syne she went to the kitchen to see how the cakes came, they were brown and steaming, set on the table, and Meikle-bogs, shy, like a big, sly steer, was sitting and eating one by the sink. And because she just couldn't thole him at all, he made her want to go change her vest, Chris smiled at him and was extra polite, and hoped that he'd stay to tea with Else, and helped Else pile the things on a tray; and they carried it through and found Robert and the laird already deep in the talk that was planned by Robert himself when he first saw Segget.

Mr Mowat's English bray sounded so funny that Else gave a giggle and near dropped the tray. *Is the creature foreign?* and Chris said *No;* and Else said no more, but went solemnly in, and took only a keek or so at the creature, a little bit thing in baggy plus-fours. And he said *Oh, thenks!* and *I say!* and *How Jahly!* Else nearly giggled again, but she didn't, till she got to the kitchen and there was Meiklebogs, and she gave him a poke, *I say, how Jahly! You old devil, I've a good mind to make up to the laird. What would you do then, eh, would you say?*

Meiklebogs smiled canny and said he would manage, and Else stared at him and wondered again why she'd ever allowed the old brute to come near her since she'd wept in his bed that night of the Show; she supposed she was still in a kind of a daze at finding the old brute as coarse as they'd said.

Chris sat in the sitting-room and listened to Mowat, and handed him tea, he said he'd come back to look after the mills and Segget in general, the curse of the age was its absentee landlords, not social conditions or unrest or suchlike. He was Jahly well sure he could buck up the village – didn't Mrs Colquohoun approve of that, now? he'd want her approval ever so much. And he flashed her a long, bright, toothy smile, he'd fine teeth and knew it; and Chris said, *I don't know. I'll wait and see what the bucking consists of. My father was a crofter and he used to say you should trust a laird just as far as you can throw him.*

Stephen Mowat said he thought Mrs Colquohoun's father Jahly, and glinted charming, and Chris gave him up, and cleared off the tea things and came back and listened. By then, so it seemed, Robert had told of his plans, and was sitting now harkening to Mowat's reply. And the reply was: The thing that was needed everywhere was Discipline, hwaw? and order, and what not. The hand of the master – all the Jahly old things. He had been down in Italy the last few months and had seen things there, Rahly amazing, the country awakening, regaining its soul, its old leaders back – with a new one or so. Discipline, order, hierarchy – all that. And why only Italy; why not Scotland? He'd met other men, down from 'varsity of late, who were doing as he did, going back to their estates. Scotland a nation – that was the goal, with its old-time civilization and culture. Hwaw? Didn't Mr Colquohoun agree?

But Chris had been listening, and now she must speak, she'd been trying to think as well as to listen, it was hard enough, but words suddenly came: they both turned round with a start as she spoke. *And what's going to happen when you and your kind rule us, again as of old, Mr Mowat? Was there ever the kind of Scotland you preach? – Happy, at ease, the folk on the land well-fed, the folk in the pulpits well-feared, the gentry doing great deeds? It's just a gab and a tale, no more, I haven't read history since I was at school, but I mind well enough what that Scotland was. I've been to Dunnottar Castle and seen there the ways that the gentry once liked to keep order. If it came to the push between you and the spinners I think I would give the spinners my vote.*

Mowat said *Rahly?* staring at Chris, Robert stared as well

at her down-bent face – suddenly she'd seen so much she
didn't say, all the pageant of history since history began up
here in the windy Mearns Howe: the ancient rites of blood and
atonement where the Standing Stones stood up as dead kings;
the clownings and cruelties of leaders and chiefs; and the folk
– her folk – who kept such alive – dying frozen at night in their
eirdes, earth-houses, chaving from the blink of day for a meal,
serfs and land-workers whom the Mowats rode down, whom
the armies harried and the kings spat on, the folk who rose in
the Covenant times and were tortured and broken by the
gentry's men, the rule and the way of life that had left them
the pitiful gossiping clowns that they were, an obscene humour
engraffed on their fears, the kindly souls of them twisted awry
and veiled from men with a dirty jest; and this snippet of a
fop with an English voice would bring back worse, and ask her
to help!

And then that went by, she was suddenly cool. It was only
a speak, a daft blether of words, whatever else happened to
Segget, to Scotland – and there were strange things waiting to
happen – there would never come back that old darkness again
to torment the simple folk of her blood. Robert was speaking,
he knocked out his pipe.

*I'm afraid my wife and I think the same – as all folk worth
their salt in Scotland must think. There are changes coming –
they are imminent on us – and I once thought the folk of some
teaching would help. Well, it seems they won't – the middle
class folk and the upper class folk, and all the poor devils that
hang by their tails; they think we can last as we are – or go
back – and they know all the while they are thinking a lie. But
God doesn't wait, or His instruments; and if in Segget are the
folk of the mills, then, whatever their creed, I'm on their
side.*

Chris started and moved, she nearly had frozen, leaning up
here while the night went on, she ought to be down in her
bed, she supposed. The rain had cleared and the stars had

come out, frost was coming – there, bright down in Segget, was a mantling of grey where the hoar was set, sprinkled like salt on the cant of the roofs. Beyond them there rose a red, quiet lowe, from the furnaces stacked for the night in the mills.

She stamped her feet and drew up her collar, watching that coming of the frost below. This impulse to seek the dark by herself! She had left Robert up in his study at work, Ewan in bed, young Mowat gone, and herself gone out for a walk through the rain that was closing in the end of Remembrance Day, wet and dank, as she'd seen it come. And it might be an age ere she came here again, too busied with living to stand looking at life, with Ewan at school and the campaign of Robert to conquer Segget for God and his dream.

A pillar of cloud by day and a pillar of fire by night.

She raised her eyes and looked where the frost lay bright in the west, where the evening star wheeled down to midnight to lead her feet home.

III

STRATUS

It was funny to think, this forenoon in June, how long it had been since she climbed the Kaimes, here rose the walls, in their mantle of heather, a blackbird was whistling up in the yews, as she turned around slow she saw the light flow up and down the hill as though it were liquid, Segget below lying buried in a sea, as once all the Howe had lain, Ewan said. Still weak, Chris halted and sat on the wall, her hands below her, and looked at Segget, and drew out her hands and looked at those so thin that almost she could see through them, so thin her face when she put up her hand that the cheekbones that once curved smooth under flesh now felt like twin jagged crags of rock – a long time ere she'd look comely again!

She leant her head in her hand a moment and waited for the hill below to cease reeling – maybe she'd come out too early from bed, this walk, Else had said she mustn't go far. But the Kaimes had called her after those weeks of the smell of medicines, close fires, and the pain that ran up and down her and played hide and seek with every sinew and bone that she had. So up she had come, the sun was up here, she was out of it for an hour or so, out of the winking flash of the days, to sit and look from the high places here, as Christ once had done with the devil for guide.

Idly she minded that and smiled – it came of being a minister's wife. What had the devil said to Christ then? Maybe *Just rest. Rest and have peace. Don't let them tear you to bits with their hates, their cares and their loves, your angers for them. Leave them and rest!*

Yes, He'd said that, there wasn't a doubt, just as He stood by her saying it now, telling her to rest for the first time in years since that night when she last had climbed up the Kaimes, telling her to rest and leave them a-be, her cares for Robert, for that other who came and yet never came – for that third, that stranger whom slow through the years she had grown to half-know as a traveller half-knows the face of another on a lone road at night, in the summer light of a falling star. . . How Segget would snigger if they heard her say that that stranger desired was her own son Ewan!

Being young Ewan Tavendale wasn't all fun, you'd to get up as early as half past six in the little room that looked down on Segget. But it *was* a good room, the best in the Manse, you could look of a night right into the trees when the rooks came nesting, they had a great time, fighting and mating and playing the devil. Once you nearly fell out when two rooks were at it – mating, you'd wanted to know how it was done. But that was a long time ago, when a kid, you knew all about it now, humans or rooks, mother or Robert, and there wasn't much in it, though the spinner kids of West Wynd thought so. Charlie

Cronin drew pictures in the lavatories at school, the silly ass
couldn't draw at all. So you drew some yourself to show how
things were, he turned red-faced when you drew IT so well.
Ewan, that's dirty! What was dirty about it?

You would lie and mind these things of a morning and stare
at the ceiling and hark to the rooks – moving and chattering
and swearing in the cold – how they *did* swear as the daylight
grew! Sometimes you'd wanted to swear yourself, and you'd
tried once or twice when you were a kid, but it sounded half-
witted, so you gave it up. You couldn't see sense in rubbish
like swearing, any more than in speaking in Scotch, not
English as mother did sometimes, and so did Robert, and so
did Else (but she couldn't help it). Scotch was rubbish, all ee's
and wee's, you didn't even speak it in the school playground.
And the other kids had mocked you at first, but they didn't
long, with a bashing or so.

Chris (and once Else) rigged you out of a morning, now
you did it yourself, nearly twelve years old. The clock went
birr as you looked at its face and you got out of bed and out
of your pyjamas, Charlie Cronin slept in his shirt, he said
only gentry wore things like pyjamas. You were glad you were
gentry, then, shirts got sticky. Then you'd hear the clock
going off down below, where the new girl slept, she was shy
and said *Eh?* A perfect fool, she near fainted one morning, in
summer it was, when she first came here. You'd thought you'd
go down and get a bath first before either Robert or Chris
should be at it. So you'd nipped down the stairs without anything on, and as you came back she came from her room, and
gave a screech like a frightened hen, as though she'd never
seen folk without clothes. Charlie Cronin said that his father,
old George, would take off his clothes slow bit by bit, the top
bits first, and cover himself up, and then the lower, and he'd
cover *that* – you'd supposed that Maidie herself was like that,
a fool, maybe frightened to look at herself.

So after that you had promised Chris that you'd wear some
clothes when outside your room, she'd said that she herself
didn't care – and you said *Yes, mother, I know that you don't.*

*I once saw you with nothing on coming up the stairs – a night
long ago when I was a kid. I think it was the night of a Segget
Show.*

She'd blushed, as though nearly as bad as the others, but
she wasn't: you were glad that your mother was Chris. She
didn't know that you called her that, to yourself, not aloud,
aloud you said *Mother*. But Robert, just *Robert*, he wasn't your
father. Robert was fun when he wasn't at work, with the kirk
or the spinners or his Labour plans – summers he took you
and Chris on your bikes out on far jaunts up and down the
Howe, to Edzell, to Brechin, to Garvock Hill where they boiled
the sheriff but not Leslie the smith – you asked Robert what
he meant by that say, and he and Chris laughed like a couple
of fools.

But out on picnics he changed and was young, and would
teach you to throw and do the high jump, he could jump like
anything, Robert, and box. Everybody knew that in Segget
now, they hadn't at first, especially the spinners, and had
mocked at Robert till he taught them manners. Charlie Cronin
had been jealous of him and of you, that was at first when you
first went to school, the first day he came swaggering up and
said *Oh, you're the dirt from the Manse, are you?* And you
said *I'm not dirt, I'm Ewan Tavendale,* and he mocked at you
till you hit him a bash, right on the nose, and he bled and bled,
though it was only a baby bash, you were both of you just
babies yourselves. But you won that fight all the same, Mr
Geddes had watched it all from a window; and he went to the
Manse and told Chris about it; and she asked that night *Did
he hurt you, Ewan?* and you said *Ay,* all the kids had said *Ay;*
and Chris said *Oh, Ewan, that was real like your father!*
Father had been killed by the Germans in France.

Time for breakfast: and there was Robert, busy with letters,
and Chris, looking sweet. But she always did that, even when
she was angry, she could do nearly anything, answer you anything, she couldn't run maybe as fast as you could and she was
a perfect fool about flints, but she always told the truth about
things, most grown-up people told lies half the time. You

didn't yourself, it wasn't worth the bother, explaining and trying to straighten things later.

And Chris would say *It's nearly schooltime,* and you'd look at the clock, and see that it was, and Robert would say, *He's dreaming about flints!* But you hadn't been dreaming, you'd been thinking of Chris, she'd looked different of late in a puzzling way. Now, if it had been any other woman in Segget, you'd have known — but not Chris! It made a cold water come in your mouth, as though you were going to be sick, that thought. And Chris said *What's wrong? That's a funny-loon stare.* And you said *Oh, nothing. I'll need to be going.*

You kissed Chris every morning, one kiss a day; kisses were sloppy except for that one — like the taste of honey up on a hill, clear, with the wind in the summer south. Robert cried *Ta-ta!* and you did the same, and were out in the hall, where Maidie would be, tweetering about and worrying again, wondering if breakfast were over yet. You hardly ever took notice of her, not since she'd screeched that time on the stairs. She'd call *Master Ewan, is the breakfast done?* and you'd say *I don't know* and leave her to twitter — who wanted to be *mastered* like a kid in a book?

Out from the Manse and down through the shingle, giving it a kick and a plough as you went, under the ferny tops of the yews, the rooks all wakened and screeching, or off — all but the young ones, pecking, gaping. If it was summer you passed under quick, they dropped dirt down when you least expected, they dropped it once on the Provost of Segget when he came to see Robert and he walked back home with it white on his hat and everyone laughed, and he nearly had a fit when he found out about it.

He was frightened to be laughed at, most people were, you didn't care a button one way or another, they might laugh themselves blue in the face at you, you were yourself — and what did it matter?

And there was the land and there were the touns, Segget half-blue in its early smoke, you started early and with time to spare to go round the toun and back up to the school. So you'd stop and pull up your stockings to your knees, in shorts, and the shirt and tie that Chris tied, you couldn't get the knack of the thing, she would say *Oh, Ewan, you've forgotten to tie it at all!* and you'd say *I forgot,* and she'd ruffle your hair, *Thinking about flints again, I suppose?* She and Robert were always joking about flints, and calling them wrong names, and thinking that funny.

Down by Meiklebogs the curlews were calling, you heard them above the shoom of the Mills, Robert said something about that once — *Twin daughters of the Voice of God.* You hadn't bothered to find out what he meant, though you bothered about most things right to the end, sense to find out why this went like this, and that was so, and the wheels went round, and some stars twinkled and a lot did not, why people were ashamed to be seen without clothes and didn't like girls to go out late at night, and hated capitalists, if they were spinners, and hated spinners if they were New Toun.

The curlew called and you stopped and listened, Else would hear it at the Meiklebogs, you'd liked Else a lot, though not all the time. Once she'd come to your room late in the night, harvest, and was sloppy and kissed you about, you hated slop and threw a book at her, it hit her, she stared, you were sorry a bit.

There was a seagull up on that post, try a stone at it — nearly its tail! — and there was Ake Ogilvie's shop beyond. Most mornings you loitered about at Ake's, he'd lean from the door with his compass in hand and cry *Well, then, have you learned your Burns?* 'twas a joke between you, the poetry of Burns, silly Scotch muck about cottars and women, and love and dove and rot of that sort. Ake would recite you some of his own, his green eyes twinkling and his eyebrows twinkling, with a coating of sawdust sprayed on the hairs, and his long moustache going up and down, so, and you'd stare at him and listen a while, it was good enough, better than Burns' rot. Poetry was rot, why not say it plain, when a man kissed a woman or a woman had a baby?

Down past the house of Jimmy the Sourock, the road had

a dip and a hollow for years, the rain would gather, deep, in a pool, you used to march through it, your feet close together, and watch the water soak in at the eyelets, and feel it trickling betwixt your toes: that was when you were only a kid. Then Mrs Sourock would look out and see, and cry she would tell the Mem at the Manse, that was Chris she meant, and you didn't care. It was no business of *hers* to get mad because you liked to wade in the water, especially as she herself was so proud that her husband, the Sourock, drank nothing but water, since he got that fright with the pig in his bed. And every Sunday he went down to the Square, to the service-meeting of MacDougall Brown, and sang about blood, and you thought that funny, he'd been so frightened at the blood of the pig. You'd once played truant from the kirk to go down and watch MacDougall Brown as he prayed, he opened his mouth and looked as though blind, with his eyes like glass and his teeth all black, perhaps he was frightened to go to the dentist.

A dentist came twice a week now to Segget, he hired a room at the back of Dite Peat's: and the first time he came Charlie Cronin was there, hiding and listening under the window to hear the howls when the teeth came out. And the first to come was old Mrs Hogg, she had a wart on her nose like Cromwell and hair growing out of the wart as well, and she groaned like anything, Charlie told. Then she said to the dentist *How much will that be?* and he said *Half a crown,* and Mrs Hogg said *What? Half a crown for that, just pulling out a tooth? Why, old Leslie the smith down there at the smiddy used to pull me all over the place with his tongs, and never would ask a meck for it, either.*

But you liked Mrs Hogg, she would cry as you passed, *Hello, Ewan lad, is there anything fresh?* And you'd show her the latest flints that you'd got, and she wouldn't just laugh or blither about Druids, as everyone else in Segget would do but would ask what the hunters had done with the things, and she'd say that that was amazing, just, what a thing it was to be learned and young. She'd sense, Mrs Hogg, more sense than her son, who sometimes came home on a holiday; he

spoke bad English and wore bad breeks, and patted your head
and said *Little man*, or tried to pat you, you just stepped aside.

Sometimes you'd look into Peter Peat's shop, where he sat
on a table making a suit, he'd frown and motion you to get
off, he came every Sunday and listened to Robert and hated his
sermons and Robert as well. You'd heard him one Sunday say
to the Provost the minister was nothing but a Bolshevik, just
as bad as that tink John Cronin, the porter. Bolsheviks lived
in Russia, you knew, they'd closed all the kirks and they all
worked together and they hadn't a king; and it sounded sense.

By now you'd got to the end of East Wynd, to the Square
where the War Memorial stood, the angel that looked like Miss
M'Askill, Miss M'Askill had eyes that would lift up that way
when she found something dirty drawn on a slate. In lower
East Wynd of a winter morning half the lane was frozen to a
slide, you took a long run from Peter Peat's shop and shot
down the Wynd on the frozen slide that came from the leaking
drains of Segget. By the Moultrie shop you'd to plan your turn,
else you'd batter yourself on the wall of their house, as you'd
done your second winter in Segget, the whole of Segget seemed
fallen upon you, and your face had shifted, you sat on the
ground and thought you had lost it and felt it all over, it still
was there, grown bigger than ever, growing bigger and bigger
every moment, it seemed.

It was while you were sitting there, licking the blood, it
trickled from your lips and tasted salt, that old Mrs Moultrie
came out and found you, she'd heard the bang as you struck
the wall, she said to Chris when she took you home she
thought that it was a cart and horse. But you liked her in spite
of clyping to Chris, her face, brown, old, and tired and quiet as
she bathed you and *whished* as though you were a baby, till
you sat up and said *I'm fine. Many thanks*. Old Moultrie was
sitting in his corner, glaring, reading a Bible, and you said
Good day.

He'd taken no notice at all before that, he glared some
more, but you didn't mind, you saw he really was awfully shy
underneath all the hair and the horns, so you said, while Mrs

Moultrie went out for a towel, *Do you like the Bible? There's a lot of rot in it.* He stood up, shaking all over, funny, and asked, *And you're the minister's bairn?* And you shook your head, *Oh no, I'm not. Robert's only my stepfather, didn't you know? My father was a crofter down in Kinraddie. Much better than being a minister, I think.*

Funny, he was friendly enough after that, and started telling you stories of Segget, when there weren't so many of the gentry dirt sossing about with their motor-cars. And you listened, polite, because he was old, a pity besides that he was so shy. But Mrs Moultrie said to Chris that you were the only soul in Segget he'd treated to a civil word for years.

There was the Arms, not worth looking at, you threw a stone at a cat in the Square and watched the dog up against the angel, funny that dogs were so fond of that. They really couldn't *want to,* so often. Every day that dog of Newlands came down, as you turned in the Square to go up the Close, and did that against the Memorial stone, you'd once told Robert, and he'd laughed and laughed and said that the dog was a pacifist, maybe. But one morning you stood and watched for the dog and sure as anything along it came, and stopped, and relieved itself by the angel; and the door of the Arms opposite opened, and Mrs Melvin came out and said that you were a dirty little brute to stand and look at a dog doing that — Weren't you black burning ashamed of yourself? She was soft in the head, why should you be ashamed? Maybe she was drunk, but you didn't say anything, just looked her all over, from top to toe, to see if she'd fallen while she was drunk, and then raised your cap and went on to school.

Round by here you could see the Mills, in the big glass windows across the field the whirr of the wheels as they caught the sun, the spinners at work in the dust and the smell; but you liked the Mills, you'd been down there twice, with Charlie, he said the folk in New Toun were daft to speak of the folk in the Mills as only spinners, there were foremen and weavers, and a lot more besides; but they all *looked* like spinners.

To the right, in the Spring and most of the year, as you passed up The Close you would see in the park the donkey that was kept by MacDougall Brown. If you whistled one note, high up in your throat, you'd found that the donkey would bray every time. So nearly every day as you passed you whistled that note and the donkey brayed, and you laughed, and he'd bray some more and come trotting and push his long nose through the fence and snuffle, but he never bit you as once Mabel Brown. Mrs Brown spoke funny, and she called her May-bull, and had a long story how the donkey once *bat May-bull* when she went to play in the park.

There was the smiddy and it once was great fun, when you were a kid, to lean up by the door and look at old Leslie blowing the bellows, he'd turn round and sweat, *Ay man, is that you?* He called you *man*, but he blithered a lot, you would hardly heed at all what he said – about Chris, was she ill-like of late, would you say? and *The minister'll be gey fond of her, eh?* and *D'ye mind your own father that was killed out in France?* And you said you didn't know to all of these questions, because you couldn't be bothered with them, and he said, *Eh man, when my father died I just roared and howled – ay, loon, I'd a heart.* And you said *Like the Roarer and Greeter, Miss Moultrie?* And he stopped and stared with his mouth fallen open, and muttered that you were an impudent get.

You'd take the West Wynd through the Old Toun then, with its crumbling white houses and its washing to dry, there was always washing to dry, never dried. You knew a lot of the kids in West Wynd, they'd be finishing porridge and pulling on boots, and they'd cry *Wait, Ewan!* but you'd never wait, except for young Cronin, he'd come slouching out and say *Ay, Ewan,* and you'd say *Hello, Charlie,* and go on together not saying a thing till he'd ask, as always, *Have you done your sums?* Then you'd know that he hadn't done his and would bring out your book so that he might copy.

Funny that he couldn't do things like sums, you could nearly do them with both eyes shut, and lean back and go off on a think on flints while the other scholars were finishing theirs;

and Miss M'Askill would cry out, *Ewan! Have you finished already? Show me your sums*. And you'd show them to her, she'd stand over close, with an arm around your shoulder, like so; and you'd move away, though as slow as you could; and she wrote in your report to the Manse that you were brilliant, but you hadn't enthusiasm; you supposed because you hadn't enthusiasm for cuddling.

It had been different in the first two years, the youngest room with Miss Jeannie Grant, Miss Grant was pretty and laughed at you, and at everyone else, and kept her cuddles for Charlie's brother, or so you supposed. She was going to be married some time to him, Jock Cronin, that was only a railway porter, Chris said that job was as good as another. But you didn't think much of John Cronin, yourself, he didn't believe what he himself said, he just said things and then tried to believe them – you knew that well while you watched him sit, with Robert, up in a room at the Manse, and talk of Segget and socialism coming – it was all a fairy-tale, and he knew it, why didn't he say the things that he thought?

You said that to Chris and she took your two shoulders, and shook her head and looked at you, strange, *Oh Ewan, you're hard and cool as – grey granite! When you too grow up you'll find facts over much – you'll need something to follow that's far from the facts*. And she said something else, about a pillar of cloud, and was suddenly angry, *Don't stare at me so!* And you said *I'm sorry*, and she shook you again. *So am I, Ewan – but oh, you're so cool!*

Well, you saw nothing to make you excited, except now and then a broad-flake flint. It was worth reading history to get at these people, the makers of flints and their lives long ago. Though most of the histories were dull as ditchwater, with their kings and their battles and their dates and such muck, you wondered how the people had lived in those times. But especially before the history-book times you wanted to know how men had lived then and had read all the books you could find in the Manse, and got money from Chris to send and buy others, the lives of the people ere history began, before the

Venricones came to the Mearns. And young Cronin would listen and say *What's the use? Father says that the only things we should learn are how to fight the caPITalists.* You didn't know about them, you asked who they were, and Charlie said *Folk like that mucker Mowat.*

Mr Mowat lived sometimes in Segget House, but most of the time he was down in London, sleeping with whores, Charlie Cronin said. You asked what whores were and he told you about them, what they did, how they slept for money with men. You said that you didn't see why they shouldn't, and Charlie said you'd a dirty mind, and would soon be doing the same as Mowat. That was rot, you hadn't any use for girls, they could only giggle and drift along roads, with their arms twined, and screech about nothing. Or they played soft games in their own playground, once you'd run through there for a cricket-ball and the bigger girls were playing a game, *When will my true love come from the sea*; and the silly fools pulled you in the middle and kissed and slobbered you one after the other, you stood it as long as you could, then pushed out, you didn't want to hurt the fools and you didn't; but you had felt almost sick in their hands.

You told Chris that when she heard about it, she laughed and said *All lasses aren't fools, and they think you a good-looking lad, I believe.* So you said that you didn't care about that, could you have a piece now and go up to the Kaimes?

You went often up there to seek round for flints, when they dug the Kaimes they must have dug deep, in a squatting-place of the ancient men, and mixed the flints with the building-earth. You had nearly thirty specimens already, properly labelled in a press in your room, and each described on a ticket near. And you had a catalogue, fairly complete, with diagrams of the ripples, hinge-fractures, the ovates and such, and a drawing of the best, a tortoise-core from the Leachie bends. Most of the stuff was late Bronze Age, when the hunters in Scotland had still only flints.

Dinner-times you went home by the near way, quick, stopping to throw up a stone at the rooks. Robert would sometimes be there at the table, and sometimes was out and about the Mearns, trying to raise his fund for the miners, and raising little but temper, he said. Chris never went with him at the dinner-hour, she would stay at home and help Maidie at work, Maidie couldn't cook a dinner for toffee.

Sometimes Chris would be out at night when you came back from the school for tea. So Maidie would give you your tea, like a mouse, and you'd have it and help her to clear and she'd say, *Oh, Master Ewan, I'll do it myself,* but you took no notice, just went on and helped, not heeding her blether you should do your lessons, any fool could do the lessons in ten minutes. Then you'd climb to your room and look in your press, and dust here and there that tortoise-core, and a fabricator-cone you had gotten near Brechin, and take them out and turn them with care, the light waning and dying in from the window as the day waned west from the slopes of the Howe. And sometimes you'd raise your head and look up, when the sun grew still on the peaks of the Mounth, by the glens and the haughs you had searched for flints, and think of the men of ancient times who had made those things and hunted those haughs, running naked and swift by the sunlit slopes, fun to live then and talk with those people. Robert said that they hadn't been savage at all, but golden hunters of the Golden Age.

And once Chris came up as you stood and looked at a new ripple-flake you had newly found, a summer night ere you went to bed, you'd taken everything off, to be cool, and stood by the window and traced out the whorls on the red and yellow of the antique axe. Chris opened the door, you felt the air waft, and turned and looked at her, her standing so still. You asked was anything wrong, she said *No*, giving a laugh, as though wakening up. *Only you looked like a hunter yourself, strayed and lost from the Golden Age!*

And Else went by, and looked through the door, and suddenly flushed and ran up the stairs, that was just a week ere she went from the Manse.

*　　　*　　　*

Faith, that had fairly set folk agog, when that coarse quean Else was sacked from the Manse. It just showed you the way that the world was going, dirty spinners that gave you their lip, worked hard to get, so many sweir — and ministers that couldn't look after their queans. Folk said they'd been at it a year and a half, her and Dalziel of the Meiklebogs, afore that Sabbath night in July when Mr Colquohoun came in on the pair, right bang in the Manse's own kitchen it was, Meiklebogs in the way you'd expect a man in, Else Queen in a way that no quean should be in, with a two-three bits of her rig laid by. The minister had said *This won't do, Else,* fair mad with rage at old Meiklebogs, for he himself had slept with his maid, and was over-mean to share the lass out.

Some said that that was all a damned lie, the minister had nothing to do with the quean, she'd left the Manse of her own free will. The Reverend Mr Robert Colquohoun wouldn't bed with an angel sent down from heaven, let alone a red-faced maid in his house, he was over decent and fond of his wife. But you shook your head when you heard that, faith! it clean took the guts from a fine bit tale. If he wasn't the kind to go to bed with any bit quean could you tell a man why he was chief with the Cronin dirt, socialists that said you might lie where you liked and didn't believe in morals or marriage?

And if some childe said that THAT wasn't true, you knew right well that he was a liar, you'd seen it all in the *People's Journal,* what the coarse tinks did in Russia with women — man, they fair had a time with the women, would you say 'twould be easy to get a job there?

Well, whatever the thing that took place at the Manse, and well you might wyte it wasn't just prayer — with that scowling brute, the minister himself, and his wife with her proud don't-touch-me face, and that meikle red-haired bitch of an Else — whatever happened Else left the Manse and took a fee at the Meiklebogs. And what the two of them did when alone, with the night in about and the blinds pulled down, you well might guess, though you didn't ask. All but Dite Peat, and he said one night, when Dalziel came taiking into the Arms, with that

shy-like smile on his unshaved face, and the yellow boots
that he wore for scuddling, *Ay, Meiklebogs, you'll sleep warm
now. She's a well-happed quean, Else Queen, I should think.*
Dalziel said nothing, just smiled like a gowk and drank at his
dram and syne had another, he hadn't a yea or a nay to say,
it showed you the coarse old brute that he was, and you
nearly bursting your bladder to know.

Some said they didn't believe it at all, Dalziel of the Meiklebogs a decent-like childe, and an elder of Segget kirk forbye.
So he must be, but you knew a man's nature, he needed a
woman just now and again — no, no, you didn't blame *him*
overmuch, but she fairly must be an ill tink, that Else Queen.
And you'd look at her hard the next time that you met, not a
bit of shame she would show as she passed, just cry *Ay, Fusty
Face, so it's you?* and go swinging by with her meikle hips on
the sway like stacks of hay in a gale, well-fleshed and rosy,
disgusting, you thought, you'd feel as mad as a mating tyke
at Meiklebogs and his shameless sin.

But faith! 'twas the same wherever you looked. There was
Mr Mowat up at the House, folk said he'd come back from a
London jaunt with *two* of the painted jades this time, you'd
hear their scraichs all over the House; and once the servant
went in of a morning and what do you think he saw in the
bed? Young Mr Mowat with a quean on each side, he'd slept
with the two and he fairly looked hashed, the bitches just
laughed as the servant gaped, and one slapped Mr Mowat in
a certain place and cried *Hi Solomon, here's the head eunuch!*

But you couldn't believe all the lies that you heard. Young
Mr Mowat was fairly a gent, and right fine if you met him
outbye, and speak civil; and say he Rahly was glad that you'd
met. He was maybe a bit daft about Scotland and such, and a
lot of dirt about history and culture. But couldn't a gent please
himself with his ploys, it kept him from wearying and did no
harm? When the Mills closed down for a fortnight once, they
had over-much stock already on hand, he said he was Jahly
sorry for the spinners — and he couldn't say fairer than that,
could he now? So you couldn't believe about the two queans,

and even were it true 'twas a different thing – wasn't it? – a
gent with his play, and a randy old brute like that Meiklebogs
man sossing about with a quean half his age?

Them that said Dalziel was an innocent childe fair got a sore
shock ere the year was out. Else at her new place worked out-
door and indoor, she'd to kilt her skirts (if they needed kilting
– and that was damned little with those short-like frocks) and
go out and help at the spreading of dung, and hoeing the
turnips and anything else, she was worth her own fee and a
joskin's as well.

Well, the harvest came and it came fell heavy, Else helped
at the stooking and syne at the leading. That was a windy
September day, the other childes were down in the fields, Else
and Meiklebogs managed a cart, out in the park Meiklebogs
forked sheaves, big and thick, into Else Queen's arms; and she
built them round and about the shelvins till they rose four high
and syne it was time for Meiklebogs to lead home the horse,
Jim, the roan, a canny old beast. So home they would go and
the stour would rise under the grind of the iron wheels, up
above the Mounth in its mist of blue, Dalziel would look back
now and again and see that the corn was biding in place, and
see Else as well, lying flat on the top, with her eyes fast-closed,
the meikle sweir wretch.

So he led the roan, Jim, up the Meiklebogs close, and round
to the back of the Meiklebogs barn, high in the wall a window
was cut, and he planned that this load be forked through the
window for early threshing with his new oil mill. He stopped
the horse and he backed it canny, the roan was old and he gave
it a bit groan, and Dalziel gave the roan a belt in the mouth,
the brute of a beast to groan out like that, folk would think
that it was ill-treated. The roan looked surprised, as though
he'd done nothing; and Dalziel cried to Else Queen, *Come on,
you'll have to be up and doing some work.*

She cried, *I'll soon do that, you old mucker,* she called him
the terriblest names to his face, and all he would do would be
to smile shy, and stroke at his chin, neither shaved nor un-

shaved. So he held, splay-footed, to the front of the barn, and got himself in and climbed to the loft, and keeked from the window, and there was Else Queen, standing atop of the rows of sheaves, her fork in her hand, waiting to fork. She cried *You're fair getting old in the bones!* and flung in a sheaf that near hit his face, he smiled and said nothing, they both set to work, her working as fast and as fleet as you liked, Dalziel inside was bigging the sheaves, ready for the first bit thresh at the place, the sun a blind fall on the cart outside. And once when Dalziel took a keek out he saw the sweat in a stream from Else, and her eyes looked glazed, it would take down her creash.

Well, there happened near next the kind of a thing that surely Else Queen had expected to happen, unless she were innocent as the Virgin Queen, Ake Ogilvie said: and he doubted that. And even she was hardly that now, with Burns a hundred years in heaven. – Folk said *What's that?* and Ake looked surprised – they had surely heard of their own Great Poet. Well, the creature died and he went to heaven and knocked like hell on the pearly gates. And St Peter poked his head from a wicket, and asked *Who're you that's making a din?* And Burns said *I'm Robert Burns, my man, the National Poet of Scotland, that's who.* St Peter took a look at the orders, pinned on the guard-room wall for the day; and he said, *I've got a note about you. You must wait outbye for a minute or so.*

So Robbie sat there cooling his heels, on the top of the draughty stair to heaven, and waited and waited till he nearly was froze; syne the gates at last opened and he was let in. And Burns was fair in a rage by then, *Do you treat distinguished arrivals like this?* And St Peter said *No, I wouldn't say that. But then I had special orders about you. I've been hiding the Virgin Queen away* – That was a real foul story to tell, it showed you the tink that Ake Ogilvie was, interrupting the real fine newsy tale of the happenings down at the Meiklebogs.

For when they had finished with the forking 'twas told, Dalziel took a bit of a look round the barn and saw he would need a hand to redd up. *Get up from the cart and come round,* he cried down, *I'll need you to lend me a hand in the loft.* Else cried back, *Havers! Do you think I can't jump?* And she put the end of her fork on a stone that stuck out a bit from the wall of the barn, and the prong-end under her arm, *so,* and next minute sailed through the air like a bird and landed near by Meiklebogs' side. And then she went white and then red of a sudden and Meiklebogs thought of the groan he'd heard, it hadn't been Jim the roan after all, 'twas Else had been groaning afore, as just now. And he stood looking sly as she sat on the sheaves, her face beginning to twist and to sweat, she said *I'm not well, send off for the doctor.* Then her time came on her and they heard her cry, the fee'd men out in the Meiklebogs fields, and came tearing home to see what was up. But by then the thing was nearly all done, the bairn born out in the barn, and Meiklebogs looking shyer than ever and getting on his bike to go for the doctor.

But faith! that was all he would do in the business. He wouldn't register the bairn his; and when the young doctor, McCormack, came up, and Else was moved to her room in the house, and McCormack said *Is the bairn yours?* Meiklebogs smiled shy, *No, I wouldn't say that.* And McCormack said *Whose is it, then?* And Meiklebogs never let on a word, just looked past the doctor and smiled shy and sly; and the doctor said *Huh — immaculate conception. Something in the air of the Meiklebogs. You've had other housekeepers ta'en the same way.*

Well, the story was soon all about the place, as scandalous a thing as ever you heard, Ag Moultrie, the Roarer and Greeter of Segget, knew every damned thing that had happened in the barn, more than an unmarried woman should know, she said the bairn was Meiklebogs' image, with his eyes and his nose — and Ake Ogilvie said *Ay, faith! and his whiskers as well I could warrant.* So Ag told him if he couldn't be civil and listen she wouldn't bother to give him the news; and Ake said *D'you think I'll suffer for that?* — not a neighbourly way to speak to a woman that was trying to cheer you up with some news.

Soon Else was up and about the place, and the bairn, a loon, tried to get its own back on its father Dalziel, if father he was. Its howl was near fit to lift off the roof, Else let it howl and worked in the parks; as the season wore on, were the weather fine, she'd take the creature out to the parks, and when it came to its feeding-time suckle the thing on a heap of shaws. When the fee'd men blushed and looked bashful at that, she'd cry *What the devil are you reddening for? You sucked the same drink before you met beer*, fair vulgar and coarse she'd turned to the bone, you'd never have thought she'd worked in a Manse. Dalziel would hark, with his sly, sleekèd smile, saying neither yea nor nay to her fleers, she would tongue him up hill and down dale when she liked, and call him the foulest names you could hear. But the foreman said she still went to his bed, or he to hers – ay, a queer carry-on!

Till the business of Jim the roan put an end.

That came with the second winter's close, when Meiklebogs carted his grain to the station, he'd sold the stuff for a stiff-like price, and put a young fee'd loon, Sinclair his name, on to the carting with the old roan, Jim. He fair was a willing old brute, the roan, he'd pant up a brae till an oncoming body might think from the other side, out of sight, that a steam-mill and thresher was coming that way. But he never would stop, would just shoggle on, with his great wide haunches shambling and swinging, he'd a free-like way of flinging his feet, but he wasn't cleekèd; and he fair could pull.

Ah well, it came white weather of frost, the ground as hard and as cold as iron, ribbed with a veining of frost each morning, folk that you met seemed most to be nose, and red nose at that when it wasn't blue-veined, Melvin at the Arms did a roaring trade, the water-pipes were frozen in the Manse, and the horses of all the farmers out about were brought to the smiddy to have their shoes cogged.

But Meiklebogs was over busy for that, on the Monday morning, the worst of the lot, he sent off Sinclair with the last load of corn; and afore he had gone very far the loon was all

in a sweat and a bother with his job, old Jim the roan on the
slide all the time, and the weighted cart going showding and
banging. Sinclair tried to lead the old horse by the grass that
grew stiff-withered by the side of the road; and that for a
little while eased up the beast, till they turned into Segget at
the top of East Wynd. There was devil a speck of grass grew
there, and near Ake Ogilvie's the ground was like glass, and
young Ewan Tavendale that came from the Manse had been
sliding there a half hour that morning.

So when Jim the roan came on that with the cart he did the
same as the Manse loon had done – took a run and a slide,
and cart, horse, and all shot down past Ake's like a falling
star – so Ake Ogilvie said, a daft-like speak. The lot fetched up
near the Sourock's house, the roan fell shaken, but he didn't
coup; and nothing of the harness by a miracle broke. Young
Sinclair had fairly got a fell fright and he leathered old Jim
round about the head with the reins and kicked him hard in
the belly, to make the old brute more careful in future.

Peter Peat looked out and he nodded, *That's it, nothing like
discipline for horses and men*; and he looked fierce enough to
eat up old Jim, that was bending under the ding of the blows
his patient old head – ay, a fierce man, Peter. And Sinclair,
that was only a loon and a fool, said, *I'll teach the old mucker
to go sliding about,* and gave the old roan another bit kick,
to steady him up, and got on the cart, and sat him down on a
bag of corn and cried to the roan *Come on, you old Bee!*

So old Jim went on and he fair went careful, flinging his
great meikle feet down canny, the loaded cart swinging and
showding behind, the road below like a sheet of glass. And he
went fell well till the East Wynd sloped, down and round by the
Moultrie shop, and there they found it – a slide once again!
all the lasses and lads of Segget had been there, the night
before, with their sleds and skates, and whooped and scraiched
and dirled down the wynd, on their feet sometimes, on their
backsides next, near braining themselves by the Moultrie wall,
young Ewan Tavendale the worst of them all – he fair could
slide, that nickum of a loon, with his black-blue hair and his

calm, cool eyes, he'd led the lot and could wheel like a bird just in time to miss the bit wall that was waiting there to dash out his brains.

Well, young Tavendale might, but old Jim mightn't, no sooner did his great bare feet come down on the slide than the same thing happened as before. He started to slip and the cart went with him, it half wheeled round with the weight of its load, and reeled by the wall of the gardener Grant and stotted from that, and the roan was down, braking with its feet, that did little good. Sinclair jumped off and fell on all fours. As he picked himself up he heard the crash, and the scream that rose with the breaking shafts, and he scrambled erect and looked down the lane; and the sight was sickener, old Jim the roan had run full tilt in the Moultrie wall, and one of the shafts of the cart had snapped and swung back right in the horse's belly, as though the old brute were a rat on a stake. He lay crumpled up, the cart broken behind him, young Sinclair started to greet at the sight: and the noise of the crash brought folk on the run.

Afore you could speak a fell concourse was round, old Moultrie came hirpling out with his stick, and cried *What do you mean, malagarousing my house?* and Jess Moultrie peeped, and looked white and sick; and Ag came out and then nipped back quick, no doubt in order to Roar and Greet. Will Melvin took Sinclair over to the Arms and had a drink down him afore you could wink; and young Sinclair stopped sniftering and habbering about it, he was feared he'd be sacked by Dalziel for this. *And what can I do in the middle of the season if I lose my job? I'll just have to starve. You can't get a fee for love or money, right in the middle of the winter, you can't. And that old mucker Meiklebogs –* But Mrs Melvin came into the bar and said *None of your Blasting and Blaspheming in here. You'll have to go out with your swearing, young man.*

So Sinclair went out and gaped like a fool at the folk that had come in around to see Jim. He lay with his eyes half closed and at last he'd stopped from trying to rise from the ground, the end of the shaft was deep in his belly, and there was a smell fit to frighten a spinner; folk took a good look and went canny away, you hadn't time to stand there and stare, you might be asked to help if you did, let Meiklebogs look to his old horse himself. Sim Leslie, the policeman that folk called Feet, came down and took his bit note-book out and asked young Sinclair how it all happened; and wrote it all down and looked at old Jim, and frowned at him stern; and then wrote some more – no doubt the old roan's criminal record. Syne he said he'd ride over and tell Meiklebogs, and he did, and when Meiklebogs heard of the news he smiled canny and shy, and got on his bike, and came riding to Segget to see the soss.

By the time he did it was nearly noon. Ake Ogilvie down with his gun at the place, a crowd had gathered to see the brute shot; but Dalziel wouldn't have it, *No, bide you a wee. If the beast be shot there would be no insurance*. Ake Ogilvie said *Can't you see it's in hell, with the shaft of the cart driving into its guts?* But Meiklebogs just smiled shy and said nothing, except to Feet – that the horse was his property, and he lippened to him it wasn't destroyed. And Feet said *Ay. D'you hear, Mr Ogilvie? You'd better take home that gun of yours.* And Ake Ogilvie stood and cursed at them both, and folk were shocked at the words he used, calling Meiklebogs a dirty mucker when the man was only seeking his insurance.

Well, there the roan lay all that afternoon, sossing up the road, and it wouldn't die. Folk came from far and near for a look at old Jim the roan as he lay on his side, as the afternoon waned he turned a wee, and the blood began to freeze round the shaft that was stuck so deep in his riven belly. But what with the folk that came in such crowds, a birn of the spinners down from the Mills, and the bairns as they left the school at four, the roan was splashed an inch deep with glaur and hardly twitching or moving by then. Meiklebogs had sent off a wire to Stonehive, to ask about the insurance, like: but no answer came, and he didn't expect one, he'd the corn loaded on another bit cart and went off home to the Meiklebogs, attending to his work with his shy, sleekèd smile, the insurance his if the horse died natural.

Once or twice Jess Moultrie came out to the beast and held a pail for it to drink out of, it slobbered at the warm water and treacle, syne would leave its head lying heavy in the pail, till Jess lifted the head and put it away; and all the while her face was like death, the fool was near greeting over the horse, if she couldn't stand the sight of the soss, why did she ever go near the beast?

It looked like a hillock of dirt by dark, and then Ake Ogilvie that half the day had been seeking the minister, that was off down the Howe, found him at last and told him the tale. And folk said that the Revered Colquohoun swore awful — *The bloody swine, the BLOODY swine!* — a strange-like thing to say of a horse. But Ake Ogilvie said it wasn't the horse but the folk of Segget the minister meant. And that was just daft, if Ake spoke true — that Mr Colquohoun could mean it of folk, real coarse of him to speak that way of decent people that had done him no harm. It just showed you the kind of a tink that he was, him and his Labour and socialism and all.

And he said to Ake Ogilvie *Get out your gun*, and Ake got it again, and the two came down, the roan lay still in its puddle of glaur, the cart behind and the night now close. And the circle of folk drew off a wee bit, and the roan seemed to know the thing that Ake meant, for it lifted its head and gave a great groan. The minister looked white as a drift of snow, he cried *Stand back there — damn you, stand back! Ake, aim canny.* And Ake said nothing, but went up to the roan, and folk looked away as they heard the bang.

Soon as Meiklebogs himself had heard of what happened, and he did that in less than the space of an hour, he was over at the Manse to see the minister, with the shy, sly smile on his half-shaved face. And he said *They tell me, Mr Colquohoun, that you've had my horse shot down in East Wynd.* The minister said *Do they? Then they tell you the truth.* So Meiklebogs said he would sue him for that, and the minister said he could sue and be damned — *And I'll tell you a thing that I am to do — report you for cruelty by the very first post. You're the kind of scoundrel over-common in Scotland.* And Meiklebogs for once lost his shy-like smile. *Say that of me again what you said of me now! Mind, there's a witness to hear us, minister.* The Maidie was near in the hall, he meant her, but Mr Colquohoun was blazing with rage. He said *Get out or I'll throw you out*, and made at Dalziel, and he shambled out, not such a fool as face up to a madman, a creature that fair went mad on a horse.

Nor was that the end of his troubles that day, for when he got home the news had reached Else, she was waiting in the kitchen when Meiklebogs came. He smiled at her shy, *Have you nothing to do but stand about there and be idle, then? Get my supper ready, or I'll need a new housekeeper*. The foreman had come in at the tail of Meiklebogs, and he heard every word that the two of them spoke. Else said *Is this true that I hear of the roan?* and Meiklebogs said *Ay; will you give me my supper?* and Else said *No, but I'll give you my notice. I've stuck queer things at your hands, Meiklebogs. I've been crazed or daft that I've stuck them so long. But I wouldn't bide another night in your house.* And Meiklebogs smiled sleekèd and shy. *Ah well, just gang — with your fatherless bairn.* And Else said she'd do that, but the bairn had a father, God pity the littl'un, the father it had.

She was greeting by then, she'd been fond of the roan. She hardly looked the Else that the foreman knew well, raging and red-haired and foul with her tongue, she stared at Meiklebogs as a body new waked out of the horror of an ill-dreamt dream; and she packed her things and wrapped up her bairn.

The foreman met her out in the close and asked her where she would spend the night, and he made a bit try to give her a cuddle, maybe he hoped that she'd spend it with him, her a tink-like quean, him buirdly and brave. But instead she banged her case at his legs, near couped him down in the sharn of the close, and held up through Segget and down to the station, and took the late train to her father's in Fordoun — the ill-gettèd bitch that she was, folk said, to leave Meiklebogs without warning like that, her and her blethering over a horse.

*   *   *

There wouldn't have been half the steer and stour if Mr Colquohoun had kept to himself. He'd need to leave other folk a-be and heed to his own concerns, him, that tink-cool stepson of his, for one – wasn't *he* the loon what had led the others in making the slide that mischieved the horse? He led most of the bairns in ill-gettèd ploys, folk told after that, though you hadn't heard even a whisper before. 'Twas said he would sneak in the lassies' playground, and cuddle and kiss them when they were at games, the ill-gettèd wretch, and at his age, too. Ay, Mr Colquohoun was more in need of trying to reform young Ewan Tavendale than interfering with a good, quiet childe like old Dalziel of the Meiklebogs.

Old Leslie said *Ay* – it was down at the Arms – *or getting that proud-looking wife with a bairn – damn't! is that an example to show, none of a family and married five years? Now, when I was a loon up in Garvock. . .* and folk began to hem and talk loud, and look up at the roof and hoast in their throats, and you couldn't hear more, and that was a blessing, the old fool could deave a dog into dysentery. But still there was something in what he was saying, other folk had bairns, they came with the seasons, there was no escape were you wedded and bedded.

But Dite Peat said *Isn't there, now? Let me tell you* – and he told about shops in *that lousy hole, London*, where things were for sale that a man could use, right handy-like, and what happened then? You never fathered a family, not you, you could sin as much as you liked and pay nothing. And Dite said forbye it was his belief that's what that couple did up at the Manse, that was why Mrs Colquohoun went about like a quean, with a skin like cream and a figure like that, hardly a chest on the creature at all; instead of the broadening out and about, looking sappy and squash like a woman of her age. Damn't, what was a woman in the world for, eh? – but to make your porridge and lie in your bed and bring as many bairns into the world as would help a man that was getting old? Not that the London things weren't fine for a childe when he went on a holiday, like. But if he himself were tied up, b'God, he'd take care he'd his wife in the family way – ay, every year, with a good bit scraich when it came to her time, that fair was a thing to jake a man up.

That was a dirty enough speak, if you liked. Folk looked here and there and Jim the Sourock, that had gotten religion, cast up his eyes, he had grown so holy with MacDougall's crush that he called the watery the wc, and wouldn't have it that women had bodies at all more than an inch below the neck-bone. But Hairy Hogg had come in and sat down, folk cried, *Ay, Provost, and what would you say?* And Hairy said he thought Scotland was fair in a way, and if Burns came back he would think the same; and the worst thing yet they had done in Segget was to vote the Reverend Colquohoun to the pulpit – him and his Labour and sneering at folk, damn't! he had said we were monkeys, not men.

Some folk in the bar took a snicker at that, the story was growing whiskers in Segget, but the Provost had never forgiven the minister. And Hairy said it was his opinion, from studying folk a good fifty year – and mind you, he was no fool at the job – the minister took up with some other woman. They said that the father of Else Queen's bairn was old Dalziel of the Meiklebogs, but he, Hairy Hogg, had his doubts of that. Had the minister ever cast out with the quean? No, when he'd meet her out and about he'd cry to her cheery, as though nothing had happened. If he couldn't give a bairn to his mistress, the minister, it was maybe because he was hashed other ways.

Damn't, that was a tasty bit story, now, queer you yourself hadn't thought of that. But long ere another day was done the news was spread through the Segget wynds that the Reverend Mr Colquohoun, the minister, had fathered the bairn of that quean, Else Queen, the Provost had seen the two of them to-gether, him making ardent love to the lass.

Ake Ogilvie heard the tale from the tailor, and Ake said: *Blethers, and even if it's true what has the business to do with old Hogg? He himself, it seems, has done a bit more than just lie down by the side of his wife – or that gawpus he has for a son's not his.*

That was just like Ake Ogilvie to speak coarse like that, try-ing to blacken the character of a man that wasn't there to defend himself. Peter Peat said *Well, I'm a friend to my friends, but a man that's once got himself wrong with me* — and he looked fierce enough to frighten a shark; but Ake Ogilvie laughed, *And what's Colquohoun done?* And Peter said *Him? A disgrace to Segget, that should be a good Conserva-tive. What is he instead — why, a Labour tink.* But Ake Ogilvie just said *To hell with their politics, I don't care though he's trying to bring back the Pretender, same as that snippet, Jahly young Mowat.*

But Peter wouldn't hear the gentry miscalled, and he said that Jahly would come to himself, and take his rightful place, you would see — at the head of the Segget Conservative branch. Ake said *He can take his place on a midden, if he likes — and he'll find they've much the same smell.* Peter asked what had much the same smell and Ake said *Tories and middens, of course,* and Peter Peat looked at him fierce, and left; that would learn the ill-getted joiner that would.

Well, the news reached Cronin, the old tink in West Wynd, him that was aye preaching his socialist stite; and he said that he thought the whole thing a damned lie, an attempt to dis-credit the socialists in Segget. Jock Cronin at the station heard it and said *He's all right, Colquohoun,* in an off-hand way, to let you know he and the Manse were fell thick and slobbered their brose from the very same bowl.

Ag Moultrie, the Roarer and Greeter (for short), took the news to the servants at Segget House; and it spread about there, and when young Mr Mowat came home from a trip he had gone to Dundon, he laughed out loud. *Some have all the luck. But if Mrs Colquohoun's in need of a bairn I'll give half a year's profits to provide her with one.*

And you couldn't but laugh at the joke of the gent.

Robert was away that New Year's Eve, into Aberdeen, he wouldn't say why; but Chris could guess and had laughed at him. *Mind, nothing expensive.* And he'd said *What, in drinks?*

I'm going to squat in a pub and swizzle confusion to all the dour sourocks in Segget! Chris wished that it wasn't a joke, and he would; he kissed her and went striding away down the shingle, turning about to wave from the yews, his kiss still pressed on her lips as she stood, and tingling a bit, like a bee on a flower.

It was frosty weather as the day wore on, the sky and the earth sharp-rimed with steel, no sun came, only a smoulder of grey, Chris cooked the dinner with Maidie to help, and remembered Else, she'd have been more use. Maidie still *Memmed* like a frightened mouse, and once when up and above their heads there came a crash like a falling wall, she nearly jumped from her skin with fright. Chris said *It's just Ewan, he's moving his press*, and Maidie said, *Oh, I got such a fright!* and looked as though it had lifted her liver. Chris left her and went up to Ewan's room, and knocked at the door, he bade her come in, the place was a still, grey haze with dust. She saw Ewan through it by the window ledge, he'd stooped to look in the press he'd moved, it was filled with his precious array of flints.

Chris asked what he was moving today? He said *Everything* and set to on the bed, she sat down and didn't offer to help. His hair fell over his eyes as he tugged, funny to look at, funny to think he had been your baby, been yours, been you, been less than that even – now sturdy and slim, with his firm round shoulders and that dun gold skin he got from yourself, and his father's hair. He stopped in a minute and came where she sat: *I think that'll do, I'll dust after dinner.*

So the two of them went down and had dinner alone, Ewan said he'd have everything moved in his rooms ere the New Year came and Chris asked why. He said *Oh, I like a new angle on things*, and then he said *Mother, you wanted to laugh. What about?* and Chris said *You, I suppose! You sounded so grown-up like for a lad.*

He said nothing to that, but went on with his meat, they didn't say grace when Robert wasn't there, that was funny when you came to think of the thing, Robert knew and knew that you knew he knew. But he was too sure to vex about that, sure of himself and his God and belief, except when the angry black moments came – seldom enough in this last three years. Once he'd raved *Religion – A Scot know religion? Half of them think of God as a Scot with brosy morals and a penchant for Burns. And the other half are over damned mean to allow the Almighty even existence. You know which half you belong to, I think.* Hate and fury in his face as he said it, the day after the killing of Meiklebogs' horse. Chris had looked at him cool and remotely then, as she'd learned with the years, and he'd banged from the room, to return in an hour or so recovered. *What a ranter and raver I am, Christine! I think you'll outlast me a thousand years!*

And now, on a sudden impulse, she said, *Do you ever think of religion, Ewan?*

He never said *What?* or said your last word the way other boys of his age would do; he looked up and shook his head, *Not now.* She asked when he had and he said, long ago, when he was a kid and hadn't much sense, he used to be worried when Robert was preaching. Chris said *But he never tried to fear you,* and Ewan shook his head. *Oh no, it wasn't that. But I hated the notion God was there, prying into every minute of my life. I wanted to belong to myself, and I do; it doesn't matter a bit to me now.* She understood well enough what he meant, how like her he sometimes was, how unlike! *So you think God doesn't matter, then, Ewan?* and he said, *I don't think He's worth bothering about. He can't make any difference to the world – or I should think He'd have made it by now.*

The evening came down before it was four, up in the Mounth the snow came thick, sheeting hill on hill as it passed on the wings of the howling wind from the haughs. But the storm passed north of Segget, lying lithe, Chris in the kitchen looked out at it pass, she was making, cakes and pies for the morn, Maidie tweetering about like a bird *Eh, Mem, but that's RICH, that'll be a fine one!*

Chris said *Then be sure you eat a good share, you're still thin enough since you came to the Manse. Are you sure you are well?* And Maidie said *Fine.* She blushed and stood like a

thin little bird, Chris looked at her quiet, a thin little lass —
what did she think, what did she do in her moments alone,
had she a lad, had she ever been kissed — or more than that,
as they said in Segget? Not half the life in her that poor Else
had; what would Else Queen be doing today?

Dark. As they took their tea together, Ewan and Chris, they
left the blinds drawn and could see the night coming stark outbye, growing strangely light as the daylight waned and the
frost, white-plumed, walked swift over Segget. Ewan sat on the
rug by the fire and read, his blue head down-bent over his book,
Chris stared in the fire and tired of that and finished her tea,
and wandered about and went to the window and looked at the
night. Then she looked at the clock. She would go and meet
Robert.

She turned to the door and Ewan jumped up, she said not to
bother, she was going a walk. He said absent-mindedly, *See
you keep warm*, and his eyes went back again to his book.

Outside, she went hatless, with her coat collar up, she found
at the door of the Manse a wind, bright, keen, and edged like a
razor-blade, the world sleeping on the winter's edge, about
her, dim-pathed, wound the garden of summer, she passed up
its aisles, the hoar crackled below her, all Segget seemed held
in the grip of frost. A queer thought and memory came to her
then and she turned about from going to the gate, and went
back instead by the side of the Manse, up through the garden
where the strawberry beds lay covered deep in manure and
straw, to the wall that girded the kirkyard of Segget.

Here the wind was still, in the Manse's lithe, she put out a
hand on the hoar of the dyke, it felt soft as salt and as cold as
steel; and idly, standing, she wrote her name, though she
couldn't see it by then in the dark, CHRISTINE COLQUO-
HOUN in great capital letters. And she minded how once she
had stood here before, four years or more, after Segget Show;
and she and Robert were there together and she'd thought of
the vanished folk in the yard, and planned to add to those that
supplanted. And the war-time wound that was seared on
Robert had seared that plan from her mind as with fire. . .

It seemed this night remote from her life as the things she'd dreamt as a quean in Blawearie, when she was a maid and knew nothing of men, the kind of play that a bairn would play: for her who stood here with life in her again, unexpected, certain, Robert's baby and hers.

And she found it strange in that icy hush, leaning there warm, her hair bare to the cold, to think how remote was that life from her now, even bairn for the thing that lay under her heart was a word that she'd hardly used a long time, thinking of it as a baby, in English – that from her books and her life in a Manse. She seemed to stand here by the kirkyard's edge looking back on the stones that marked the years where so many Chrises had died and lay buried – back and back, as the graveyard grew dim, far over those smothered hopes and delights, to that other Chris that had been with child, a child herself or so little more, and had known such terror and delight in that, young and raw and queer and sweet, you thought her now, that Chris that had been – the Chris far off in that vanished year who had lain in terror as nights came down with knowledge of the thing that moved in herself, the fruit of her love for the boy she had wed. Ewan sleeping so quiet and so sound in her bed. Remote and far to think she was YOU!

Quiet in the dark she wrote with her finger another name across that of her own, on the kirkyard dyke, and heard as she wrote far up in the Kaimes a peesie wheep – maybe a lost memory from those years in Kinraddie, a peesie that had known that other Chris! She heard a long scuffling through the long grass, silver beyond the rim of the dyke, some rabbit or hare, though it made her heart jump; and slowly she felt her finger rub out the name she had written in hoar on the dyke – ill-luck to have done that, she minded folk said.

A month ago since she'd known for sure, had puzzled for days with the second no-go. Robert would frown, *What on earth's gone wrong? You're dreaming, Christine!* and smile, and she'd smile, and puzzle again when he'd left her alone. So it came on her in the strangest places, she stood in MacDougall Brown's to shop, and MacDougall asked thrice what thing she might want – *Now, Mem* – and she said – *Did I want it at all?* and then came to herself at his cod-like stare. So she gave her order and went out and home, she supposed MacDougall would manage to make out that was another proof of her pride! – all Segget for some reason thought her proud, maybe because she had taken to thinking, not stayed as still as a quean in a book or a quean in a bothy from year unto year.

And when once Stephen Mowat came down to see Robert, and she gave them supper and sat by to listen, Mowat broke off the talk to say *Rahly, Mrs Colquohoun, do tell us the joke!* She said *What joke?* And he said *The one that's making you smile in that charming way.* She said *Oh, I suppose I am full up of supper!* And he'd said he thought that a Jahly untruth, joking, polished as a mart-day pig.

So at last she had known and woke one day sure; and lay and dreamt; and Robert got up – *Feeling all right?* – and she had said *Fine. Robert, we're going to have a baby.* He stared – *We?* – the thing had staggered him, she lay and watched, something moved in her heart, laughter for him, a queer pity for him – oh, men were funny and just boys to be pitied. *Well, I am*, she'd said, *but you had a share.*

He was standing half-dressed, with his fair hair on end, he sat on the bed and stared and then smiled, slowly, with that crinkling about the eyes she had loved near the very first time she met him. *Really and honest-to-God that we are?* And she'd said it was real enough, how did it happen? And he'd said he hadn't the least idea, and that struck them as funny, they giggled like children; and after 'twas Robert that went into long dreams. She'd say *What again?* and he'd say *But Christine! A baby – Good Lord, I hope it's a girl! What does it feel like being as you are – a nuisance, just, or tremendous and terrible?* And Chris had said that it made you feel sick, now and then, and Robert had laughed at that, he wasn't so easily cheated as Mowat. *Oh Chris Caledonia, I've married a nation!*

Now, standing beside the dyke in the dark, she minded that, it was true enough, somehow you did hide away the things, Scots folk had always done that, you supposed – in case they'd

go blind in their naked shrine, like a soul in the presence of
Robert's great God – God he followed unfaltering still, and
was getting Him deeper in dislike than ever, with his preaching
in Segget the cause of the Miners. These were the folk that
were going on strike, in May, unless their wages were raised.
Robert said their case was a testing case, the triumph of greed
or the triumph of God.

Chris herself had hardly a thought in the matter because of
that nameless doubt that was hers – doubt of the men and
method that came to change the world that was waiting change
– all the mixed, strange world of the Segget touns, with its
failing trade and its Mills often idle. The folk of the Mills would
hang round the room where their dole was paid by a little
clerk, they'd laze there and snicker at the women that passed,
and yawn, with weariness stamped on each face; and smoke,
and whistle, and yawn some more. Once she'd passed and
heard some of them quarrelling out loud, she had thought it
must surely be over politics; but instead 'twas the chances of
a football match! She'd told Robert that and he'd laughed and
said *Demos! – didn't you know that the chap was like that?
But we'll alter these things forever in May.*

May: and the baby wouldn't come till July, a good enough
month for a baby to be born, though Robert said if they had
planned it at all they would surely have planned it better than
that. July might be far too hot for comfort. But he didn't fuss
round her, stood back and aside, he knew it her work and that
he'd little help – oh, different as could be from the Ewan long
ago, the frightened boy who had so fussed about her – how
they'd quarrelled, how wept, how laughed in that time of the
coming of that baby that was now in the Manse – a boy, grown
up, remote from it all, remote enough with his books and his
flints, far enough off from being a baby, rather like a flint himself in some ways, but of a better shape and grain, grey granite
down to the core, young Ewan, with its flinty shine and its cool
grey skin and the lights and the flashing strands in it. Different
from that, Robert's baby and hers—

She stamped her feet and woke from her dreaming as down

through the dark she heard on the shingle the coming footsteps of Robert himself.

And next morning he said, *Let's go out a walk, up in the hills
somewhere – are you keen?* Chris said she was and well before
eight they were off, they met with Ewan in the hall as they
went, he said nothing at all about going out with them, he
always knew when he wasn't much wanted. Chris kissed him
and said they'd be back for dinner; syne she and Robert went
up by the Kaimes, and Ewan stood and looked after them –
you could hardly believe that Chris was so old.

Underfoot the frost held hard and firm in the rising sun of
the New Year's Day, that sun a red smoulder down in the
Howe, the hoar was a blanching on post and hedge, riming
the dykes, far up in the Mounth the veilings of mists were
draping the hills, except that now and then they blew off and
you saw the coarse country deep in the haughs, remote with a
flicker of red on the roofs of some shepherd's sheiling high in
the heath. Robert was walking so fast that Chris for a while
could hadly keep up with his stride, then she fell into that and
found it easy, the Kaimes was past and above it the path
opened out through the ragged fringe of the moor that came
peering and sniffling down at Segget as a draggled cat at a dish
out of doors, all the countryside begirdled with hills and their
companions the moors that crept and slept and yawned in the
sun, watching the Howe at its work below.

They passed a tarn that was frozen and shone, Chris tried
the edge with her stick and it broke, and she saw herself for a
minute then, with the looped-up hair and the short-cut skirts
and the leather jacket tight at her waist, high in the collar; and
the blown bronze of her cheeks and hair and the stick in her
hands and the fur-backed gloves, she smiled at herself for this
Chris that she'd grown. Robert stopped and looked back and
was puzzled and came and stood by her side and looked down
at that Chris that smiled remote in the broken ice. *Yes, not at
all bad. See the childe by her shoulder? Do you think the two
can be decently married?*

Chris said that she thought not, they'd something in their eyes – and Robert kissed her then, iron, his hard, quick kiss, the kiss of a man with other passions than kissing; but wonderful and daft a moment to stand, on the frozen moor, her head back on his shoulder, and so be kissed, and at last released, Robert panting a little, and they both looked away; and then they went on, swinging hand in hand for a while till they tired and needed their sticks.

Robert went first, bare-headed, black-coated, he was whistling *Over the Sea to Skye*, clear and bright as they still went on, up through the wind of a sheep-track here where the Grampians pushed out their ramparts in fence against the coming of life from below.

By eleven they were high in the Culdyce moor, winding the twist of its slopes in the broom that hung thick-rimed with unshaken frost for the sun had died away in a smoulder, the Howe lay grey in a haze below, as they climbed that haze betook itself from the heights to the haughs, Leachie towered high, its crag-head swathed with a silk-web mutch. Trusta's ten hundred feet cowered west as if bending away from the blow of the wind, the moors a ragged shawl on her shoulders, crouching and seated since the haughs were born, watching the haze in the Howe below, the flicker of the little folk that came and builded and loved and hated and died, and were not, a crying and swarm of midges warmed by the sun to a glow and a dance. And the Trusta heights drew closer their cloaks, year by year, at the snip of the shears, as coulter and crofter moiled up the haughs.

Once Chris and Robert came to a place, out in the open, here the wind blew and the ground was thick with the droppings of sheep, where a line of the ancient stones stood ringed, as they stood in Kinraddie far west and below, left by the men of antique time, memorial these of a dream long lost, the hopes and fears of fantastic eld.

Robert said that they came from the East, those fears, long ago, ere Pytheas came sailing the sounding coasts to Thule. Before that the hunters had roamed these hills, naked and

bright, in a Golden Age, without fear or hope or hate or love,
living high in the race of the wind and the race of life, mating
as simple as beasts or birds, dying with a like keen simpleness,
the hunting weapons of those ancient folk Ewan would find in
his search of the moors. Chris sat on a fallen stone and heard
him, about her the gleams of the wintry day, the sailing cloud-
shapes over the Howe; and she asked how long ago that had
been? And Robert said *Less than four thousand years*, and it
sounded long enough to Chris – four thousand years of kings
and of Gods, all the dark, mad hopes that had haunted men
since they left the caves and the hunting of deer, and the
splendour of life like a song, like the wind.

And she thought then, looking on the shadowed Howe with
its stratus mists and its pillars of spume, driving west by the
Leachie bents, that men had followed these pillars of cloud like
lost men lost in the high, dreich hills, they followed and fought
and toiled in the wake of each whirling pillar that rose from
the heights, clouds by day to darken men's minds – loyalty and
fealty, patriotism, love, the mumbling chants of the dead old
gods that once were worshipped in the circles of stones,
christianity, socialism, nationalism – all – Clouds that swept
through the Howe of the world, with men that took them for
gods; just clouds, they passed and finished, dissolved and were
done, nothing endured but the Seeker himself, him and the
everlasting Hills.

Then she came from that thought, Robert shaking her arm.
Chris, you'll be frozen. Let's climb to the camp. He had once
been here with Ewan, she hadn't; the moor shelved smoothly
up to its top, as they climbed in view Chris saw two lines of
fencing climbing each slope of the hill, new-driven and stapled,
the fences, they met and joined and ended up on the crest. But
before that meeting and joining they plunged through the
circles of the ancient camp that had been, the turf and the
stones had been flung aside, Robert told that the hill had been
recently sold and the lands on either side as well, and two
different landowners bought the hill and set up those fences
to show their rights – what were dirt like the old heathen

forts to them? Symbols of our age and its rulers, these clowns, Robert said, and the new culture struggling to birth – when it came it would first have to scavenge the world!

Then he started talking of the Miners, of Labour, of the coming struggle in the month of May, he hoped and believed that that was the beginning of the era of Man made free at last, Man who was God, Man splendid again. Christ meant and intended no more when He said that He was the Son of Man, when He preached the Kingdom of Heaven – He meant it on earth. Christ was no godlet, but a leader and hero—

He forgot Chris, striding up and down the slope, excitement kindled in his harsh, kind eyes. And Chris watched him, standing, her stick behind her, her arms looped about it, saying nothing to him but hearing and seeing, him and the hills and the song that both made. And suddenly she felt quite feared, it was daft – as she looked at the scaling heights high up, the chasms below, and her Robert against them.

She put out her hand and caught him, he turned, something in her face stopped questions, all else, the pity and fear that had been in her eyes. He didn't kiss her now, his arms round about her, they were quiet a long moment as they looked in each other, they had never done that that Chris could remember, seeing herself globed earnest, half-smiling, and with trembling lips there in the deep grey pools that hid away Robert – never hers for long if ever at all, unceasing the Hunter of clouds by day. The men of the earth that had been, that she'd known, who kept to the earth and their eyes upon it – the hunters of clouds that were such as was Robert: how much was each wrong and how much each right, and was there maybe a third way to Life, unguessed, unhailed, never dreamed of yet?

Then he said *Now we surely know each other*, and she came from her mood to meet his with a laugh, *If we don't we've surely done shameful things!* And they sat in the lithe of the heath-grown dyke and ate chocolate Robert had brought in his pocket, and Chris fell fast asleep as she sat, and awoke with Robert sitting still lest he wake her, one hand around her and

under her heart, but far away from her in his thoughts, his
eyes on the sailing winter below and his thoughts with the
new year that waited their coming down through the hills in
the Segget wynds.

Chris watched the coming of that Spring in Segget with her
interests strange-twisted back on themselves, as though she
re-lived that Chris of long syne, far from the one that had
taken her place, that Chris of kirks and Robert of books —
they sank from sight in the growing of the Spring, quick on the
hills, on the upland parks, you saw the fields of Meiklebogs
change as you looked from the window of that room in the
Manse that John Muir had set with Blawearie gear. It was there
you intended the baby be born, the only sign of insanity yet,
said Robert, laughing, and helping you change.

He seemed to have altered too with the Spring, the black
mood came seldom or never now, nor that red, queer cough
that companioned it. You'd hear him of a morning go whistling
away under the yews, on some kirk concern, blithe as though
the world had been born anew. It wasn't only the coming of
the baby that had altered him so and kindled his eyes, all the
air of the country was filled with its rumour, that thing awaited
the country in May, when the Miners and others had threatened
to strike. Robert said that more than a strike would come, the
leaders had planned to seize power in May.

The red-ploughed lands steamed hot in the sun as Meiklebogs' men drove slow their great teams in the steam of the
waiting world of Spring, the rooks behind them, Chris stood
still and watched, and remembered, and put her hand up to
her heart, and then lower, by belly and thigh: and slow, under
her hand, that shape would turn, May close and July coming
closer now, she felt fit and well, contented, at peace.

Ewan knew now, he had stared one morning; and then asked
if she was going to have a baby. Chris had said *Yes, do you
mind very much?* and he had said *No,* but hadn't kissed her
that morning, she watched him go with a catch of breath. But
by night he seemed to have got the thing over, he put cushions

behind her when she sat at tea, grave, and with care, and Robert winked at her. Ewan saw the wink and flashed his cool smile; and they all sat silent in front of the fire, with its smouldering glow, they had no need to speak.

Then Maidie knew, as she watched Chris at work, and tweetered the news to some quean outbye, and the quean gasped *Never!* and told Ag Moultrie, the Roarer and Greeter, met in the street. And Ag had nearly a fit with delight, and before that night came down in Segget there was hardly a soul in both touns but knew the minister's wife had taken at last — ay, and must be fell on with it, too, by her look, so the lassie Moultrie had said. Had Ag seen her? you'd ask, and they'd tell you Ay, she'd fairly done that, and Mrs Colquohoun had told the bit news to Ag Moultrie herself; and syne broke down and just Roared and Grat on Ag's shoulder.

Old Leslie said 'twas Infernal, just, you'd have thought a minister would have more sense. He never had thought it decent in a minister to show plain to his parish he did *that* kind of thing; and he minded when he was a loon up in Garvock— Those nearest the door of the smiddy nipped out, Ake Ogilvie near was killed in the rush, and he found Old Leslie habbering to himself, hammering at a horseshoe, and far off in Garvock. *What's up then, Leslie?* Ake Ogilvie asked, and Leslie said *What, have you not heard the news?* and told of the thing that was on at the Manse, and might well have begun to tell of Garvock, but that Ake, the coarse brute, said *Well, what of it? Didn't your own father lie with your mother — the poor, misguided devil of a childe?*

Syne out he went swaggering and met with John Muir, and asked if he'd heard what the scandal-skunks said? Muir gleyed and said Ay, and it made him half-sick, and Ake said the same, they were both of them fools, and cared nothing at all for a tasty bit news.

John Muir went home, never told his wife, she found out herself nearly three days late; and fair flew into a rage at that, to be so far behind with the news. *Did you know the news of Mrs Colquohoun?* she spiered of John and he gleyed and said *Ay.*

And she asked could he never tell her a thing, her that had to
bide at home and cook, and wash and sew and mend all the
time, with himself and two meikle trollops of daughters, working her hands to the very bone? And John said *Well, it's nothing
to me if Mrs Colquohoun has been ta'en with a bairn – I'm not
the father, as far as I know.*

Mrs Muir reddened up. *Think shame of yourself speaking
that way in front of the lassies.* Tooje was standing with her
meikle mouth open, drinking it up, afore she could close it her
mother took her a crack in the gape. Tooje started to greet
and Ted in the garden heard the greeting, as aye she would do,
and came tearing in, and started to greet to keep Tooje company; and John Muir got up with his pipe and his paper and
went out to the graveyard and sat on a stone, and had a fine
read: decent folk, the dead.

In the Arms Dite Peat said *Wait till it comes. She's the kind
that takes ill with having a bairn – over narrow she is, she'll
fair have a time. I warrant the doctor'll need his bit knives.*
Folk thought that an unco-like speak to make, he'd a mind as
foul as a midden, Dite Peat: but for all that you went to the
kirk the next Sabbath and took a gey keek at Mrs Colquohoun
– ay, God! she fairly was narrow round there, more like a
quean than a grown-up woman, with her sulky, proud face and
her well-brushed hair, she'd look not so bonny when it came to
her time.

Then Hairy Hogg heard it and minded the story of what Mr
Mowat had said he would give – to take the minister's wife
with a bairn. *You well may depend that was more than a speak.*
Folk had forgotten it but now they all minded, it was said in
Segget it was ten to one the bairn wasn't the minister's at all,
young Mr Mowat had been heard to say he'd given half of a
whole year's profits for lying with that proud-like Mrs Colquohoun. MacDougall Brown said 'twas a black, black sin, and he
preached a sermon in the Square next Sabbath, about scarlet
priesthoods living in shame; and everybody knew what he
meant by that, his son Jock wabbled his eyes all around, and
Mrs Brown shook like a dollop of fat; only Cis looked away and

turned red and shy, and thought of Dod Cronin and his hands
and lips.

The spinners didn't care when the news reached *them*,
though an unco birn came now to the kirk that had never
attended a kirk before, the older men mostly, disjaskèd, ill-
dressed, with their white, spinner faces and ill-shaven chins,
like raddled old loons, and they brought their wives with
them – the minister was fairly a favourite with them. So might
he be, aye siding with the dirt and the Labour stite that the
Cronins preached; and twice he had interfered at the Mills and
forced Mr Mowat to clean out his sheds. But the younger
spinners went to no kirk, just hung about of a Sabbath day,
and snickered as a decent body went by, or took their lasses
up to the Kaimes as soon as the Spring sun dried the grass.

Most of the gossip Chris heard of or knew, and cared little
or nothing, folk were like that, she thought if you'd neither
books nor God nor music nor love nor hate as stand-bys, no
pillar of cloud to lead your feet, you turned as the folk of farm
and toun – to telling scandal of your nearest neighbours,
making of them devils and heroes and saints, to brighten your
days and give you a thrill. And God knew they were welcome to
get one from her, she found herself liking them as never before, kindled to new interest in every known face, seized
again and again in the Segget wynds – looking at the rat-like
little Peter Peat, at MacDougall's bald head, at the lizard-like
Mowat – with the startling thought, *He was once a bairn!* It
nearly put you off having one sometimes; and then again you'd
be filled with such a queer pity, as you passed, that Hairy Hogg
would go in and say to his wife – *That Mrs Colquohoun she
goes by me and SNICKERS!* and his wife would say *Well
damn't, do you want her to go by you and greet?*

So April was here, with its steaming drills and the reek of
dung in the Meiklebogs parks; and in Segget backyards a
scraich and chirawk as the broods of the winter gobbled their
corn, you could hear the ring of the smiddy hammer across
the still air right to the Manse – above it, continuous, the
drum of the Mills. Young Mr Mowat had new orders on hand

and most of the spinners were at work again. But early that
week that he put them on Stephen Mowat came down to the
Manse, with a paper in his hand and a list of names. He wanted
Robert to join the list, the OMS, a volunteer army, that was
being prepared all over the country to feed the country in the
Miners' strike. And he said that they didn't always see eye to
eye, him and Colquohoun, but that this was serious: you
Jahly well couldn't let a push like the miners dictate to the
country what it should do. And he said that Rahly Robert must
join, and Mrs Colquohoun as well, if she would; and he smiled
at her charming, and showed all his teeth.

Robert said *Well, Christine, what do you say?* and Chris
didn't much care for she didn't much hope. Then she looked at
Mowat, elegant, neat, in his London clothes, with his tended
hair and his charming look; and the saggy pouches under his
eyes. And it seemed she was looking at more than Mowat, the
class that had made of the folk of Segget the dirt-hungry folk
that they had been and were – made them so in sheer greed
and sheer brag. You had little hope what the Miners could do,
them or the Labour leaders of Robert, but they couldn't though
they tried make a much worse mess than Mowat and his kind
had done, you knew. So you just said *No*; Robert smiled at
Mowat. *That's Chris's answer, a trifle abrupt. And I can't help
the OMS myself – you see, I've another plan afoot.* Mowat
said that was Jahly, what was the plan? And Robert said *Why,
do all that I can to hinder the OMS or such skunks as try to
interfere with the Strike.*

Chris had never admired Stephen Mowat so much, he kept
his temper, charming, polite, she and Robert watched him
stride from the door, down under the yews, and they later
heard he had gone to the Provost and gotten his help, and the
same from Geddes, and the same from Melvin that kept
the Arms. Near everybody that counted would help, except
the spinners, the Manse, and Ake Ogilvie – Ake had told Mr
Mowat they could hamstring each other, strikers and Government, for all that he cared. And neither would MacDougall
Brown give his name, he said his living depended on spinners:

and if all the world renounced its sin the cares of the world would be ended tomorrow.

And all the time he was saying this he was mixing sawdust under the counter, canny-like, in a bag of meal.

Chris put the whole thing out of her mind, busied in making the baby's clothes, busied in going long walks by herself, the last day in April she took Ewan with her, across by Mondynes, till they saw far off, crowning the hills, the roofs of Kinraddie. *You were born over there twelve years ago,* she thought aloud as they sat to rest, Ewan with his head cupped up in his hands, his arms on his knees, his blue-black hair rumpled, untidily tailed, in the glow of the sun. He said, *Yes, I know,* and then looked at her sudden — *but I say! I never really thought of that . . . Or anyway, never as I thought just now.* She asked how was that, and he looked down the Howe. *Well, that I once was a part of you; though, of course, I know all about how babies come.*

And for almost the first time in years he seemed troubled, her boy, the fruit of herself, so cool, so kind and sure and so stony-clear, troubled to a sudden, queer brittle pity. *Mother!* And he looked at her, then away, then came and cuddled her tight for a moment, his arms round her throat Chris nearly was stifled: but she didn't move, didn't say a word at that strange embracing on the part of Ewan.

And May and tomorrow waited their feet as they turned back quiet up the Segget road.

Ewan in his bed; in the May-time dark Chris wandered the sitting-room of the Manse, looking again and again from the window at the mist that had come and grew thicker each minute. Beyond her vision the yews, the hedge: she could see but a little space from the window, a space translit by a misty star, the lights far up in Segget House.

What had happened to Robert — had he been in time?

And at last she could bear it no longer, went out, into the hall and put on her coat, and opened the door and went down through the path, through the slimy, slow crunch of the shingle, mist-wet. A light gleamed faint in the house of John Muir and a dog barked loud from old Smithie's shed as he heard her footsteps pass in the mist, it came draping its cobwebs across her face, she put up her hand and wiped off the globes, from her lashes, and stopped and listened on the road. Nothing to be heard, the mist like a blanket, had Robert come up with the spinners in time?

They had gone to blow up the High Segget brig, a birn of the spinners and one of the porters, the news had been brought to the Manse by John Cronin, panting – *They've gone to blow up the brig and prevent the trains that the blacklegs are running reaching beyond this, or south from Dundon.* Robert had jumped up – *When did they go?* and Cronin had said *Ten minutes ago, I heard of it only now in Old Toun, this'll mean the police and arrest for us all.* Robert had said *Oh, damn the fools and their half-witted ploys – blowing up brigs! Right, I'll be with you,* and hadn't waited his coat, had told Chris not to worry and kissed her, and ran, long-striding down through the shingle, Cronin at his heels and the mist coming down.

Where were they now, what had happened at the brig?

She pressed on again, that fear for an urge – a fool to be out, maybe Robert would miss her. The mist was so thick she could hardly see a thing on the other side of the Wynd, she kept the leftward wall and held down, past the locked-up shop of little Peter Peat, the shop of the Provost locked up as well, and Dite Peat's as well, all three of them specials enrolled by Mowat to help Simon Leslie. But the station folk and the spinners were out, so Robert had told her, and here in Segget, as all over the country, the Strike held firm.

Had he and Cronin reached the brig in time?

Now she was down in the Square, so she knew, the lights of the Arms seeped up through the mist, the Arms crowded with spinners as usual, few of them knew of the thing at the brig, John Cronin had said the folk who had gone to blow up the place were no more than boys, and daft at that, with their blasting-powder gotten or thieved from the quarry at Quarles.

As Chris crossed the Square she met in the mist two men who were holding up to East Wynd, Sim Leslie was one, and a man with a brassard, one of the specials, she thought it Dite Peat. They peered in her face and Sim Leslie coughed, and the man with the brassard laughed a foul laugh. Chris felt her blood go cold at that laugh, she heard them engage in a mutter of talk as she hurried down the road to the station.

There were lights down there, but still as the grave, she stood and looked down, her heart beating fast. And so, as she stood, slowly, quietly, under her heart her baby moved. She gasped a little, she must go more slow, she shouldn't be out in the mist at all. Robert and Cronin must have reached them in time.

But even yet she could not go back. She stood and listened in the mist and heard the fall of it on the grass, on the hedge, beyond the wall where she stood and leaned – soft, in a feathery falling of wet, blanketing sound away from her ears. She ought to go home, but how could she, unsure?

In that minute, far to the south the mist suddenly broke and flamed: she stared: the flame split up through the mirk from the ground. Then there came to her ears the crack and crinkle of such explosion as she'd heard before up in the Mounthside Quarles quarry. She knew what it meant; and started to run.

Beyond the railway lines was the path that wound by the lines till it reached Segget brig. Here the hawthorns brushed her face and the grass whipped wetly about her legs as she ran, not thinking, trying hard not to think, to run fleetly, and gain the brig, as she must – Robert was there – Oh, and those fools!

The second explosion laid hand on the night and shook the mist as a great hand might. Then it died, and Chris found the true dark had come, it had seeped through the mist like spilt ink through paper, and she couldn't run now, but walked and stumbled, and heard no more for it seemed an hour.

Till far behind her there rose a whistle, a long-drawn blast remote in the night.

She stopped at that and turned about, a whin-bush lashed
her face as she turned and then stood listening and looking
beside her. And far away north up the side of the Mounth a
line of lights twinkled suddenly bright, and moved and slowed
and came to a stop.

Clenched hand at her throat, for that seemed to help, she
gasped and stared at the cluster at halt – some Dundon train
that had halted at Carmont, in five minutes more it would be
in Segget, and the brig was down, and it wouldn't know—

Running again she felt that change, slow and dreadful and
sick in her body, her arms held out as she kept the path; and
she cried to the thing unborn in her womb, *Not now, not now*;
and it moved again. Then up the line she heard the skirl of
the starting train, its windows flashed, it purred from sight
as it climbed through the woods – she never could do it, try
though she might!

Yet, so at last, running, she did; and gained the road with
the station below. Down there was a flurry and scurry of lights,
behind on the road a scurry of feet. She turned at that sound,
saw a drift of men, she seemed to know one: and cried out
Robert!

The night quietened away in a mist of faces and a kindled
lantern and Robert's voice. So later Chris minded, and then
the next hours closed suddenly up as a telescope closes. One
minute she was standing, her teeth in her lip, harkening Robert
tell how he'd gained the brig, just in time, they'd done no more
than test off the powder, he and Cronin had stopped them at
that; and the next she was up in the Manse with Robert, as
she stood in the hall and he closed the door the hall rose up
and spun twice round her head, she stared at the grandfather
clock in the hall, for a minute she couldn't breathe, couldn't
move. Something suddenly flooded her mouth, she sopped the
stuff with her handkerchief – red, and saw as last thing
Robert's startled scowl as he leapt to catch her; and then he
quite vanished.

She opened her eyes in bed the next time, sick and weak
with the May light high and pouring into the room in a flood,

somebody she didn't know near the bed. Then the somebody turned and looked and Chris knew her, she whispered *It's Else!* and Else said *Shish! You mustn't move, Mem,* and crinkled her face as though she would cry. Chris would have laughed if she hadn't been weak, so she closed her eyes for another rest, maybe another day, maybe a minute, and woke, and the dark was close outbye, the first thing she heard as she came from the dark the rake and tweet of the rooks in the yews.

She looked round about and saw Robert and Ewan, Robert was over by the window, hunched, with his shoulders and head black-carved in the light, Ewan was sitting by the side of her bed, a hand on his knee, his head down-bent, looking at a little flint in his hand. She coughed: and both of them turned at the sound, and she coughed again and saw with surprise the stuff that spilt from her mouth on the sheet, not red, it was brown, and she suddenly saw, vividly clear and distinct, it was awful, horror and horror in Robert's face.

Night, with a setting of stars, all alone, in the May-time dark, she knew it still May. There was a hiss of rain on the roof, light rain, and all the house set in silence but for that whisper of the falling rain. She lay and suddenly knew the Thing close, a finish to the hearing of rain on the roof, a finish to knowing of that hearing at all, the world cut off, she felt free and light, strung to a quivering point of impatience as she waited and waited and the night went by — ready and ready she waited, near cried, because the Thing didn't come after all. And grew tired and slept; and the Thing drew back.

Lord, Chris, you've given us a devil of a time!
She lay and looked at him and suddenly she knew, wakened wide, she said *And what happened to my baby?* Robert said *You mustn't worry about that. Get well, my dear* — he was thin as a rake, and near as ungroomed, his hair up on end, she asked if Maidie had been doing the cooking, for him and Ewan — and where was Ewan? He said that Ewan was at school today, seeing the doctor had found her much better. As for

Maidie, she'd proved no use at all, and he'd sent for Else, Else
had done fine. . .

So it hadn't been a dream Chris lay and knew as the hours
went by, and Robert went out and Else came in; and later the
doctor and all fussed about her; below the sheets her body felt
flat, ground down and flat, with an empty ache; and her
breasts hurt and hurt till they saw to them, she hadn't cried
at all when she knew what had happened, till it came for them
to see her breasts, for a minute she nearly was desperate then.
But that was just daft, she'd given plenty of trouble, said the
Chris that survived all things that came to her. So she gave in
quietly, and they finished at last, and she slept till Ewan came
back from the school, and came up after tea, and looked in
and smiled.

Hello, mother, better?

He came to the bedside and suddenly cuddled her; for a
minute she was hurt with the weight of his head on her
breast, though she put up her arms about him. Then something hot trickled on her breast, and she knew what – Ewan
to cry! that was dreadful. But he did it only a minute while
she held him, then drew away and took out his handkerchief
and wiped his eyes, and sat down, calm, but she didn't care,
reaching out and touching his hand as he sat. Funny she should
ever have feared she would lose him, that already she'd done
so, him no longer a baby, remote from her thoughts or from
thought of her. How nearer he was than any there were! She
said *You must tell me Ewan, what happened. When was the
baby born, was it dead?*

So he told her the baby was born that morning after the
spinners were to blow up the brig. Robert had gone for the
doctor and Ewan had stayed at home and tried to look after
her, though he didn't know much of the things he should do:
as for Maidie, the girl was a perfect fool. At last the doctor and
Robert arrived, Robert sent off a wire to Else at Fordoun, and
they put Ewan out of the room – he was glad, even though it
was Chris, he'd a beast of a headache. The baby had been born
then, it wasn't born dead, though it died soon after, or so

Ewan heard. Else said that it was a boy, like Robert, but Ewan hadn't seen it: that was days ago, two or three days before the Strike ended.

Chris remembered: *What, is it ended, then? Who won?* and Ewan said the Government, Robert raved the leaders had betrayed the Strike, they'd been feared that they would be jailed, the leaders, they had sold the Strike to save their skins. Robert hadn't believed the news when it came, that was the morning that Chris was so bad and the two of them had sat in her room—

Chris lay still and said *Thank you, Ewan,* with a little ghost of a laugh inside to know that he called her Chris in his thoughts, as she'd thought he did; and soon, wearied still, she slept again, sleeping till supper-time, it brought Else up with a tray and hot bottle and all things needed, she cried, right pleased, *You're fine again, Mem?* and Chris said she was, she had to thank Else with others for that.

Else said *Devil a thanks — if you'll pardon a body mentioning Meiklebogs' cousin in a Manse. I liked fine to come 'stead of biding in Fordoun, with the old man glunching at me and my bairn.* Chris asked how the baby was, and Else kindled, *Fine, Mem, and fegs you should see how he grows.* And then suddenly stopped and punched up the pillows, and set Chris up rough, and began to chatter, like a gramophone suddenly gone quite mad, with her ears very red and her face turned away.

Chris knew why she did it, she'd thought of that baby she'd carried out dead from this room a while back, she was feared that Chris might take ill again were anything said to mind her of babies. But Chris had never felt further from weeping, appalled at the happening to Robert, not her.

Else told how the Strike had ended in Segget, folk said that the spinners who went out that night and tried to blow up the brig would be jailed. But there was no proof, only rumours and scandal, and the burnt grass in the lee of the brig. Sim Leslie, him that the folk called Feet, had come up to the Manse like a sow seeking scrunch, but the minister had dealt with him short and sharp and he tailked away home like an ill-kicked cur.

The spinners and station folk wouldn't believe it when the news came through that the Strike was ended, they said the news was just a damned lie, John Cronin said it, and they wouldn't go back, he and the minister kept them from that till they got more telegrams up from London. And Mr Colquohoun and Ake Ogilvie the joiner, John Muir and some spinners had organized pickets to keep Mr Mowat's folk from getting to the Mills. Syne they heard how the leaders had been feared of the jail, and the whole thing just fell to smithereens in Segget. Some spinners that night went down the West Wynd and bashed in the windows of the Cronin house, and set out in a birn to come to the Manse, they said the minister had egged them on, him safe and sound in his own damned job, and they'd do to the Manse as they'd done to the Cronins.

But coming up the Wynd they met in with Ake Ogilvie, folk said that he cursed them black and blue; and told them how Chris was lying ill and wouldn't it have been a damned sight easier for Mr Colquohoun to have kept in with the gentry, instead of risking his neck for the spinners? The spinners all sneered and jeered at Ake, but he stood fast there in the middle of the road, and wouldn't let them up, and they turned and tailed off. A third were on to the Bureau again, and Jock Cronin sacked from his job at the station, and Miss Jeannie Grant hadn't gone to the school, though all the nine days she'd been helping the spinners: and when she went back Mr Geddes said No, and folk told that she would get the sack, too.

Chris said *So it ended like that? Else – was my baby born dead, and was it a boy?* Else went white and wept a little at that, Chris lay and watched and Else peeked at her, scared, she looked strangely un-ill with that foam of bronze hair, and the dour face thin, but still sweet and sure. Else said that it wasn't, it lived half an hour, the minister came up and baptized it Michael, a bonny bairn, tiny and quiet, it yawned and blinked its eyes just a minute – *oh, Mem, I shouldn't be telling you this!*

Chris said *But you should. Where is it buried?* and Else said 'twas out in the old kirkyard, there were only the minister and Muir and herself, the minister carried the coffin in there, and read the service, *bonny he did it, if it wasn't for that fool John Muir that stood by, like a trumpet, near, blowing his nose. And when the minister came to the bit about Resurrection — I don't mind the words—*

Chris said *I do,* and heard her own voice tell them with Else near weeping again: *I am the Resurrection and the Life. He that believeth in me, though he were dead, yet shall he live.*

Else gulped and nodded. *And after he said that — he didn't know what he was saying, Mem, with his bairn new dead and his Strike as well — he said AND WHO SHALL BELIEVE? quiet and queer. . . I shouldn't be telling you this, but oh! you'll have to hurry and get well for him!*

Coming out of those memories given to the years, Chris moved and looked at the waiting Segget, quiet in the lazy spray of June sun, the same land and sun that Hew Monte Alto had looked on that morning before Bara battle. You were waiting yourself in a halt before battle: all haltings were that, you thought, or would think if you weren't too wearied to think now at all.

But that would pass soon, you'd to get better quick — quick and quick for the sake of Robert. Better, and take him out of himself, Ewan would help, maybe Segget even yet—

She rose slow to her feet and smiled at herself, for that weakness that followed her when she stood up, with the drowse of the June day a moment a haze of little floating specks in her eyes. Then that cleared, and a cold little wind came by, she looked up and saw a thickening of clouds, rain-nimbus driving down upon Segget.

IV

NIMBUS

Now, with the coming of the morning, the stars shone bright
and brittle on the Segget roofs, the rime of the frost Chris saw
rise up, an uneasy carpet that shook in the wind, the icy wind
from the sea and Kinneff. Under her feet the dark ground
cracked, as though she were treading on the crackle of grass,
and as she passed through the Kaimes' last gate – far up, in
the dimming light of the stars, there fell a long flash from the
arc of the sky, rending that brittle white glow for a moment,
its light for a second death-white on the hills. Then she saw
the sky darken, and the corpse-light went: behind the darkness the morning was coming.

So, walking quick to keep her feet warm, and because she'd
but little time left for this ploy, she gained the Kaimes and
halted and looked – not at them, but up at the heights of the
hills, sleeping there on the verge of dawn. Nothing cried or
moved, too early as yet, but a peewit far in the hidden hollow,
she minded how it was here she had come – almost at this
very hour she had come – the very first night she had lain in
Segget. And here she climbed from those ten full years, still
the same Chris in her heart of hearts, nothing altered but
space and time and the things she had once believed everlasting and sure – believed that they made her life, they made her!
But they hadn't, there was something beyond that endured,
something she had never yet garbed in a name.

She put up her hand to her dew-touched hair, she'd climbed
bare-headed up to the Kaimes, she had seen a grey hair here
and there 'last night. But it felt the same hair as she felt the
same self, its essence unchanged whatever its look. Queer
and terrible to think of that now – that all things passed
as your life went on, but the little things you had given no
heed.

The wind goeth towards the south, and turneth about unto the north; it whirleth aloud continually, and the wind returneth again according to his circuits.

That was Ecclesiastes, she thought; stilled; the dawn pallid on her coiled, bronze hair.

In Segget below a cock crew shrill, she turned and looked down at the shining of frost, remotely, and saw it gleam and transmute, change and transmute as though Time turned back, back through the green and grey of the years till that last time here when she'd climbed the Kaimes, her baby new dead and herself a live ache—

She had shown as little of the ache as she might, in spite of the waste, she had hated that. So she told to Robert and he laughed and said *You sound like a woman in an Aberdeen joke,* his eyes with the beast of the black mood in them. *Waste? Good God, do you think that is all?*

He flung away from her and walked to the window, beyond it the smell and blow of the hay in the sleeping parks of Dalziel of Meiklebogs. Then suddenly he turned – *Christine, I'm sorry. But I'm weary as well, let's not speak of it more.*

And she left it at that, he'd drawn into himself, lonely, he sat for hours in his room with impatience for either her pity or help. So she buried herself in the work of the house, and sought in her pride a salve for the sting of the knowledge she counted for little with Robert, compared with his cloudy hopings and God. She could be strange and remote as he could...

And it came with hardly an effort at all, they were hurrying nods that met on the stairs and went to bed at uneven hours; yet sometimes a hand seemed to twist in her heart as she watched him sit at his meat in silence, or at night when she woke and he lay asleep, with it seemed the tug of lips on her breasts and the ghostly ache of her empty womb – silent the yews in the listening dark.

Segget crowded the kirk the first Sunday in May after the

General Strike collapsed, to hear what that cocky billy Colquhoun would say of his tink-like socialists now. But he never mentioned the creatures at all, he preached a sermon that maddened you, just, he said there was nothing new under the sun: and that showed you the kind of twister he was. Hairy Hogg, the Provost, came out of the kirk, and said that the man was insulting them, sly, trying to make out that the work they had done to beat the coarse Labour tinks was a nothing. Instead, now the Strike was ended so fine, you'd mighty soon see a gey change for the good, no more unions to cripple folks' trade, and peace and prosperity returning again: and maybe a tariff on those foreign-made boots.

But damn the sign of either you saw as that year went on and the next come in, there was little prosperity down at the Mills, they were working whiles, and whiles they were not, young Mr Mowat went off to London and syne from there he went off on a cruise, as a young gent should; but he fair was real kind. For he wrote that he'd soon be back home again, and would see about pushing the Segget trade, that would mean more men – *but no union men.*

It wasn't his wyte that he had no work, in spite of the spinners and their ill-ta'en grumblings. For they grumbled still, though their union was finished – faith! that was funny, for you'd got from the papers that the men would be fine if it wasn't for the unions – the Tory childes nearly broke down and wept on the way the unions oppressed the workers. The Cronins had all been sacked from the Mills and no more of a Sunday you'd hear them preach about socialism coming, and coarse dirt like that. Jock Cronin, that had once been a railway porter, was down now in Glasgow, tinking about, it fairly was fine to be rid of the brute. Folk said that that Miss Jeannie Grant had gone with him, some childe had seen her, down there at a mart, all painted and powdered, she'd ta'en to the streets, and kept Jock Cronin, he lived off her earnings. Ay, just the kind of thing you'd expect from socialists and dirt that spoke ill of their betters, and yet powdered and fornicated like gentry.

But young Dod Cronin, that was a mere loon, he heard the news, he worked out at Fordoun, and he went to the smiddy and tackled old Leslie, with the sweat dripping down from his wrinkled old chops. And Dod said *What's this you've been saying of my brother?* and old Leslie said *What? And who are you, lad?* And Dod said *You know damn well who I am. And if ever I hear you spreading your claik about my brother or Miss Jeannie Grant, I'll bash in your old face with one of your hammers.*

Old Leslie backed nippy behind the anvil and said *Take care, take care what you say! I'm not a man you must rouse, let me tell you.* And he told later on that never in his life had he heard such impudence — 'twas Infernal, just, he'd a might sore job to keep himself back from taking that Cronin loon a good clout. Now, when himself was a loon up in Garvock — And you didn't hear more, for you looked at your watch, and said you must go, and went at a lick; and left him habbering and chapping and sweating.

Young Dod was as mad as could be on the thing, he went up to the Manse and clyped the Colquohoun; and Else Queen, that was back there again as the maid, told that the minister said he was sorry, but what could he do? Young Cronin shouldn't worry, you could only expect a smell from a drain.

Else said the minister was referring to Leslie: and folk when they heard that speak were real mad. Who was he, a damned creature that sat in a Manse, to say that an honest man was a drain? There was nothing wrong with old Leslie, not him, he'd aye paid his way, a cheery old soul, though he could sicken a cow into colic with his long, dreich tales and his habberings of gossip.

He'd aye been good to his guts, the old smith, and faith, he grew better the longer he lived. At New Year he took a bit taik down the toun, into the shop of MacDougall Brown; it was late at night and what could Brown do but ask the old smith to come ben for a drink — not of whisky, you wouldn't find that at MacDougall's, but of some orange wine or such a like drink, awful genteel, though it had a bit taste as though a

NIMBUS 169

stray pig had eased himself in it. Well, Leslie went ben, and
there sat the creash, MacDougall's wife, and Cis, the fine lass,
and the other bit quean that folk teased and called Maybull.
Mrs Brown was right kind and poured out the wine, syne she
went and took out a cake from the press, there was more than
half of the cake on the plate, and Mistress Brown cut off a thin
slice, genteel, and held out the plate to the smith.

And what did he do but take up the cake, not the slice, and
sit with it there in his hand, habbering and sweating like a
hungered old bull, and tearing into MacDougall's cake, Mac-
Dougall watching him boiling with rage – faith! speak about
washing in the blood of the Lamb, he looked as though he'd
like a real bath in the smith's.

Well, old Leslie finished his bit of repast, and got up,
though he hadn't near finished his story, about Garvock, but
he never yet had done that, though you'd known him fine this
last fifty years. But it was getting fell late-like by then and he
thought he'd better go take a taik home, Mrs Brown had gone
to her bed, and Maybull, and the fine lass Cis had gone as well.
MacDougall showed him out to the door, and cried goodnight,
and banged it behind him; and old Leslie was standing sucking
at a crumb that was jooking about in an old hollow tooth,
when what did he see round the end of the dyke that sloped
to the back of MacDougall's shop, but a body slipping over in
the dark.

Old Leslie wondered who it could be, and stepped soft in the
dark down the lithe of the dyke. Near to the end he stooped
and stopped, and heard the whisp-whisp of some folk close by.
And he knew one voice, but not the other, 'twas the voice of
Cis Brown and he heard her say *Not tonight – Mabel is sleeping with me.* The voice that the smith couldn't put a name to
said *Damn her, why doesn't she sleep with the cuddy?* Cis
laughed and sighed and syne Leslie heard the sound of a kiss,
disgusting-like, he himself had never all his married life so
much as pecked at his old wife's face: and once when she saw
him without his sark, he'd been changing it, careless-like by
the fire, she nearly had fainted, and so near had he, they'd

never been so coarse as look at each other, shameless and bare, in their own bit skins...

Well, where was he now with this story of Cis? — Ay, her slobbering her lad by the dyke. In a little bit while they were whispering again, and the smith tried hard to hear what they said, they spoke over low, the tinks that they were, to make an old man near strain off his neck from his hard-worked shoulders to hear what they said. Syne that finished and Leslie heard footsteps coming and dodged in the shadow of the post-office door. And who should loup over the wall and go by but that tink Dod Cronin, that had so miscalled him, him it had been that was kissing Cis Brown!

But folk said that that was just a damned lie, Cis Brown was as douce and sweet a quean as you'd find in the whole of Segget, they said — old Leslie telling the tale in the Arms was nearly brained by Dite Peat himself. Dite said he liked a bit lie fell well, just as he liked to soss with a woman, especially a woman he'd no right to, but he wasn't to hear that kind of a speak of Cis Brown, he was fairly damned if he was. And others cried *Ay, that's right, that's right!* and Feet, the police-man, said to his father *You'd better away home*. Off the old smith went, the coarse old brute; still habbering his lies and swearing he'd seen Dod Cronin and that fine quean Cis together.

Chris heard the tale, but she paid it no heed, with long months of resting her strength had come back, she was out in the garden of the Manse each dawn, digging and hoeing as the Spring came in. Funny to think 'twas nearly a year since she'd walked this garden, her child in her body, and stood over there and looked in the kirkyard, and thought of the folk that had once been bairns, and died, and nothing of them endured. And now she herself walked free and young, slim as of old, if her face was thinner, but warm and kind, warm blood in her body, she could see it rise blue if she looked at her hands loosen their grip from the shaft of the graip, and her hair was alive, that had gone a while dead, and crackled its fire as she combed it at night, long hair that still came near to her knees. And the baby she'd brought in the world last year—

But she'd not think of that, not here in the sun, the rooks a long caw out over the yews, sailing, sun-winking, dots in the sun, the clouds went wind-laden down through the Howe, all the Howe wakening below them to hear the trill and shrill of the springs of Spring. So busied Chris was as the days grew warm, she'd found in a garden what once in the fields, years before, on the windy rigs of Blawearie, ease and rest and the kindness of toil, that she saw but little or nothing of Robert – no loss to him, with his bittered face, and no loss to her now, they went their own ways.

Ewan was shooting straight as a larch, narrow and dark, with a cool, quiet gaze, and a sudden smile that came seldom enough, but still, when it did – Else said she could warm her hands at that smile. He was out all hours of the day, was Ewan, still at his flints, he'd raked half the Howe, he'd been down by Brechin and Forfar for flints. He was known in places Chris never had seen, the dark-faced loon from the Manse of Segget, that would ask if he might take a look at your fields, and would show the arrows and such-like of old that the creatures of hunters had used in their hunts. And the farmers would say, *Faith, look if you like,* and Ewan would thank them. Charming and cool, a queer-like loon, not right in the head, folk that were wice weren't near so polite.

Sometimes, as the light of the Spring days waned he'd come back from school and find bread and milk, and bring them out to the garden to eat, and set them down by a bed or a drill and take the hoe or the fork from Chris, and start to work with quick, even strokes, the down of a soft fine hair on his cheeks, Chris would sit with her knees hand-clasped, and watch him, the ripple of his smooth dark skin, he'd long lashes as well, that were curled and dark, he worked with a cool and deliberate intent at digging the garden as he did at all else. Once Chris asked him, one of those evenings in April, what he would do when he had grown up.

He stopped at the turn of a drill and looked at her, he was

leaving school and going to Dundon, up to the college in the summer term. He said *I'd like to be an archæologist, but I don't suppose that I'll ever be that.* Chris asked *Why not?* and he said that he thought it unlikely you could be that without lots of money. He would just have to face up to things as they were, jobs scarce, and all the world in a mess.

Chris wondered what were his thoughts on the mess, he had read nearly every book in the Manse, had he read the books on Socialism yet? She asked him that and he said that he had, indifferently saying it, one of the books – by a Ramsay Mac-Donald, all blither and blah. Charlie Cronin, who had now left the school was a socialist, the same as MacDonald, they were both very muddled, they had no proofs and they hadn't a plan, it was spite or else rage: OR BECAUSE THEY WERE FEARED.

Chris looked at the fairy featherings of clouds that went south on the hurrying wind of the Howe, the green of the hedges trilled low in its blow, you could feel in your body the stir of the blood as the sap stirred sweet in the hedge, you supposed. Spring and the time of young folk and dreams, following cloud-pillars as they sailed the Howe! . . . And maybe Ewan was doing no more in that he refused all clouds and all dreams!

She said *What are YOU going to do with the mess?* and he put down his cup and said *Oh, nothing,* and started to weed in the strawberry patch: *Unless I just must,* and he whistled to himself, calm and cool, with his dark, cool face, he whistled and hoed in the evening light. And Chris felt for him a tenderness, queer, not as though she were only his mother but as though he were all young life in an evening of Spring – thinking the world would dare hardly intrude in their lives and years, but would stand back and bow, and slip to one side to let them go by. . . She held out a hand – *Help me up, son, I'm stiff. Growing old, I suppose*; he stopped and looked at her, his gravity suddenly drowned in that smile. *I thought just now you looked like a girl. There are some at school who look older than you.*

But he gave her his hand and she jumped to her feet, light

enough still, and they looked at each other; and Chris put up her hand to his throat, making on that the button there needed re-sewing, it didn't, but she wanted to touch that cool throat. He let her, standing there quiet and alert, like the deer she had seen come down from the haughs, with brindled pelts, in the winter-time — not feared and not shy, cool, quick and alive, under her fingers a little vein beat as she fastened his collar, and Ewan said *Thanks*, and went on with his weeding, Chris went to the house and looked at the clock and made tea for Robert.

He was off at Stonehaven, a meeting of ministers, called together to discuss the reason why every kirk in the Howe grew toom, a minister would sometimes rise of a Sunday and preach to a congregation of ten, in a bigging builded to hold two hundred. So Robert told Chris as he wheeled out his bike, that morning, under the peep of the sun; and Chris had said *Well, they surely know why? Do they need a meeting to find out that?*

Robert had looked at her withdrawn, remote, the brooding anger not far from his eyes. *Do YOU know the reason?* Chris had said *Yes, the reason's just that the times have changed.*

His unchancy temper quite went with him then, *By God*, he sneered, *isn't that profound?* Chris flushed, with an angry retort on her lips; but she bit it back, as so often she did, and turned indoors as he wheeled down the Wynd — what a fool she had been to say what she'd said! Like telling an angry blind man he was blind. . . She would keep to herself, she was nobody's serf.

But sometimes she ached for kind eyes and kind hands. One night she had turned to him, kissing him then, and he'd shrugged away from her — *Not now, Chris, not now.* She had said in her hurt, *And maybe not again — when YOU would again*, and had turned her back and pretended to sleep, but had wept a little instead, like a fool. Spring was here, she supposed it was that, daft to desire what no one could give except with a flame of desire in the giving.

So she waited this evening, with pancakes new baked, they might live poor friends, with love and lust by, but she still ate his meat and she owed him for that. Else had the day off to go down to Fordoun, her baby bade there in its grandmother's care. In the cool of the kitchen Chris stood for a while and watched Ewan kneel to a thrawn-like weed, and saw him twist it up ruthlessly, sure; she sighed with a smile at herself for that sigh. Were she sure of herself as Ewan of himself, she might go her own way and not heed to any, have men to lie with her when she desired them (and faith, that would sure be seldom enough!) do and say all the things that came crying her to do, go hide long days in the haughs of the Mounth – up in the silence and the hill-bird's cry, no soul to vex, and to watch the clouds sailing and passing out over the Howe, unending over the Howe of the World; that – or sing and be glad by a fire; or wash and toil and be tired with her toil as once she had been in her days on a croft – a million things, Chris-alone, Chris-herself, with Chris Guthrie, Chris Tavendale, Chris Colquohoun dead!

She lighted the lamp as she heard Robert come and carried it through to the hall for him to see to hang up his coat and his hat. He said *You look very sweet, Christine, there with the lamp*, and held her a moment, lamp and all, Chris felt her heart turn, with gladness – then, queerly, she felt half-sick. . .

He loosed her and followed her into the room, soft happed in shadow in the loglight's glow, she put down the lamp and looked at him again. There was something about him that wasn't him at all – a *filthy* something, she thought, and shivered. He said *Not cold?* and smiled at her kind – ROBERT with eyes like a kind milch cow!

She went in a daze and brought in the tea, they sat and ate by the open window, the world all quiet out and about, except, sharp-soft in the fading light, the click and scrape of the tools of Ewan as he redded and bedded by the kirkyard wall. And again, as she looked at Robert, Chris shivered – *What's ta'en you Robert – Robert what is it?*

He raised up his head and she saw his eyes smile. *Just something you'll think is quite mad when you hear...*

And he told her then of the thing that had come as he rode from the ministers' meeting at Stonehaven grinding his bike through Dunnottar's woods, he had looked once or twice from the road to the woods and saw them green in the April quiet, the sunset behind him – *very quiet, Chris.* He had ridden up there till the way grew steep, the old bike was near on its last wheels now: and just as he gained the neard edge of the woods he got from his bike and looked back at Stonehaven, in that corridor of trees the light fell dim, a hidden place, no sun came there. And, as he stood there and breathed in the quiet, he saw the Figure come slow down the road.

He came so quiet by the side of the road that Robert hadn't heard His coming or passing, till he raised his head and saw Him quite close, tired, with a white strange look on His face, no ghost, for the hair blew out from His head and he put up His hand to brush back the hair. And Robert saw the hand and the pierced palm, he stood frozen there as the Figure went on, down through the quiet of Dunnottar's woods, unresting, into the sunset's quiet, a wood-pigeon crooned in a far-off tree, Robert heard the sound of a train in Stonehaven, he stood and stared and then leant on his bike, trembling suddenly weeping in his hands.

Outside, the next day broke quick with wind, a grey quick drive that was bending the trees, blowing its blow in the face of the sun, Chris went to her room and dressed in short skirts, the rig she'd once worn – it seemed years before – that day she and Robert climbed up the Mounth. She'd no fancy at all for that walk today, she found a stick and went down through the shingle, and looked back as she passed in the whisp of the yews. Ewan in his room, he stood near the window, some everlasting flint in his hands. She waved to him, but he didn't see, then at the turn of the dyke the wind caught at her breath and her skirts and her hair.

Ake Ogilvie looked from his shop as she passed, and gave

her a wave and bent over his desk, his poetry maybe, Robert
said it was awful, the angry sneering of a poet born blind. . .
But Chris hurried on from the thought of Robert, swinging her
stick, the wind in her face, the Sourock's wife looked out as
she passed, and stared after the creature, that Mrs Colquohoun,
like a slip of a quean she was, not decent, her that had had her
two bairns, one dead, the other upgrowing and nearly a man.
She said later on she was black-affronted as Mrs Colquohoun
reached the bend of the Wynd, the wind blew up the creature's
short skirts, all about her, and instead of giving a bit scraich
and blushing to the soles of her feet as she should, she just
brushed them back and went hastening on — what was *her*
hurry, no hat on her head, and her fine silk breeks and nought
else below?

(And folk said *What, had she nothing else below?* and the
Sourock's wife said *Not a damned stitch, fair tempting the
childes, half-naked like that, not to mention tempting her
death with cold.*)

Past the shop of Dite Peat and Hairy Hogg's front, Alec, the
son of the Provost, stood there, he had lost his job in Edinburgh, Alec, Chris liked him better than when she first met
him, she cried *How are you?* and he raised his cap; and Chris
sped on, Alec said that night when he looked in on Else, that
Mrs Colquohoun looked more of a boy than a grown-up woman
who had a fine son. Else said *She both looks them, and makes
them, my lad*, whatever she meant by that, if she knew; but
she kept him at sparring distance, did Else.

Down at the edge of the Moultrie shop, where Jim the roan
had had such an ill end, Chris found herself in the lithe of the
dyke that shielded the plots of the gardener Grant. It was here
she nearly ran into Cis Brown, running, with sober face and
blown hair, Chris held her and laughed and they steadied
themselves, Chris asked *And how are things at the college?*
Cis coloured up sweet, she said they were fine. She loitered a
moment and Chris looked in her face and caught there a
glimpse of a desperate trouble.

Something (what Chris of them all?) made her say *I'm off*

for a long walk down through the Howe, I'm restless today,
would you like to come?

At noon that day they stopped at a place, a little farm high in
the Reisk, over-topped by the wave of its three beech trees,
standing up squat in the blow of the wind that came in a
shoom from the Bervie braes. They were given milk there, and
new-baked cakes, and rested a while, Chris glad of the rest,
Cis lying back in her chair with her face flushed to colour from
the walk they had come. They had come down the Howe from
the Segget haughs, past Catcraig, out on the Fordoun road,
Fordoun a brown, dull lour to the north, and so swung on down
past Mondynes, Kinraddie to the left, and then reached the
brig, Chris stopped and peered in the water below and minded
how once she'd done that, long before, in a summer, and seen
the school-bairns plash, naked and dripping, in the shadowed
shallows. Now the water flowed under, free and unvexed, east,
to twine to the Bervie mouths, Cis leaned beside Chris and
stared down as well, and then said *There is something I want*
to tell you.

   And Chris said, gently, *I think I know what.* Cis flushed up
a moment and bit at her lip, she wasn't afraid, only troubled,
Chris saw. And she said *We'll go on, to the right, I think;* and
so they had done, and climbed up the brae to the Geyrie's
moor, and looked back from there and saw all around the
steaming teams a-plod in the parks, shoring the long red drills
of clay. Up in the hills the mists had come down, as they
watched they saw a rain-cloud wheel out, down from the
Mounth on the roofs of Drumlithie, white-shining there on the
road to the South. Back and still back, line on line, rose the
hills, the guardian wall of the Mearns Howe, it came on Chris
as she stood and looked she'd never been beyond that wall
since a bairn. The peewits were flying in the parks outbye, in
the wind that came facing up from the east was the smell, a
tingle that tickled your nose, of the jungle masses of whins
that rose, dark as a forest, on the Geyrie's moor.

   Chris said that she thought they might take that way, Cis

said *Is it safe?* she had heard it was nearly impassable with bog holes in the earth where a cart could lair, they sat on a gate and looked into its stretch, dark brown and green in the hand of Spring. And Cis' shyness and constraint had gone, she was calm and young, they smiled one at the other, and Chris said suddenly, *Oh, we're such fools — women, don't you think that we are now, Cis? To worry so much about men and their ploys, the things that they do and the things that they think!*

Cis said *But what else is there to do? They count for so much —* and sat and thought, grave, shy and sweet as a wing-poised bird. *Or maybe they don't as much as they think, but there wouldn't be children without them, would there?* Chris laughed at that and jumped down from the gate. *I suppose there wouldn't, but still — we might try! Let's go through the moor:* and so they had done.

There they saw the cup of the Howe rise up to the Barras slopes that led to Kinneff, on their right, dark-mantled, lost in its trees, Arbuthnott slept on the Bervie banks, clusters of trees, with the sudden gleam in the wind and the sun of the polished gear, bridles and haimes, on the straining shoulders of the labouring teams. Like going back into your youth, Chris thought, and sighed at that thought and Cis asked why, and Chris said *Because I am getting so old*, and Cis said *That's silly, I sometimes think you're the youngest of all the folk in Segget.* And was shy, *Please don't ever cut your hair, though I've had mine cut: it's lovely, your hair.*

Chris said that she thought it wasn't so bad, and they came to a little bare patch in the moor, where the whins drew aside their skirts and stood quiet, and right in the middle a great stone lay, maybe a thing from the antique times, and Chris sat on it and clasped her knees, and Cis looked at her and then sat at her feet, Chris with her golden eyes closed in the sun, the run and wheep of the wind in her hair, the sun on her face: she could listen to it now, aloof and sure and untroubled by things. And she said to Cis *Is the boy Dod Cronin?*

So she'd heard it all as she sat knee-clasped, there, in the play of the wind and the sun, a tale so old — oh, old as the

Howe, everlasting near as the granite hills, this thing that
brought men and women together, to bring new life, to seek
new birth, on and on since the world had begun. And it seemed
to Chris it was not Cis alone, her tale – but all tales that she
harkened to then, kisses and kindness and the pain of love,
sharp and sweet, terrible, dark, and the wild, queer beauty of
the hands of men, and their lips, and the sleeps of desire fulfilled, and the dark, strange movements of awareness alone,
when it came on women what thing they carried, darkling,
coming to life within them, new life to replenish the earth
again, to come to being in the windy Howe where the cloud-
ships sailed to the unseen south. She fell in a dream that went
far from Cis, looking up and across the slow-peopled parks at
the scaurs of the Mounth and its flying mists, beyond these the
moving world of men, and back again to those clouds that
marched, terrible, tenebrous, their pillars still south. *A pillar
of cloud by day and a pillar of fire by night.*

She said *I must think, I'll get Robert to help*; and Cis said
The minister? and looked still more troubled. *Oh, Mrs Colquohoun, what have men to do with it, it's not their concern,
they don't understand. Dod doesn't – he's frightened – for me
or himself, but he doesn't know this, how queer it all is, and
sickening, and fine – maybe I'm sickening myself to say that?*

Chris said she thought she was sweet to say it, and put her
arm round the shoulders of Cis, and the girl looked up, and her
lips came to Chris'; and Chris thought at that moment that
no men could kiss – not as they should, they'd no notion of
kissing. . . Oh men, they were clumsy from the day they were
breeked to the day they took off their breeks the last time!

The wind was coming in great gusts now, driving the riven
boughs of the broom, in times it rose to a scraich round about
and the moor seemed to cower in its trumpet-cry. Cloud Howe
of the winds and the rains and the sun! All the earth that,
Chris thought at that moment, it made little difference one
way or the other where you slept or ate or had made your bed,
in all the howes of the little earth, a vexing puzzle to the howes
were men, passing and passing as the clouds themselves

passed: but the REAL was below, unstirred and untouched, surely if that were not also a dream.

Robert with his dream of the night before, that Face and that Figure he had seen in the woods. Chris had listened to him with her head bent low, knowing she listened to a mad-man's dream. And Robert to dream it! Robert who once followed a dream that at least had the wind in its hair, not this creep into fear and the fancies of old. But she'd seen then, clear and clear as he spoke, the Fear that had haunted his life since the War, Fear he'd be left with no cloud to follow, Fear he'd be left in the day alone, and stand and look at his naked self. And with every hoping and plan that failed, he turned to another, to hide from that fear, draping his dreams on the face of life as now this dream of the sorrowing Face. . . And she'd shivered again at the filth of the thing, not looking as she heard that crack in his voice, he was saying he could almost have touched the Figure – *God, Chris, it was HIM, whom I've never believed! I've thought Him only a Leader, a man, but Chris – I've looked on the face of God. . .*

She'd sat and said nothing till that was impossible, so to sit silent, and raised up her eyes, misty with pity, yet repulsion as well. Robert had said quiet, *And you don't believe?* And she said *I don't know, I don't know – oh, I'll try!* And gripped his hand tight that he mightn't ask more—

She jumped up then from that seat in the moor – *Come on, I'm so hungry!* and the two of them went on through the whins with the scud of the clouds overhead, that parched their faces in the sharp sun-fall, a snipe was sounding up by the Wairds as they came to the shaven lands of the Reisk, shaven and shorn in the greed of the War. So, as they climbed they came on the farm, with the three beech trees, and, beyond the horizon, poised and glistening, the tumbling sea.

And when they had finished with drinking their milk and eating their cakes Chris offered to pay. But the farmer's wife shook her head, she'd not have it, she'd heard of Chris from her son, she said, he lived in London and wrote horrible books: but he and Chris were at college together. Chris couldn't mind much of the son at all, she supposed they'd met some time or another, but she didn't say that, she and Cis cried their thanks, and went on down the road, it was afternoon then, the sun had wheeled round and was on the west slant.

Down in Arbuthnott they found a bus and with that were carried down the road to Bervie, where the old brig hung by the lazy drifts of smoke from the Mills that lay in the hollow – mills half-idle, as were those of Segget, Bervie above them, a rickle and clutter. They got from the bus and looked at the shops, then went down to the sea by a straggling lane, the sea was pounding into the bay where no boats came because of the rocks – it frothed and spumed like a well-beaten egg, out east a fisher boat went by, into the mist and the Gourdon smell. Chris sat on a rock and looked at the sea, very wakeful, but Cis went to sleep in the sun, till Chris waked her up and they went back again, and found a new bus to take them to Stonehaven, where they'd get yet another to take them back, up the long roads, to Spring-green Segget.

And so, by the fall of night, they came back; and Chris was tired, but her mind made up. Not even for Robert could she change and pretend, though she'd not say a thing that would hurt, could she help. She had found in the moors and the sun and the sea her surety unshaken, lost maybe herself, but she followed no cloud, be it named or unnamed.

Next Sabbath the minister stood up in the pulpit and preached from the Sermon on the Mount of Segget, he said that the Christ still walked the earth, bringing the only message that endured – though all else faded, that was undying, they must search out the Christ, each soul by himself, and find in himself what the world denied, the love of God and the fellowship of men.

Folk listened and thought the man a fair scunner, damn't! you wanted a minister with spunk, whatever had come over this childe Colquohoun, bleating there soft as a new-libbed sheep? Once he'd glowered as though he would like to gut you, and thunder his politics, and you'd felt kittled up, though

you didn't believe a word that he'd said. But this Sunday he
blethered away in the clouds, folk came out and went home
and were real disappointed, minding the time when he'd said
from the pulpit, right out, that Hairy Hogg was a monkey –
damn't! he'd fair fallen away since then.

And some of the spinners that came to the kirk, they were
few enough now, remembered the name they had called the
minister a long time back, they said that Creeping Jesus was
back, he'd got feared at the gentry, the same as some others.
Old Cronin himself it was that said that, and by others he
meant his own son Jock that had led the Strike but a two years
back, and had aye been a right coarse brute, folk thought,
though fair the apple of his father's eye. But Jock had gotten
on well in Glasgow, where he'd lived in sin with Miss Jeannie
Grant, he'd gotten a job on a union there and went lecturing
here and went blethering there, in a fine new suit and a bowler
hat, and spats, right trig, and brave yellow boots. And he'd
married Miss Grant, a three weeks back, and they had a fine
house on the Glasgow hills; and wherever he went Jock Cronin
would preach alliance between all employers and employed
and say to the folk that came to hear him that they shouldn't
strike, but depend on their leaders – like himself; and take a
smug look at his spats.

When news of that came up to old Cronin, he cursed his son
in a sickening way, and he said he'd never guessed he had
fathered a Judas that could sell out the workers for that – not
even for silver or a hungered guts, but spats, and a house on
the Glasgow hills, and a craze for a white-legged quean in his
bed.

Folk took a good laugh when they heard the news, Jock
Cronin was showing some sense, they said, he fair had changed
since the days when he'd go and break up the meetings of Mac-
Dougall Brown. Next MacDougall himself got a sore stammy-
gaster, and so did the whole of Segget; it gasped. That tale of
old Leslie's had had the truth in it, though you'd hardly believe it again when you heard it – it was all a damned lie and
Cis a fine quean.

But then, when you met with her out in the street, and looked, and heard the news from the Manse, she and Dod Cronin to be wed in a week – your throat went dry, you went into the Arms and had a bit dram and swore at the bitch, all the folk said she was a foul creature, but they said it with something catching their throats, they'd been proud of Cis, all Segget had been, and here she was showing herself in that way, no better than that tink Else Queen at the Manse.

Ake Ogilvie said it was only nature, Cis or Else or the whole jingbang, what ailed the folk of Segget, he said, was that they'd seen Cis as *they* might have been – clean – and they'd liked her for what they had lost. He spoke that speak to John Muir, the roadman, Muir gleyed and skeuched and chewed the thing over, it didn't make sense, Ake seldom did.

He went out to dig a bit grave after supper, the moon far up out over the Mounth, the sunset still far, though the lines lay long, in long slants across the hayfields of summer, and smoke drowsed low on the Segget roofs. In the kirkyard the grasses lay scythed as he'd left them, and he walked through that grass, there was some of it clover, bonnily scented with dead men's manure. So he came to the kirkyard corner and stopped, and lighted his pipe and spat on his hands, and started in to dig the bit grave, for one of the old spinner wives of West Wynd.

All the land here about was thick with old graves, he'd soon have to stop or start carting the bones to a pit and bury them out and apart, to leave room for the rest of Segget down there, eating and sleeping and having its play, all coming to stour and a stink at the end. And Muir gleyed down at the grave and dug, and minded of Cis and the speak there was, Dod Cronin had been found a job in Dundon and he and the lass were moving up there, the best they could do to get out of their shame. God knew there wasn't much shame in the thing, a lot overrated, this bedding with a quean – you worked yourself up and you got damned little, and where did it end then, all said and done? Down here with the clay and the grass up above, be you rich, be you poor, unwedded like Cis, or as

bonny as Mrs Colquohoun was bonny, or a shameless limmer
like one of the queans that young Mr Mowat would bring to
the House.

He fair was a devil among women, young Mowat, gents were
like that, Peter Peat said; but he'd time yet to settle down
bravely in Segget and take his natural place at its head: and
that was the Segget Conservative branch. Maybe he *had* had
more queans than he should, but he'd settle down bravely yet,
you would see. Ake Ogilvie said, *No doubt – in his sharns*, a
tink-like speak, just what you expected, he was jealous as hell
of the gentry, Ake, nearly as bad as that creature Moultrie
that was now over stiff to crawl out at all.

One of the Mills had been idle for months, though young
Mr Mowat had come back from his sail. He was no sooner back
than a birn of the spinners went up to the House in a deputation. But when the deputation got there, and the servant had
shown them into the hall, and they stood there twisting their
caps, fell shy, they heard the crackle of a falling bottle and a
hooting and laughing as though lunatics were loose; and out
of a side-door a quean came running, without a stitch on,
nothing but a giggle, she looked back and laughed at young
Mowat behind her, running and laughing with his wee frog
face; and up the stairs the two of them went.

Well, the deputation blushed from head to heel; syne one
of them, the oldest operative there, said *That's where the cash
goes we make in the Mills*, and they looked from one to the
other, old, hungry, and some of them were gey bitter, most on
the dole, on starvation's edge; and they stood in the rich,
warm hall and looked round, at the log-wood fire and the
gleam of deer's heads, and the patterned walls and the thick,
soft rugs. But the rest said nothing to the speak of the first,
they knew it was useless trying to complain or to start that
kind of socialist stuff that the Cronins of old had preached in
the Mills, you'd seen the end of that with the Strike, young
Mowat was the only hope of the Mills.

He came down at last and was charming, polite, and said it

was Jahly to see them again. And he stood with his back to the
fire and said *Hwaw?* and read them a lecture on the awful
times, he said that taxation was killing the country, all they
could hope at the coming election was that the Conservative
folk would get back, stronger than ever in position and
power, and reduce taxation on men like himself. Then perhaps
he would manage to open the Mill. And he smiled at them,
charming, with his horn-rimmed eyes, but he offered no drink,
instead rang a bell, and the servant childe came and ushered
them out; and young Mr Mowat said it had been Jahly; and
that showed that he had a real good heart.

Now, that was the first Peter Peat had heard about young
Mr Mowat and the wishes he had that the Tory Party should
get back again, they'd been holding office but a bare five years
and hadn't yet had time to set things right, being busied with
breaking strikes and the like, and freeing the working men
from their unions, and seeing that we had a real strong navy,
and trying to get the coarse foreign tinks to reduce their
armies, a danger to Europe. . . Peter Peat had these facts at his
fingertips and went up to the House to see Mr Mowat, and ask
a subscription for the Segget branch. And Mr Mowat said it
was Jahly to see him, Rahly Jahly, and sipped at his wine, and
the quean did the same, exploding a giggle, sitting bare-legged
on the back of his chair.

Yes, he believed in Devolution for Scotland, but not this
mad nationalism now rampant, only the Unionist Party would
see that Scotland got her just dues in the end. And he told
Peter more of the coarse new Nationalists, not the flower of
the country's gentry, as once, Scotland had lost her chance
once again, the new leaders a pack of socialists and catholics,
long-haired poets, a fellow called Grieve, and Mackenzie and
Gunn, hysterical Highlandmen. Well, he had Jahly soon
finished with *them*, and would be glad to give a donation some
time to the branch of the Unionist Party in Segget.

And Peter Peat was fell happy at that — ay, the old blood
flowed in the gentry's veins.

*   *   *

The Autumn came, the Election results, and Segget was fair stammy-gastered at them, the Labour tinks had gotten in power, led by that coarse brute Ramsay MacDonald. You minded him and the things he had said, long before, when the War was on? – that we shouldn't be fighting the Germans, no, no, but leave them a-be, they were much too strong. Ay, that's what he'd said and here he was now, at the head of the country, lording it about, and not even maybe saying Sir to the King. But others said the creature would fairly swank now, and get the King to make him a lord, or a duke or some-thing: and Ake Ogilvie said he'd heard the title was Lord Loon of Lossie.

But that was just one of his ill-natured speaks, damn't! was he against this Government as well? – after going to all that stour to vote Liberal, instead of decent and Tory like others. Hardly any of the spinners had voted at all, they just hung about and smoked their bit fags, or dug in their gardens back of the wynds, or stared at the Mills with their hungry eyes. But Ake Ogilvie had said he was voting Liberal, and had can-vassed Segget for the Liberal childe, doing him a sight more harm than good, he said there was good in none of the parties, Labour or Tory or Liberal or any: but the Tory name fair stank in your throat, it was built on the purses and pride of the kind of half-witted loon that mismanaged the Mills; the Liberals were damn little better, he knew, but they *had* a great name that was worthy a vote.

Hardly a soul paid heed to his blethers, just smiled at him canny and said *Well, we'll see*; and got ready for the polling day to come to ride to Laurencekirk in the Tory cars. Ake Ogilvie borrowed a Liberal car, and its driver, and waited in Segget Square; and the Tory cars piled black with folk, getting off to vote for the gentry childes that had promised them reischles and reischles of tariffs; but not a damn soul looked near Alec Ogilvie, sitting with a sneering look in his car. And then the door of the Moultrie shop was flung wide open and who should come out, hoasting and hirpling slow on his stick, but that thrawn old billy, Rob Moultrie himself, leaning on a

stick and his old wife's shoulder, he hobbled and hirpled over
to the car, near bent down double, Jess Moultrie beside him.
Ake jumped from his seat and helped the two in, and stood
back with a queer-like grin on his face – were these all who
championed Liberty Mere?

But there was a fourth; Ake had grown tired and was crying
to the shover that they might as well go, when he heard a hail
and looked over his shoulder. And there was Mrs Colquohoun
of the Manse, crossing the Square, running like a lad, with a
spray of blood on her dark, soft skin. *Sorry I'm late, Ake*, she
said, and jumped in; and Ake got in himself and could nearly
have cuddled her.

But the Liberal man got a mighty few votes, the Tory got in,
as you knew he would do, if the rest of the country had done
half as well, where would these tinks of socialists have been?
Selling spunks in the London streets, or that coarse brute
Ramsay MacDonald tracts. And the Provost said in the Segget
Arms 'twas an ill day this for our Scottish land. What was it
the poet Robert Burns had written? – an ancestor, like, of the
Hoggs, Rabbie Burns. *A man's a man for a' that*, he wrote, and
by that he meant that poor folk of their kind should steer well
clear of the gentry and such, not try to imitate them at all,
and leave them to manage the country's affairs.

Deeper and deeper as that year slipped by, Robert slipped from
the life of his parish, he hadn't bothered to vote at all, he
locked himself up long hours in his room, dreaming or reading
or just sitting still – alien to Chris as that Figure he'd met in
the dark at Dunnottar woods.

Nor was that meeting the only one, there were others haunting the paths of his feet, times when he'd known that Presence
in his room, once in the midst of a sermon he stopped, not
staring or wild, but all the kirk watched him, and he watched
the door, and his eyes moved slow as though following a figure
that came down the aisle; and folk turned round and stared
where he stared, and saw nothing at all but the winter gleam
of the cold kirk floor, and beyond that the glass of the far,

stained window that looked on the tossing boughs of the trees. Chris half-rose from her seat in that silence, she saw the sweat bright on Robert's still face. Then his eyes left the aisle and he wiped his forehead, and went on in an even voice with his sermon.

For outside these moments he was quiet and kind, with a kindness Chris hated – for it was not his. It was something borrowed from his unclean dream, not Robert at all, a mask and a pose, a kindness he followed with Fear for an urge. And a dreadful loneliness came upon Chris, and a shivering hate for that cloud he followed, that sad-faced Figure out of the past, who had led such legions of men to such ends up and down the haughs and hills of the earth. Christ? So maybe indeed He had lived, and died, a follower of clouds Himself.

That Figure she minded from school-time days, and even then it had not moved her, it seemed a sad story, in mad, sad years, it was over and done: and it left her untouched. And it left her so still, it was only a dream that could alter nothing the ways of the world. . . Oh, why wasn't Robert like other ministers? – easy and pleased and hearty and glib, with no religious nonsense about them, they led hearty lives and ate well at table and took the days as they found them come, and didn't leave their wives to think daft thoughts, and cry here, quiet, in the dark, like a child, sometimes with the fear of a child for the dark.

But she just had to meet it: and her life was still hers. So she worked through that autumn tending the garden, till almost the earth rebelled from her touch, she thought with a smile, and welcomed the winter. New Year's Eve came in a bluster on Segget, in snow and a breaking of sleet for sharp hours, there were spinners starving down in Old Toun John Muir told Chris as he came in on Sunday. And he said that another twenty were sacked, it was likely the second Mill would close down.

Robert heard that story as well, and listened, and said not a word, who once would have flamed into curses and anger on the cruelty of men. But now he stood up in the pulpit and preached, his text the saying of Christ, *Feed my lambs*. And Chris sat and listened to the gentle voice, and shivered as though at a filthy thing. And she looked round quiet at the people he preached to – the Provost Hogg with his heavy face, John Muir, with his skeugh and his puzzled eyes, Peter Peat the tailor, red-eyed, like a rat, and the mean, close face of the publican, Melvin. What hope in appealing to them for help? – were there but a flicker he had sold his soul to that fancy and Figure for something at least. But they heeded as little the whine of his Christ as the angry threat of his Struggling God.

And that New Year's night as she lay by Robert, in the quiet and the dark, she knew fear again, fear for the new year come to birth, for the man who lay so quiet in his sleep, beside her, turned away from her touch, low in the grate the coals were drooping, in a little red glow, she watched them sink and fade and grow grey as the dawn came dim over a world that was wrapped in white; and out in the yews the frozen rooks stirred: and down in the kitchen Else Queen did the same.

That year brought plenty of changes to Else, before it began there were rumours about her. Ag Moultrie one morning was going by the Manse when she saw the door of the kitchen open, and out, as quiet as an ill-getted cat who should come stepping but that loon Alec Hogg? And he turned and gave a bit nod of his head, and Else Queen looked out and nearly saw Ag, but she dropped down smart in the lithe of a bush and watched the two part, and was fairly ashamed – to think that the son of a man like the Provost should have taken up with a harlot, just. And the more Ag thought of it, the more she was shamed, till she just broke down and fair Roared and Grat.

Well, she passed the news on in a neighbour-like way, and folk were fair shocked, and snickered at the Provost – ay, that was a nasty smack in the face for old Hairy Hogg: had he heard the news yet? And when it came out that he hadn't, just yet, there were half a dozen that took him the news, you yourself were nearly killed in the rush, there was never such a birn of boots needing mending, Dite Peat went in with a pair, and his brother, and Bruce the roadman, and syne Will Melvin. And old Hairy sat like a monkey and blew on how well he could sutor, and Dite Peat said *Ay, and we hear you'll be sutoring soon for a marriage. Or is it a christening?* And they all took a sly bit look at the Provost; and he habbered and said *What?* and so he was told.

Well, he couldn't believe that speak about Alec, the loon might be a bit of a fool and had lost his work in the Edinburgh office, the place had closed down, that wasn't his wyte: but he wasn't such a fool as take up with a quean that once warmed the bed for that wastrel Dalziel. And as soon as young Alec came home that day from some gardening work he had gotten outbye the Provost cried out, *Come into the shop*, and told him the coarse-like speak in Segget. Alec Hogg said, *Well, then, there's something in it. I like Else well and I mean to marry her*. When he heard him say that old Hairy near burst, and he asked Alec Hogg did he want to bring them, respectable folk, in shame to the grave? And Alec said No, he didn't think so, he only wanted to bring Else to tea. And the Provost said 'twould be over his dead body if he did.

When that got around folk fair took a laugh – faith, man! that would fair be a funny-like sight, Else Queen stepping over old Hairy Hogg's corpse, and the old ape, dead or alive, you could swear, taking an upward keek as she passed. Else and Alec were watched fell close after that, and once, when they took a walk up the Kaimes, that Spring, a windy Sunday in March, and sat in the lithe to have a bit crack, there was nearly a dozen that kept on their track, and Ag Moultrie, the Roarer and Greeter of Segget, was up in the Schoolhouse watching the pair with a spy-glass she'd borrowed at racing speed. And the childes that had crept up the Kaimes to watch near froze to death, for they didn't dare move, and Alec and Else did not a damn thing, they didn't even kiss all the time they were there; and you could well warrant if they didn't kiss then, it was only because they had come to a pass when neither kisses nor cuddles contented.

Well, Alec couldn't marry, he hadn't a meck, Else's wages went to the keep of her bairn, Dalziel of the Meiklebogs wouldn't pay a penny. When Else had written and asked him for that he had just smiled sly, and torn up the letter. So things might well have stood as they were but for the tink row that broke out in the house of Smithie, the whiskered old roadman of Segget.

He hardly had seemed to alter at all, except that his whiskers looked more and more still like the birns of hay he would pinch from the parks. He still bade on with his daughter and goodson, Bruce, folk said he had hell for a life, though the house was his and all the gear in it, the kye in the byres and the kirns in the creamery. But he'd come home still of an evening from work and get no friendly greeting from any unless 'twas the kye, and only from them if he brought them their meat: otherwise, they would sulk. In his house his daughter would say, *Oh, it's you? Then clean your nasty big feet on the mat.* And old Smithie would glower at her sore, but say nothing, it was years since the old bit creature broke out.

But one Saturday afternoon in April, just as old Smithie had stopped from his chapping out on the road that led to Stone-hive, and had wiped his long whiskers and took a keek round, a lorry came down the road and went skeugh, and nearly went into the west-side ditch. Well, the lorry-driver swore like a tink, which wasn't surprising, he probably was one, and cried on old Smithie to give him a shove. And he shoved, and old Smithie, they shoved and they heaved, and swore at the lorry, and chaved a good hour, 'twas a lorry-load of crates of whisky and beer going north to Dundon, the lorry-man told. And he said that he hoped that their guts would rot, them that would drink but a drop of the stuff.

Well, at last they got the wheel from the ditch, and the lorry-driver said he was bloody obliged. He looked at his watch and said he must go, but syne he reached back in a small bit crate. *Here, I pinched two bottles of this for myself, but you try one, it's a fine-like drink.* And he said some more and syne he drove off, leaving the bottle in old Smithie's hands.

Old Smithie took a bit keek at the thing, a fattish bit bottle of an unco-like shape; and he took off the cork and gave it a lick. That tasted as unco as the bottle looked, sugary and sweet, and old Smithie thought, *Well, damn it, he surely thinks I'm a bairn, it's a lemonade drink this Benny Dick Tine.*

So he held the bottle to his mouth for a suck, and down the stuff gurgled, and old Smithie paiched, and wiped his long whiskers and curled up his nose – feuch! it was sickening; but he fairly was dry. So he drank down a half of the lemonade stuff, and corked the bottle and put it in his pouch, and got on his bike and rode home to Segget.

God knows what happened atween there and Segget, he rode through the Square at the awfullest lick, and nearly killed Melvin opposite the Arms. He was singing that his heart was in the Highlands, not here, Will Melvin sore vexed to see him like that, if the coarse old creature wanted to get drunk why couldn't he come down and get drunk at the Arms? Will Melvin cried *Hi!* and louped like a goat, and Smithie cried back *That'll teach you, I hope, to bide out of my way, you whiskied old wife!* Syne he wheeled round and up the East Wynd like the wind and narrowly missed running into the dyke, and swung the bike over to the other bit side, and nearly killed a lone chicken there; and vanished through Segget in a shower of stour, with Will Melvin and the angel gaping together.

Ake Ogilvie told that he saw him go by, like a Valkyr riding the wings of the storm – whatever that fool of a joiner meant. But the next thing that happened for sure was the Smithie got off at the door of his house and went in. His goodson Bruce sat canny by the fire and hardly looked up as he heard Smithie's step. Then Smithie said *Just a minute, you, the sweir swine there, and I'll deal with you!* and Bruce looked round and there was old Smithie, with a bottle upended, sucking like mad. And then he had finished and flung off his coat, the daft old tyke, and let drive at Bruce, and near knocked him head first into the dinner that was hottering slow on the swey by the fire. Well, Bruce got up, he would soon settle this, and his wife, old Smithie's daughter, cried out *Crack up his jaw — don't spare the old tink!*

But God! she nearly died at what followed. Old Smithie had fair gone mad of a sudden, he didn't heed the bashings of Bruce, not a bit, but took him a belt in the face that near floored him, syne kicked him right coarse, and Bruce gave a groan and caught at himself, and as he doubled up old Smithie took him a clout in the face with a tacketty boot, and for weeks after that it looked more like a mess in a butcher's shop, than a face, that thing that the childe Bruce wore. Bruce was blinded with blood, he cried *Stop — I can't see!* But old Smithie had gone clean skite, what with his wrongs and the Benny Dick Tine. *Oh, can't you? Well then, you can damn well feel!* And he took Bruce and swung him out through the door, and kicked him sore in the dowp as he went, and threw a chair at him, and Bruce had enough, he ran like a hare, half-blind though he was, and the Muirs all stood next door and gaped, Mrs Muir and Tooje and Ted, all but John, he sat indoors and gleyed quiet up the lum.

The next thing the Muirs saw was Mrs Bruce herself, kicked out like her man and running like him, and syne the bairns, and syne they heard sounds inside the house like a wild beast mad. Then old Smithie started to throw out the things that belonged to his daughter and his goodson Bruce, a sewing machine and their kists and clothes, a heap in the stour outside the door. Bruce had cleared his eyes by then and come back, but old Smithie saw him and chased him away, with a breadknife, and came back and danced on the gear, he looked like the devil himself, said Ake, who had come up to see what the row was about — if you could imagine the devil in whiskers raising worse hell than was usual in Segget.

Well, he closed the door next and after a while some folk went over and chapped at the door, but they got not a cheep, and waited for Bruce, he'd gone to the smiddy to borrow an axe. He came back with a fair-like crowd at his heels, Feet the bobby came with him as well, and just as they started in on the door Ake Ogilvie cried *No, damn't! that won't do.* And he said to Bruce *Is this your house, or his?* Bruce told him to mind his own mucking business, and was raising his axe to let fly at the door when Ake Ogilvie said, *All right, then, all right. It's up to you, Feet. You're supposed to defend the law here in Segget. Here's a man that has locked himself up in his house, and you're standing by and aiding and abetting a burglar trying to get into the place.*

That hadn't struck folk afore, now it did, they cried, *Ay, that's right,* and Bruce glared around; and Feet scratched at his head and took out his note-book. And he said to Bruce that he'd maybe best wait, he himself would call on old Smithie for a change, to open the door in the name of the Law. But all that they heard after Feet had cried that were the snores of old Smithie asleep on his bed.

He wasn't seen in Segget till the Sunday noon, when he crawled out to give some meat to his kye. But he never left the house but he locked up the door, the Bruces got tired of trying to dodge in, they said they couldn't bear the old brute, anyhow, him and his stink, and they flitted to Fordoun, and Bruce got a job on the railway there; and old Smithie at last had his house to himself, thanks to the lorry-man's Benny Dick Tine.

And what all this clishmaclaver led to was Alec Hogg getting the job on the road that had once been Bruce's, and the seat by the fire in old Smithie's house that was Bruce's as well. For young Alec Hogg was a skilly-like childe, right ready and swack and no longer polite, he called a graip by its given name. As for looking around for slop-basins these days, he'd have eaten tea-leaves like a damn tame rabbit, and munched them up with contentment, too.

And he said to old Smithie as they mended the roads there was nothing like a damn good taste of starvation to make you take ill with ideas you'd held, he had starved down south when he lost his job, and near starved when he managed to get back to Segget, his father, the old mucker, would glunch and glare at every bit mouthful he saw his son eat – *his* hands had never held idleceit's bread. He'd sneer at the table, the monkey-like mucker. *And what have your fine friends, the Fashers, done for you?* And it was but the truth, they had done not a thing; as for Fascism's fancies on Scotland and Youth – well, starvation's grip in your belly taught better. Scotland and its young could both go to hell and frizzle there in ink for all that he cared.

And old Smithie thought that a fell wice speak, and so did John Muir, and they'd sit and crack, the three of them by the side of the road, and watch the traffic go by to Dundon, the cars with gentry, the buses with folk. And John Muir would gley *Ay, God, and that's sense. I was once myself a bit troubled about things – fair Labour I was, but to hell with them all. Poor folk just live and die as they did, we all come to black flesh and a stink at the end. . . And like fools we still go on with the soss, bringing grave-fodder into the world. For I hear that you're courting Else Queen, are you, Alec?*

Alec reddened up a bit and said maybe he was; and John Muir said Well, and he might do worse, since women there were you'd to bed them sometime. And he asked when Else and Alec were to marry, and Alec said *Christ, I haven't an idea – we've no place to bide though we married tomorrow.*

And 'twas then that old Smithie said *Have you no? You're a decent-like childe and I like you well. Let you and your wife come bide in with me.*

Else came to Chris and told her the news. Chris said she was glad – *and I know you'll be happy.* Else tossed her head, *God knows about that. There are worse folk than Alec – at least, so I hear. And as for being happy – och, nobody is!*

Chris laughed at that and said it wasn't true, but she wondered about it in the fresh-coming Spring, maybe it was Else had the sense of the thing – not looking for happiness, madness, delight – she had left these behind in the bed of Dalziel; only looking to work and to living her life, eating and sleeping and rising each dawn, not thinking, tiring by night-time and dark — as Chris did herself in the yard of the Manse. And Chris raised her head as she thought that thought, and heard the trill of a blackbird, shrill, and saw the spirt of its wings as it flew, black sheen of beauty, across the long grass: and the ripple and stilly wave of the light, blue sunlight near on the Manse wall. And she thought that these were the only glad things — happiness, these, if you found the key. She had lost it herself, unlonely in that, most of the world had mislaid it as well.

She minded then as she worked at that tree, an apple tree, and set smooth the earth, and reached her hands in the cling of the mould, that saying of Robert's, long, long ago, the day he unveiled the new-hallowed Stones up by the loch on Blawearie brae — that we'd seen the sunset come on the land and this was the end of the peasants' age. But she thought, as often, we saw more than that — the end forever of creeds and of faiths, hopes and beliefs men followed and loved: religion and God, socialism, nationalism — Clouds that sailed darkling into the night. Others might arise but these went by, folk saw them but clouds and knew them at last, and turned to the Howe from the splendid hills — folk were doing so all over the world, she thought, back to the sheltered places and ease, to sloth or toil or the lees of lust, from the shining splendour of the cloudy hills and those hopes that had followed and believed everlasting. She herself did neither, watching, unsure: was there nothing between the Clouds and the Howe?

This life she lived now could never endure, she knew that well as she looked about her, however it ended it could not go on; she was halted here, in these Segget years, waiting the sound of unhasting feet, waiting a Something unnamed, but it came. And then—

She stopped in her work and looked down at herself, at her breast, where the brown of her skin went white at the edge of the thin brown dress she wore, white rose the hollow between her breasts, except where it was blue-veined with blood; funny to think that twice in her life a baby had grown to life in her body and herself changed so to await that growth, and still she looked like a quean, she thought, breast, hips, and legs, and she liked her legs, even yet, as she looked at them with a smile, at the line of herself as she squatted to weed, nice still to cuddle spite her sulky face!

Had she lived in the time of the golden men who hunted the hills by the Trusta bents there would have been cuddles enough, she supposed, fun and pain and the sting of the wind, long nights of sleep in a heath-hid cave, morns shining over the slopes of the hills as you stirred by your man and peered in his face, lying naked beside you, naked yourself, with below the Howe just clearing its mists as the sun came up from an alien sea – the Howe unnamed and shaggy with heath, with stone-oak forests where the red deer belled as the morning grew and the Bervie shone; and far over the slopes of the Howe you could see the smoke rise straight from another cave, and know your nearest friends a day off; and you'd not have a care or a coin in the world, only *life*, swift, sharp, and sleepy and still and an arm about you, life like a song, and a death at the end that was swift as well – an hour of agony, or only a day, what woman feared death who had borne a child? And many enough you'd have borne in the haughs and been glad enough of their coming in that day, undreaming the dark tomorrows of the Howe that came with the sailing ships from the south. . .

And, kneeling and cutting at a wallflower clump that had grown over-large for its portion of earth, Chris smiled as she thought of her talk with Else on this matter of humankind itself growing over-large for *its* clump of earth. Else had stood and listened with red-tinted ears, and stammered and blushed, it was funny and sad, Chris knew how she felt, she had once felt the same. Else said *Oh, Mem, but I couldn't do that – it wouldn't be right to do anything like that!* Chris said *It's surely better to do that than have the bairns that you can't bring up?* Else shook her head, *They'll just come, and we'll manage. But I couldn't do things to myself like that.*

Robert had overheard Chris as she talked, he had heard the talk through the kitchen door, coming down the stairs in his

silent way. And when he and Chris were alone together, he said
You shouldn't have said that, Christine, gentle and quiet and
even of speech. Chris had shivered a little and drawn further
away. *Why not?* she asked, and he said *Because we have no
rights in these matters at all. We have meddled too much with
our lives as it is; they are God's concern, the children who
come.*

For a minute Chris hardly believed what she heard, she had
stared at him, at his masked face; they themselves had done
this thing he denounced...

All the next afternoon, as it seemed to Chris, she heard the
rumour and hum of the wedding, down in the hall of the
Segget Arms. It had turned to a day sunblown and clear,
the earth was hard as she weeded the beds, clumps of begonias
under the dykes, back of the Manse the chickens of Muir were
deep in a drowsy scraiching, well-fed. Chris went and looked
over the wall and watched, and laughed a little at the courting
play of an over-small cock with a haughty, shamed look, as
though it thought mating a nasty thing, but yet was right
eager to make half a try. There were lots of folk who had
minds like his!

Robert and Ewan were both at the wedding, Robert returned
as soon as he might, Chris heard him climb up the stairs to
his room. The noise went on far into the night, stirring in
sleep towards the Sunday morning Chris heard the light step
of Ewan go by. Next morning he wasn't stirring as usual, and
she carried a cup of tea to his room, and knocked and went in
and he still slept fast, lying straight, his dark hair thick as a
mop, she stood and looked at him and tickled his arm, and he
woke up lightly, as he always woke. *Oh, it's you, Chris!* and
stared a moment: *I'm sorry, Mother!*

She said *Oh, I'm Chris as well, I suppose,* and sat on the
side of the bed while he drank, the morning growing in the
yews outside, promise of another day of summer yellow on
the ivied walls of the Manse. She asked how the wedding had
gone, and he yawned, so grown-up, and stretched while she

caught the cup; and he said that the wedding had gone off fine,
except that folk were afraid of Robert, he'd changed so much,
with never a laugh. Ewan had heard Dite Peat say of Robert—

Chris said *Yes, what did he say of Robert?* and Ewan lay
and looked at her, calm and cool. *He said that Robert had lain
with Else, he knew bed-shame in a man when he saw it.*

Chris said *You didn't believe that, did you?* Ewan yawned
again, *I don't know; he might. Though I shouldn't think it
likely, he has you to sleep with; and you must be very nice,
I should think.*

Chris felt the blood come swift in her cheeks, and a moment
the wildest feeling of fear; and then that went by, she'd be
honest as him. She said *Oh, I think I am nice to sleep with.
You've to be terribly in love with someone for that – it makes
all the difference, as you'll know some time.*

He said, politely, *Yes, I suppose so,* he hadn't much interest
in the matter at all; and told some more of the fun at the
wedding, the Provost and MacDougall Brown had both sung,
the Provost banking and braeing, bass, MacDougall strong on
the Blood of the Lamb. There had been lots to eat and lots
of dancing, Ewan had danced with most of the women, rather
fun, though most were too fat round the hips, the hips were
the things that counted, he'd found. He'd told Else that and
she'd said she was shocked, but he didn't suppose that she
was, very much.

And then Alec Ogilvie and Dite Peat had quarrelled, it seems
they had hated each other for years, and kept away from each
other for years, neither one nor the other sure that he'd win.
It was round about seven o'clock that it happened; they went
out to the back of the Arms to fight, Ewan didn't hear till
the fight was near done and went out and saw Dite Peat on
the grass, his eyes closed up and rather a mess, Ake Ogilvie
being helped into his coat and wiping a trickle of blood from
his nose. And Ewan had felt a bit sorry for Dite – goodness
knew why, the *dirtiest* rat.

Chris asked what time he'd reached home and he said *Not
till this morning some time, nearly two. I took a friend of*

Else's to Frellin, the servant-maid at the Manse up there. Chris
asked was she nice and Ewan gave a shrug. *I thought her
rather a boring young beast, she wanted me to make love to
her — up to a point, I suppose, I don't know*. Chris asked *And
did you?* and Ewan said *No, but I thought I would try to teach
her a lesson. You know I've got strong wrists? — I get them
from you — so I held her with one hand and smacked her with
the other, and patted her all neat and nice again, and put her
in through the Frellin Manse gate, and came home to my bed:
I felt a bit tired*.

Folk said he fair was a nickum, that loon, young Ewan Tavendale that came from the Manse, and went to the college at
Dundon each day, cool and calm you'd see him swing by, no
hat on his head be it sun, be it sleet, folk said he was proud as
dirt: and for why? He was only the son of a crofter, just, killed
in the War, and only his luck his mother had married into a
Manse. He never went by with a loon-like slouch, or reddened
up, loon-like, over the lugs, if he met with a covey of queans
in the Square — damn't, there was something unnatural about
him, a sly young brute, you could well believe. And what
though they said he did well at college? No doubt his stepfather, the minister Colquohoun, did all his lessons and he
got the credit.

Then the speak got about from the Frellin Manse that he'd
taken a lass from the wedding of Else, the lass that idle young
thing Jeannie Ray, and she'd thought to have a bit play with
the loon — she often would play about with the loons and get
them sore in a way to have her, syne leave them looking and
habbering like fools. But she'd got a sore stammy-gaster with
Ewan, the coarse young brute assaulted the quean, and left
her greeting on the Manse door-mat. And she told the news to
a crony in Frellin, and the crony giggled and passed it on, and
it reached Ag Moultrie, the Roarer and Greeter, and she nearly
exploded with shame and delight. And next time she met in
with Ewan she cried, *Ay, Ewan, what's this that I hear about
you and that lass Jeannie Ray down at Frellin Manse?* And

the loon said *I'm sorry I don't know what you've heard, Miss Moultrie, but no doubt Segget soon will. Good morning.* And he smiled, polite, and passed on, not a bit ashamed, and left Ag to gape. And not only that, she felt a bit feared, it was fair uncanny, a loon like that.

And a queerer thing followed, her father was dying, Rob Moultrie that said he wasn't her father, the coarse old brute still tormented his wife with the speak that Ag was no daughter of his. Well, he was down and fast sinking at last, about time that he was, the snarling old sinner. And near to the last, when he'd got gey low, he said that he'd like to see the young man, Ewan Something his name was, up at the Manse, he'd like to see him and nobody else. Ag sat by his bed and she heard the bit blither, and she said to him, soothing, *You're wandering a bit. He doesn't know you, the young man at the Manse.* And Rob Moultrie said *Go get him at once, you goggle-eyed gowk, with your claiking tongue. He's more kin of mine that you'll ever be, you with your half-dozen fathers or more.*

So Jess Moultrie trudged away up through Segget, and gave in the message, and young Ewan came down, and went in and sat by the bed of old Moultrie, not feared as a loon at the breath of death, but cool and calm, as though it were nothing. Folk sat outbye and couldn't make out the words that the two spoke one to the other, except that they heard Ewan Tavendale say *Yes, I've noticed that,* and *Yes, that's worth knowing.* And he shook hands with Rob when at last he stood up, and didn't make on, as any other would, that old Rob would soon be up and about, instead he shook hands and wished him Goodbye, and went out as calm as he had come in – ay, a heartless young mucker if ever there was one, whatever could Moultrie have wanted with *him?*

Rob wouldn't hear of the minister coming, and died without a prayer in the house, and that was queer in a childe like him, fell religious and fond of his Bible. Ag cried that her father had died unblessed; and when he was dead she just Roared and Grat.

They buried the old tyke on a hot, quiet day, Mr Colquohoun thinner and quieter than ever: but he had a fine voice as he read out the words, lower than once it had been, more genteel, he fairly had quietened down, had Colquohoun. Once on a time at a burial service folk said the minister would speak out as though he fair meant that the dead would rise up some day, and live once again, and it made your hair crawl – it was all in the Bible, no doubt, and right fine, but you knew the whole thing just a stuttering of stite. But now the minister spoke earnest and low, with a kind of a whine that you heard undisturbed as they lowered old Moultrie down in the clay, with his ill-led life and his ill-getted ways, his hatred of gentry, his ill-treating of Jess. Well, that was his end, and you felt undisturbed, all but John Muir, as he told Ake later.

For it came on him when the folk had gone, and he worked there alone in the stilled graveyard, and watched the figure of Colquohoun move off, that something was finished and ended in Segget, more than old Moultrie, older than him. And a queer qualm came in the pit of his wame, he stopped in the sun to gley in a dream, 'twas as though they were shadows in the sunblaze he saw, nothing enduring and with substance at all, kirk and minister, and stones all around graved with their promised hopes for the dead, the ways and beliefs of all olden time – no more than the whimsies a bairn would build from the changing patterns that painted the hills.

And faith, there were more than enough of those changes, folk woke to the fact of ill changes in Segget, you'd to count your silver now ere you spent it, there wasn't a soul but was hit some way, prices so high and the spinners, the dirt, with hardly a meck to spend in shops. Whiles one of the Mowat mills still joggled along, as it wore to Autumn you'd see its smoke like a lazy snake uprise in the air. But it joggled half-hearted, there was fell little traffic, the stationy, Newlands, said so little jute came in he wondered the Mill kept going: and he tried to get spinners to do what he did, bawl for the Blood of MacDougall's Lamb; and no doubt he fair was a pious childe, though you thought yourself that praying for blood was hardly the way to start a jute mill.

The Segget wynds were crowded with spinners, lolling about in the sun, the dirt, you turned one moment from cursing the brutes for their sweirty and living off the like of yourself, and the next you had nearly moaned your head off that there wasn't a thing they now bought in your shops. Dite Peat was the first to feel the bit nip, he'd never done well with the spinners, Dite, since that time long back he'd mishandled his father. But up until late he'd managed to live, with trade from the rest of Segget New Toun, though most from the countryside out around. Well, he found that the farms were failing him now, cottar folk got their meat from the vans on the roads, and all the farmers had gotten them cars and went into Stonehaven or even Dundon: in the end Dite Peat was rouped from his door. It lent a bit of excitement, that, Dite's stuff sold up while he stood and looked on, still bearing the marks of the knocks he had got in that tink-like fight with the joiner of Segget.

Folk wondered what would become of him now, it was said he hadn't a meck of his own: and though when it seemed he owned a bit shop folk bore with him and his dirty jokes, they weren't such fools as to do that now and cold-shouldered him everywhere that he went. And down in the Segget Arms one night when he started in with his dirty tales, Alec Hogg was there and he said *You shut up, we're sick of you and the things you can do – though you can't keep your shop-roof over your head.* Dite bared his rotten brown teeth like a dog, but other folk were crying *That's right*, and he didn't dare make a set at young Hogg. That was near the end of the brute in Segget, he went to Meiklebogs and asked for a fee, folk told that Dalziel had ta'en him on cheap – Dalziel whose new housekeeper was in the old way; faith! with Dite Peat at the Meiklebogs as well, the question of fatherhood in the future would be more of a complication than ever.

For bairns came thick as ever they'd come, folk cut their costs in all things but cradles, down in Old Toun they squawked into life, the bairns, in rooms that were packed out already. The less the work the more of the creatures, they bred fair disgusting old Leslie would say, and it showed you the kind of dirt that they were, living crowded like that, four-five in a room, in houses that were not fit for pig-rees. 'Twas Infernal, just: the men should be libbed: now, when he himself was a loon up in Garvock—

But his trade at the smiddy was failing as well, though he habbered and blethered as much as ever, you'd fell often hear the anvil at rest and look in and see old Leslie sit there, sitting and staring down at his pipe, it gave you an unco-like feeling to see him. There were fell few jobs came down from the Mills and a mighty few from the farms outbye, with their new-like ploughs that needed no coulters, if they broke a bit they looked in a book and sent away to the makers for't. Not like the days of the crofter childes, when in and about from Kinraddie, Arbuthnott, and half the hill-land betwixt Segget and Fordoun, the folk of the lost little farms would ride with plenty of trade in a small-like way.

The only creature that seemed to flourish as the harvest brought a dour end to the weather and the clouds rolled slower over the Howe was Will Melvin that kept the Segget Arms, him and that sharp-tongued besom his wife, the spinners would go down to the Arms and get drunk, instead of biding at home in their misery and cutting their throats, as decent folk would.

Mr Mowat came suddenly home to Segget and sacked every servant he met in the House; he said that he Jahly well must, he'd no choice, he was taxed to death by those Labour chaps. Then he went to the kirk, the first time in years, and sat and listened to a dreich-like discourse – God! there was something queer with Colquohoun. But he kept his eyes, Mr Mowat, folk told, on Mrs Colquohoun and not the minister, as she sat in the choir with her sulky-proud face, and her swathings of hair, ay, she'd fairly fine hair, herself looking up at the pulpit as though she didn't know Mr Mowat looked at her – and didn't know as everybody else did in Segget, that he'd been the father of that bairn of hers that died away a three-four years back.

Mr Mowat never went near the Manse now, he hadn't done that since the days of the Strike, nor the Geddeses either since Mrs Colquohoun had raised a row at the WRI. And what do you think that row was about? A socialist creature had offered to come down from Dundon and lecture on birth-control: and all the folk were against it at once, except the tink bitch the minister had wed. . . And what might IT be? you asked, and folk told you: just murdering your bairns afore they were born, most likely that was what *she* herself did.

She did her own work in the Manse nowadays, they had had to draw in their horns as well, no other maid took the place of Else. And the Sourock's wife was fairly delighted, she said getting down on the floors to scrub would be an ill-like ploy, she would warrant, for the brave silk knickers that Mrs Colquohoun wore. For the Sourock's wife had never forgiven the minister's wife her bit under-things, and the way she voted at the General Election.

But syne news came that fair raised a stir, the Labour Government thrown out at last, and that fine-like childe, Ramsay MacDonald, was in with the Tories, and said they were fine. And them that had wireless sets listened in, and Ramsay came on with his holy-like voice and maaed like a sheep, but a holy-like sheep, that the country could yet be saved: and he'd do it. Ay, he'd grown a fine chap and had got back his guts, you were pleased to hear as the maa went on, now he had jumped to the gentry's side. And no doubt you would see fine changes in Segget.

But Chris watched that and the life in Segget with a queer apprehension holding her heart. One evening she climbed up to Ewan's back room, where he sat at a little desk he had there, reading a text-book, his head in his hands. He jumped up when she came and found her a seat, polite and kind, though remote with his book till she asked him what the book was about. So he told her the stuff was geology, he was studying the strata of the last Ice Age that came in Scotland long years ago, when the bergs came drifting down by Dundon and folk looked out from their mountain eyries and saw the peaks and the glaciers come. Chris sat and listened, hands clasped round her knees, looking at Ewan's head in the light, smooth and dark and yet shot with gold, the pallor of the lamplight upon his hair – grey granite below as grey granite above.

Then her mind switched away to what he was saying, she thought *And the thing is happening again* – all over the world the Ice was coming, not the ice-time that ended the Golden Age, but the Ice of want and fear and fright, its glacier peaks on the sky by day, its frozen gleam on the sky by night, and men looked out bewildered to see it, cold and dank, and a dark wind blew, and there was neither direction, salvation, nothing but the storming black lour of the Clouds as the frosts and the fog of this winter came. . .

Ewan had twisted around, he said *Mother!* sharp, and jumped to his feet and shook her. Chris came to herself with a start, and stared. *What's wrong?* she asked, and he said *You looked – fey.*

She seldom heard a Scots word from Ewan, he brushed them aside as old, blunted tools, but the word had come on his lips as though sudden he'd sought in English and English had failed. She laughed and said *Did I?* and ruffled his hair, and he grinned at her, quiet, he'd been quick, but not feared – he'd do strange things yet in the world, Ewan, who hadn't a God and hadn't a faith and took not a thing on the earth for granted. And she thought as she held him (he endured that, polite) he was one of the few who might save the times, watching the Ice and the winter come, unflustered, unfrightened, with quiet, cold eyes.

And she smiled at that and her prideful dreamings for the child of her womb, an idle woman's pride: and bade Ewan goodnight and went down to the kitchen to leave it neat for the morning's work. 'Twas then that there came a knock at the door and Else Queen that was now Else Hogg stamped in, with the washing she did each week for the Manse, she cried *Well, Mem, have you heard the news?*

Chris asked *What news?* and Else sat down and gasped, *I fair had to run to tell you. It's about Mr Mowat — but surely you've heard?*

The story, she said, was all over Segget, Mr Mowat was ruined and hadn't a penny, the whole of Segget mortgaged to the hilt. The last time he came back from London he'd tried to raise a bit loan at any damn price; and he'd gone to his Dundon bankers and tried, and they'd said they must see the jute in his Mills. So they sent a man down, Mr Mowat met him and dined him and wined him up at the House, it minded old Sinclair, the last of the servants, of the good old days when young Jahly Mowat would come back with a half-dozen whores in his car. Ah, well, the banker childe was fell canny, he drank but little, and that with suspicion; but Mr Mowat soaked like a drouthy fish, and then said *Right O, we'll go down to the mills.*

There were two main storage sheds at the Mill, one was near empty, said young Mr Mowat, the other well filled with new bales of jute. And Mr Mowat showed the first of the sheds, there was only a bale or so in the place, but when they came to the other bit shed, and the sliding doors slid back in their slots, there were the bales packed up to the roof, so tight they nearly bulged through the door. *You see, we've a Jahly good stock at the Mill,* said Mr Mowat, and the bank man agreed.

So the bank childe went back to Dundon and reported, and they loaned Mr Mowat a five hundred pounds. And the creature vanished, none knew where he'd gone; and this last week or so the bank grew suspicious. It sent a man down to Segget yes-treen, and he went to the Mills, and what did he find, down there at the shed that had seemed so packed? That there was no more than a curtain of bales, stacked up to the roof at the shed's near end, the rest of the shed was as toom as your hat, Mr Mowat had swindled the bank to the end: and now the bank had ta'en over the Mills.

Chris asked what that meant and Else didn't know, except that all the folk left at the Mills had been sacked that evening and the Mills closed down. And folk were saying they never would open, it wouldn't be worth it, with trade so bad; and nobody knew what the spinners would do that had waited for years for their jobs to come back.

And the winter was coming. Down in Old Toun a weary indifference lay on the wynds, they paid no heed to the new Election, Chris herself didn't bother to vote – were the liars and cheats called Labour or Tory they'd feather their own nests and lie to the end.

Rain held the sky at November's end, she saw the streaming parks of Dalziel lift and move under the freezing haze that sailed and swam by the base of the Mounth, the curlews had ceased to cry on the Kaimes and of nights the sounds of the trains came blurred, those nights that the great lighted buses would lighten, suddenly, firing the walls of the room where she lay by the side of Robert unsleeping, him sleeping so sound that he sometimes seemed dead. How to sleep, how to sleep, when your mind took hold, in the dark, of the plight of the Segget wynds?

They had brought in a thing they called the Means Test, spinners who had had the dole over-long were told that their relatives must keep them in future. Chris had stopped by the door of Ake Ogilvie's shop, and he told her that things were black in Old Toun, the Wilsons had been cut off the dole altogether because their old grannie had the Old Age Pension – the three of them to live on ten shillings a week. How could they pay their rent on that?

Since the Mowat creditors took over the place they were forcing the payments right through the nose, they'd already had Feet up at the eviction of a two-three families out of their houses, if houses you could call them – they smelt like pigrees. Old Cronin had been cut off the Bureau as well because young Charlie was fee'd up at Frellin, and stayed at home to look after his father: and how could they live on the pay of a loon? And there were worse cases than these, far worse, God damn't! you had never much liked the spinners, but the things that were happening near turned you sick, it was kicking in the faces of the poor for no more than delight in hearing the scrunch of their bones.

Chris said *They won't stand it, there'll be revolution*, and Ake sneered *Revolution? They'll starve and say nothing. Or 'Come and walk on my face and I'll give you a vote!'*

Then the news went round that old Cronin was dead, found dead in his bed by his young son Chae, Chae blubbered the old man had no firewood for days, and nothing but a pot of potatoes to eat. Folk wouldn't believe that blither at all, it couldn't be true, for it made you shiver – no, no, 'twas only another damned lie, that kind of thing never happened in Segget. Would you find that news in the *Mearns Chief?* – you wouldn't, so you knew that it couldn't be true, the *Chief* said week by week we were fine, and Scotland still the backbone of Britain, and the Gordon Highlanders right gay childes, not caring a hoot though their pay was down, and Progressives just the scum of the earth that planned to take bairns out of the slums and rear them up in Godless communes, and a woman Naomi Mitchison coarse, for she said not a word about Christ in her book. . . Ay, the *Mearns Chief* was aye up-to-date, and showed you a photo of Mrs MacTavish winning the haggis at a Hogmanay dance.

That son of old Cronin's, Jock was his name (you surely minded when *he* was in Segget?) had done right well for himself, folk said. He was now a National Labour supporter, one of Ramsay's new men down in Glasgow, and would likely get into the Parliament soon: and he was starting on a lecture tour – *The Country First, Parties Must Wait.* By that, of course, he meant the political parties, not the kind he would hold in his Glasgow house – he spoke and acted the gent to the life.

But Charlie said his old father had seemed to shrivel up when he heard of the tour; and the last time Charlie had been to his father he hardly had spoken a sensible word, just muttered over some one of his socialist books, by Ramsay MacDonald, till the light grew dim, so faint that he couldn't have seen to read.

He told that to Ewan when he came to the Manse to arrange the burial in Segget kirkyard, he and Ewan hadn't met for a long time past, chief enough though they'd been at the school together. And Charlie was shy and he said to Ewan, *I hear, Mr Ewan, you're clever at college*, and stood and shuffled his great glaured boots, and his hands were heavy and calloused and cold, holding the clumsy cap in his hand. Ewan said *I'm all right. Sit down. Like some tea?* and went ben to the kitchen where Chris made a cake. *It's young Charlie Cronin, and mother, he's hungry.* Chris said she'd bring some food on a tray, but Ewan said *No, you see he would guess I know he was hungry and that would offend him. I'll take in some and we'll eat it together.*

So he did, though he'd only new-finished his dinner, Chris peeped at the two of them, sitting and talking, with a tinge of pride and wonder for Ewan, and a twist of pity in her heart for his friend, with his shy red face and his clumsy hands. Then she went back to her work, and they ate; and when Charlie Cronin at last went away she heard Ewan make a dive for the bathroom and be suddenly, exceedingly, very sick there. She took him a glass of water to drink, and he smiled and drank and said that was better: white-faced and black-haired, but still cool enough. Chris thought at the time 'twas because of the food he'd eaten to keep the Cronin lad company; but she wasn't sure later, for she found out that Charlie had told him black tales of the things in Old Toun.

And that night she went up to his room and found Ewan, staring out at the fall of sleet, a pelt and a hiss in the moving dark, his head in his hands, not reading as usual. She touched him, quiet, and he started a little.

Oh, nothing, he said. *I'm fine, don't worry. I was trying to remember old Cronin's face.*

He was turning to look in the face of Life.

That was the Sunday; on Monday folk woke to a blinding pelt of rain-sheets on Segget and down and across the steaming Howe where the churned earth lay with its quagmired pools, the hills corona'd dark with their clouds. Robert went early up to his room and Chris was making the dinner in the kitchen when she found John Muir at the kitchen door. He looked

stranger than ever she had seen him look, John Muir, and
forgot to call her Mem. He said a gey thing had happened last
night: and gleyed at her queer and gave a queer cough.

Chris said, *What's happened? Sit down, you look queer.* And
he sat and told her the unco-like tale.

She had heard of the Kindnesses? Well, they were folk that
bided down in Segget Old Toun. At least they had done till a
three days back, Kindness himself, was an ill-doing childe, and
weeks behind with his rent, folk said. His wife was a lass from
Kinraddie way, she'd a bairn only a three weeks old, and had
near gone daft when the landlord's folk came down to the
house to turn them out. Sim Leslie had gone to see it was done
and thought nothing of it, he was used to that now.

Well, out they'd been turned, their bit gear in the streets,
you minded that Saturday streamed with sleet, and the house
they'd been in was at Segget's tail end, and few folk saw the
thing that went on, or cared to be out in weather like that, and
Kindness himself was a surly brute. He got sacks and happed
up the most of his gear, and prowled Segget for hours to look
for a place. But he wasn't well known and he wasn't well liked,
so he came back at last somewhere about midnight, and broke
in a window and put his wife in, she had stood in the lithe all
those hours in the sleet with her bairn in her arms and must
near have been dead. She sat in the kitchen the rest of the
night, Kindness himself had brought in a chair, then he prowled
some more, for he couldn't sleep.

But worse was to come with the Sunday morning; the
policeman, Sim Leslie, that folk called Feet, came on them
early and miscalled them for tinks, and took Kindness's name
in his little note-book, as though the fool didn't know it by
now, and said there would be a court-case about this. Syne he
turned them out and boarded the window and went off and
left them, and a neighbour nearby took in the wife and bairn
for a while. But she hadn't an inch of space to spare, and at
last, as the night came, Kindness came back and said he'd

gotten a place where they'd bide, he didn't say more, a surly bit brute.

Well, his wife went with him through the pelt of the sleet, and got to the end of Old Toun to the place, and that was an old deserted pig-ree, from the time when folk in Segget bred pigs, long ere the Mills or the spinners came. You could get inside if you got down and crawled, Kindness had taken a mattress in there and a stump of a candle and some of their things. Mrs Kindness was feared at the dark and the sounds that the old ree made as the night wore on, but they put out the light at last, fell tired, and went to sleep in the sound of the rain.

It must have been somewhere near morning they woke, Mrs Kindness woke up with her bairn screaming, not just the cry of a bairn in unease but a shrill, wild cry that near feared her to death. She tried all she could to comfort its wail, then the light began to peek in the pigsty and they saw the reason for the bairn's screams, the rats in the night had gnawed off its thumb.

John Muir cried *Mistress, don't take on like that!* and caught Chris' arm and put her in a chair. And then as he straightened up from that he saw the minister stand in the door, he'd come quietly down as he came these days, and he looked like Chris, he had heard it all. But he only said *John, where are they now?*

Muir skeughed and said that he didn't well know, he'd heard that folk had ta'en meat to the ree, and Kindness was off for a doctor, 'twas said, walking all the way to Stonehive. Robert said *Walking?* – his face looked queer – *WALKING? Chris, I'll go for those folk. Will you get a room ready before I come back?*

She worked as quick as she could when he'd gone out into the shining pelt of the rain. But it nearly was noon ere Robert came back, the woman looked only a slip of a quean, Robert carried the bairn, it had ceased to cry, whimpering and weeking soft like a kitten. The woman stopped and looked at Chris with the shamed, strange eyes of a frightened beast, Chris squeezed her hands for a moment, just, and was rough, and told her where her room was, and was rough that she mightn't break down and weep. And she took the bairn and bathed the torn thumb, though it nearly turned her sick as she worked; and the bairn weeked like kitten hurt. Then she carried it up to its mother, waiting, in the spare bedroom with the blazing fire.

She left them there and came down to find John Muir come back with the Kindness gear. He told her the minister was off to Stonehaven, on his bike, to try and overtake Kindness, the minister himself would hold on for the doctor.

Kindness reached back to the Manse about three, and an hour or so later Robert and MacCormack, Robert soaked and shivering from his ride in the rain. The doctor went up and bade a long time and then came down to the hall and Chris. He shook his head and snibbed up his bag.

I came over-late. Poison and shock. The woman didn't know it though she had it beside her. The baby's been dead this last hour or more.

In the dead of the night three nights after that, Chris woke, she was sharply and suddenly awake. Robert beside her coughing and coughing. She got up and padded to his side of the bed, and he had not known that her warmth had gone, all his body was in such a heat; but he saw her against the light from the windows. He said *I'm all right, go back to your bed* and instantly fell to his coughing again.

Chris put on a dressing-gown and went down, and made and brought up a hot lemon drink, he drank it and thanked her, she put out the light, his body still burned as she lay by his side. But presently the cough died away and she slept, and didn't awake till the morning came, Robert's cough awoke her, that and the sound of the wind as it swept the snow down on Segget, piled up on the edge of another New Year.

With the coming of the day the wind rose and rose and rattled at the window-hasps of the house, the skirl of it in the old roof-tops and wailing down the long, winding chimneys. Robert kept to his bed, Chris had made him do that, almost by force, he had suddenly smiled — smiled so that her bowels had seemed turned to water, with that flare of the hot old love that was gone. *If I was a man again, I'd hold YOU, you wretch of a woman to bully me like this!* Chris said *You'll be welcome to hold me as you like — when that cough's better, not until then.* He stroked her arm, the flame in his eyes: *Strong and comely still — I've neglected you, Chris!* Then he coughed for a while and when he came to, lay quiet, listening to the day go on.

The Kindnesses had gone to friends in Dundon, and left no relic but a snow-happed grave, and this cough that Robert had got in his throat, and that memory that woke you, sick in the night, of the rats that fed on a baby's flesh. And men had believed in a God and a Christ, men had believed in the kindness of men, men had believed that this order endured because of its truth and its justice to men. . . Robert was sound beside you in sleep, but once he moved and muttered in dreams. He said *Oh, I can't, I can't — oh, my god!* Chris happed him close and again sought sleep, and the next day came, and he woke to that coughing, and Chris saw a spray of blood on the pillow.

She said *I must send for a doctor, Robert,* fear in her heart, though none in her voice. But he shook his head, his eyes grown remote. *I'll be all right, I'll look after myself.* And after he'd eaten a slice of toast and had drunk some tea, he didn't cough more, and asked for a pad of paper and pencil, he wished to write out his tomorrow's sermon.

Chris knew he wouldn't be able to speak it, a week at least ere he'd rise from his bed; but she took him the paper and pencil to quiet him, and stood by a while till at last he looked up — *Yes, Christine?* his eyes far from her again. So she turned to her work with a daft, dull pain, daft ever to think that THAT could come back.

Ewan helped her that morning, scrubbing the hall, bringing in coal, the wind still raged, a steely drive that was edged with sleet; as the day wore on it froze up again. When she went up that afternoon to Robert's room the door wouldn't open a while though she pushed, then it did, and the stinging air smote her face, the window wide open, the room ice-cold, Robert

lying half-naked asleep in his bed. He woke as he heard the
sound of her come, his face was flushed in spite of the cold,
he said that he'd tried to sleep and couldn't, he'd felt choked
and opened the window and slept. Where had the pad for his
sermon gone?

Chris went down to Ewan to wire for the doctor. When he
came in the evening he sounded Robert's lungs, Robert lying
quiet, his eyes far away; and the doctor was puzzled, though he
chatted and joked. But later, downstairs, he said to Chris,
*There's something queer in Mr Colquohoun's lungs — oh no,
this cold's not on to them yet. Was he ever gassed in the War,
do you know? There's the strangest contraction in both upper
lungs. I'll be back fell early the morn's morning, keep him in
bed and keep him warm.*

Ewan went up about six and came back and said that Robert
was sleeping again, but there was blood on his pillow, fresh.
Chris got up to change it, she ached in each limb, but Ewan
said that he'd done that already, and Robert wasn't waked up
from his sleep. *Sit down and rest*, and he forced her to sit, and
they sat a long time looking into the fire, hearing the blast of
the wind over Segget. But near eight or nine when they went
to their beds the wind seemed to die in the cry of the yews,
Ewan went to the window and called Chris to look. So she did,
and stood by his side in the dark, and looked on a sky that was
burnished in steel, rimed with a pringling frost of stars, nothing
moved or lived, the yews stood black, the garden hedges rose
up in the silence as if to listen to the void star-glow. . . Ewan
said *You'll catch cold*, and blinded the window, and above their
heads they heard Robert cough.

Next morning John Muir came early to the Manse, he said that
he'd tell the congregation there wouldn't be a service; and
Chris agreed. But then, as they stood together in the hall they
heard the sound of an opening door, and looked up, and Chris
gave a gasp and cried, *Robert!* He was coming down slowly, his
hand on the rails, he said *I'm all right; I MUST take the
service.* He'd a handkerchief up to his mouth, saying that, and

stopped and coughed, and Chris wrung her hands. *Robert, go back to your bed – you must.*

He shook his head, he was fully dressed, even shaved. *I'll take the service as usual. There's nothing in a cough to stop me, is there? AND I HAVE SOMETHING TO SAY TO THE FOLK.*

Chris had stood enough, now she knew at last if she didn't win now she never would win. She said *Robert, for me. I've never asked much – for me, and I'll never ask another thing: Will you please go back?*

Ewan had come out of his room and looked down, and he saw Robert's face for a moment twist, as if in pain, then it altered again, back to the dark, dreaming look that they knew. *It's you or the kirk, Chris, and I'm the kirk's man.*

For a second it seemed to Chris she'd be sick, she gave the funniest dry laugh at that thought, with that gripping in her stomach and that pain in her throat. Then that went by, she was suddenly cool, she heard herself say, *All right, here's your coat*; and found a coat for him in the hall, and a muffler, and wrapped it about him, as she finished with that he stared at her queer, the ice broke round his eyes. He said suddenly, *Chris – my dear, dear Chris!* and kissed her with that look, not with his lips, not in front of John Muir, and she smiled at him, white. Then he went out across the chill blow of the wind, his feet rang sharp on the frozen ground. Chris caught Ewan's arm and shook it – *Go with him! I'll come as soon as ever I'm dressed.*

She fled and changed in a flurry and was down, and across through the snow-wrapped garden before the kirk bells had ceased from their sudden clamour. She raised her eyes as she hurried through the kirkyard, and saw the Mounth as though suddenly halted, watching, and staring down at Segget, the far peaks under their canopy of cloud, the nearer bare but for a snow-pillar she saw rise up from the Leachie bents and whirl in the icy blow of the wind.

Folk said that the kirk at Segget nowadays was a fine bit place to go for a sleep, the Reverend Colquohoun was as quiet as a cow with his blethers of Jesus and Brotherhood and Love and the Sacred Heart that still bled for men. You could pop a sweetie or so in your mouth and take a bit snore as the sermon went on; even Hairy Hogg confessed it was quiet, they had fairly tamed that creature Colquhoun, with his coarse-like suggestings the Hoggs came from monkeys, when instead they were all descended from Burns. And Ake Ogilvie said *Well, monkeys for me!*

They were both of them there, both Ake and the Provost, that Sunday, and Mistress Hogg came as well, she was failing a bit, but still as sharp-tongued, she had said to her son when he married Else Queen – *Ay, you're keen on the bowl in spite of the slop.* She sat by her man, Else and Alec sat near, and it tickled you a bit to see Meiklebogs – behind, ill-shaved, smiling shy to himself, he had come back to kirk since Colquhoun quietened down.

The kirk began to fill up a bit, old Leslie came in, he was getting fell done, and you thought as you watched him paich down the aisle he never would finish that story about Garvock. And damn't! you felt almost sorry about that, worse folk than old Leslie, his son Sim for one, promoted now, he was leaving Segget, if it wasn't he had such feet as he had you'd have said he'd grown overbig for his boots.

That fair was a hell of a clamour Muir raised, Will Melvin came in in the middle of the ring, like a pot-bellied cat, his thin mistress behind, they were making money like dirt, folk said, *Dirt unto dirt, 'twas the way of all flesh* was Ake Ogilvie's speak about that – aye the same, he'd miscall both the good and the bad in Segget, and didn't seem to see any difference at all 'tween an ill-doing brute like that tink, Dite Peat, and his brother, Peter, that owned his own shop.

There was wee Peter Peat up near the choir, looking round him right fierce to see folk were quiet, his mistress beside him, and the Sourock's wife, the Sourock himself would be down in the Square, singing about Blood in MacDougall's band – he'd never gotten over that mess in his bed when Dite Peat had left the pig he had killed.

God! the frost was fair driving the folk to the kirk; you moved over a bit to let a childe in: young Cronin, you saw, from the Manse at Frellin, the only one of the spinners that had come; the coarse creatures hadn't a care for religion. Charlie Cronin blushed and opened his Bible and sat like a duck on the edge of egg-laying, fell decent-like and shy; and you thought to yourself that Geddes, the headmaster, might well take a lesson, there he was, all asprawl in his pew, showing no respect or example at all; and that nasty bit sneer on his face as he sprawled.

Syne you saw the choir was beginning to fill, Miss Ferguson first; God! how she still blushed. Ake Ogilvie said she'd have a blush on her face if ever they exhumed her corpse from its coffin. Beside her Miss M'Askill sat down with a jerk that couldn't have been good for her spine, you'd have thought, specially as the bottom of that looked ill-padded. She hadn't got a man, and there seemed little chance that she ever *would* now, things as they were – damn't, Segget affairs were fair in a state, you could only hope, with the National Government, they'd alter some time afore Segget was dead. Ramsay Mac-Donald had said that they would, if we all went poorer, ate less, and spent more – ay, fair a fine childe, with a right clear mind. Ramsay MacDonald, as the English knew well, they couldn't breed the like of Ramsay in England: though Ake Ogilvie said they smothered them at birth. But that was just one of his tink-like says, the English aye needed the Scots at their head, right holy and smart at the same bit time.

John Muir had finished with his ringing at last, and went gleying down the aisle as of old, one shoulder first, and brought in the minister. Faith, he looked white, you'd heard he'd been ill, some cold or such like, a nothing at all. He climbed to the pulpit and coughed and sat down, and looked down the kirk – damn't a queer-like look, near the kind he would give in the days long syne when he was so keen on changing the world.

Syne you saw that you'd fair been mistaken in that, he was praying, with his head laid down in his hands; you felt a bit

better to see him like that, decent and douce, as a minister
should be – not trying to alter things as he'd done – who the
hell wanted alterations in Segget? Folk were fine, if it wasn't
that there wasn't any work, and meat a bit scarce, and you
hadn't a notion what your bairns would find to do in the
world, when they grew up and found it full up of the ill-getted
bairns of spinners, and such. Ah well, they'd just have to gang
their own gait, with the help of some guts and the rock of
Christ's kirk.

Young Ewan Tavendale came in and sat down, and looked
round the kirk and up at the pulpit as though he owned both
and was frightened at neither – faith, folk were right, an impudent get, with no respect for God or man. Then, as the playing on the organ stopped, the far door opened to Mrs Colquohoun, white-faced and proud, like a proud quean still, hurrying
to take her seat in the choir. Half-way to that she stopped and
looked up, at her man who sat so quiet in the pulpit – folk
saw the look and kittled to interest, could the two of them
have had a row in the Manse?

The minister gave out the psalm, but so low you hardly heard
the words that he said; and you spent so long looking up the
passage that the singing was over afore you had found it. Syne
the minister was praying, you bent your head, a fell dreich
prayer and only half-heard. But then as he finished and gave
out his text folk fairly louped in their seats as he spoke, his
voice had a ring like a sudden bell;

*My text is from the twenty-third chapter of St Luke, verse
forty-two: AND HE SAID UNTO JESUS, LORD, REMEMBER
ME WHEN THOU COMEST INTO THY KINGDOM.*

*It is nineteen hundred years since that cry was heard, it is
sixteen hundred years since the holy Catholic Church was
established in temporal power. In the early days after the
death of Christ His return was hourly awaited – His followers,
scanty, assured, looked to His coming within a few months or
years at the most, they were certain He would come again and*

redeem the evil of the world that had murdered HIM. And the years went by: and He tarried still. But that Hope and that Promise it was that bore the Cross to triumph at last in Rome, all over Europe; that uplifts it still. And still the Christ tarries and the world remains.

LORD, REMEMBER ME WHEN THOU COMEST INTO THY KINGDOM.

In Segget a week ago tonight, in this Christian village, a man and a woman were driven from their home and had no place to lay their heads. In the night a rat came and fed on their child, eating its flesh in a sacrament of hunger—

LORD, REMEMBER ME WHEN THOU COMEST INTO THY KINGDOM.

In the years when the Great War ended the world seemed to turn in its sleep and awake, a new promise cried all about the earth, the promise of the Christ fulfilled in Man – fulfilled in the movements of pity and hope that men called by many names, meaning the same. Against ignoble oppressions and a bitter tyranny the common people banded themselves at last – in a Christ-like rage of pity to defend their brothers who sweated their blood in the mines, to give warmth and light and ease to us all. And the leaders of the great Nine Days, days filled with the anger and pity of the Christ who drove the money-changers from the Temple courts, looked in their hearts and found there fear, heard the crunch of the nails that were driven in through the shrinking hands of Christ. And they sold Him again, his promise in Man, each for their thirty pieces of silver.

LORD, REMEMBER ME WHEN THOU COMEST INTO THY KINGDOM.

This year, when hunger and want filled the land, the coun-

sellors of the nation told for our guidance that more hunger
and poverty yet must come, an increasing of stripes in the
name of the Law, of Good Government, Order, in this Christian
land, in this nineteenth century since the Christ died and came
into that Kingdom of the Soul which the Churches proclaim
that He came into—

LORD, REMEMBER ME WHEN THOU COMEST INTO THY
KINGDOM.

AND IT WAS ABOUT THE SIXTH HOUR, AND THERE
WAS A DARKNESS OVER ALL THE EARTH UNTIL THE
NINTH HOUR.
AND THE SUN WAS DARKENED, AND THE VEIL OF THE
TEMPLE WAS RENT IN THE MIDST.

So we see, it seems, in the darkened sun, in the rending veils
of the temples and kirks, the end of Mankind himself in the
West, or the end of the strangest dream men have dreamt – of
both the God and the Man Who was Christ, Who gave to the
world a hope that passes, and goeth about like the wind, and
like it returns and follows, fulfilling nothing. There is no hope
for the world at all – as I, the least of His followers see –
except it forget the dream of the Christ, forget the creeds that
they forged in His shadow when their primal faith in the God
was loosed – and turn and seek with unclouded eyes, not that
sad vision that leaves hunger unfed, the wail of children in
unending dark, the cry of human flesh eaten by beasts... But a
stark, sure creed that will cut like a knife, a surgeon's knife
through the doubt and disease – men with unclouded eyes may
yet find it, and far off yet in the times to be, on an earth at
peace, living and joyous, the Christ come back—

His voice had sunk near to a whisper by then, so that folk in
the back of the kirk couldn't hear, all the kirk sitting and
staring in silence. Then he started again, he said, very clear,
and once again, slowly, terrible to hear, as a man who cried

from his soul on a friend who had passed beyond either helping or help:

*LORD, REMEMBER ME WHEN THOU COMEST INTO THY
KINGDOM!*

Chris was never exactly sure of what followed. But she got
from the choir stalls and ran up the aisle, the frozenness gone
that had hemmed her in — took scarcely a second to move
from that moment when Robert had stopped, the queer look
on his face. For he stared down the kirk as though Someone
stood there. And then a bright crimson thing came on his lips,
and down at the kirk's far end a loon screamed.

John Muir reached the pulpit as quick as she did, she saw
Ewan, swift and dark, stand up. Ake Ogilvie as well, the rest
of the folk stared and stared in a frozen silence, from them to
the silent figure up there. Chris ran up the pulpit-stair, opened
the door, Robert's head had fallen forward in his hands, and
all the pages of the Bible below she saw soaked in the stream
of blood from his lips.

And somehow it did not matter, she had known, she put out
her hand and put back the hair, from his forehead, gently; and
looked at the faces of the congregation. She wetted her lips
and tried to speak, to be cool and tell them the minister was
dead, and the service was ended, would they please go? And
then at last she heard herself speak, in strange words not her
own, unbidden to her lips:

It is Finished.

Now, with the broadening of the day, she could see the peaks
of the Mounth wheel one by one into the line of the flow of
the light, dun and sun-riding they rode down the Howe. Trusta
towered first and north and north the peaks came fast, sun
on the Howe and day on the Howe, her last day in Segget ere
she went elsewhere, to new days and ways, to changes she
could not foresee or foreknow. Round her the new year

wakened to life, she saw the steam of a ploughing team, a
curlew was calling up in the broom.

She moved and stretched in weariness then, the morning
weariness before you right woke, so standing she minded the
way that Robert would bless the folk of Segget on Sabbath.
And, queerly, her hands shaped into that gesture, with Segget
rising in its driftings of smoke, and the hills behind, and all
time before.

Then that had finished; she went slow down the brae, only
once looked back at the frown of the hills, and caught her
breath at that sight they held, seeing them bare of their clouds
for once, the pillars of mist that aye crowned their heights, all
but a faint wisp vanishing south, and the bare, still rocks up-
turned to the sky.

Lewis Grassic Gibbon
Sunset Song 80p
Book One of *A Scots Quair*

Chris Guthrie knew love and hate in the same breath.

Hate for the ceaseless toil of a life in the Mearns that brought her mother to tragic despair . . .

Love for the tumbling land of her heritage – a love shared by Ewan, with whom she finds ecstatic union . . .

Grey Granite 80p
Book Three of *A Scots Quair*

Living in a new world of factories, pubs, strikes, marches, riots, tanner hops, picture-houses and picket lines, Chris's hopes for the future lie in the burning love between her son Ewan and Ellen Johns – a love as tempestuous as the times . . .

'All three novels are magnificent pieces of writing' J. M. Reid, GLASGOW HERALD

'By far the best Scots writer since George Douglas Brown. *A Scots Quair* is likely to be read for many years to come' DAILY TELEGRAPH

Guy McCrone
Antimacassar City 75p

The first part of Guy McCrone's trilogy of Victorian Glasgow introduces the Moorhous family of Ayrshire – Mungo, the farmer, Arthur, the merchant who is the first of them to move to Glasgow, the young and sensitive David, Phoebe, the half-sister from the Highlands who grows up into a gallant and stormy beauty.

'A very human and readable story' GUARDIAN

The Philistines 75p

The Moorhous family become established in Glasgow town. They are swiftly drawn into turmoil when the dashing and impulsive David falls in love with Lucy Rennie, a professional singer whose trade places her far beneath his family in the social order – especially when he is already engaged to the charms and riches of another . . . Book Two of the classic *Wax Fruit* trilogy.

'The authentic stuff of life' TIMES LITERARY SUPPLEMENT

The Puritans 75p

Grown up into a beautiful and elusive creature of the world, Phoebe is drawn away from Glasgow. Destiny sweeps her and her husband to Vienna, the romantic and enchanting capital of the Hapsburgs in its heyday of the 1880s. The third part of Guy McCrone's panoramic *Wax Fruit* trilogy.

'Recaptures the atmosphere of the period most effectively' GLASGOW HERALD

Grace Metalious
Peyton Place 90p

Teeming with incident and vitality, this richly diverse novel of
American small-town life first appeared amid a storm of controversy.
It became a record-breaking TV series and remains one of the great
bestsellers – a story of corruption and compassion, high hopes and dark
secrets, ripe sensuality and rigid inhibition.

Joan Biggar
The Maiden Voyage 60p

Aboard the *Lady Edwina Douglas* on a grim October day in 1860,
Hannah Blackshaw set forth to find a new life half-way across the world.
Between yesterday and tomorrow lay a harrowing voyage across the
wide oceans, but also friendship with the red-haired Jessie and a
new-born love for the young teacher, Jamie . . .

You can buy these and other Pan books from booksellers and
newsagents; or direct from the following address:
Pan Books, Sales Office, Cavaye Place, London SW10 9PG
Send purchase price plus 20p for the first book and 10p for
each additional book, to allow for postage and packing
Prices quoted are applicable in the UK

While every effort is made to keep prices low, it is sometimes
necessary to increase prices at short notice. Pan Books reserve the
right to show on covers and charge new retail prices which may differ
from those advertised in the text or elsewhere.